A H

The kitten meowed [illegible] turned around to see it hanging by its [illegible] halfway up the curtains. Laughing, she lifted it down, cuddling it under her chin. "What shall I call you? Or did Ramsey name you already?"

"No, I haven't."

She looked over her shoulder to see him standing in the doorway, the candlelight refecting in his dark eyes.

"I love my present," she said, turning so he could see the kitten in her arms.

"I'm glad." He entered the room, closing the door behind him. Johnna felt that strange flicker of excitement that he always brought out in her, but he only held out his hand to the kitten.

It mewed excitedly and tried to launch through intervening space. Johnna caught it with a juggling motion. "Here now, slowly," she said. Its back claws had caught on her dressing gown. She drew breath between her teeth as one dug through her clothes and scratched her waist. Johnna tugged free of the little claw and the kitten ran over her shoulder to fling itself on Ramsey.

"She likes you," she said, smiling at the picture he made. . . .

—from *The Birthday Kitten,* by Cynthia Pratt

Valentine Kittens

Jo Ann Ferguson

Valerie King

Cynthia Pratt

ZEBRA BOOKS
KENSINGTON PUBLISHING CORP.
www.kensingtonbooks.com

ZEBRA BOOKS are published by

Kensington Publishing Corp.
850 Third Avenue
New York, NY 10022

All Kensington titles, imprints and distributed lines are available at special quantity discounts for bulk purchases for sales promotion, premiums, fund-raising, educational or institutional use.

Special book excerpts or customized printings can also be created to fit specific needs. For details, write or phone the office of the Kensington Special Sales Manager: Kensington Publishing Corp., 850 Third Avenue, New York, NY 10022. Attn. Special Sales Department. Phone: 1-800-221-2647.

Zebra and the Z logo Reg. U.S. Pat. & TM Off.

First Printing: January 2005
10 9 8 7 6 5 4 3 2 1

Printed in the United States of America

CONTENTS

Belling the Kitten

Jo Ann Ferguson

Chapter One

Peace.

Serenity.

Quiet.

Yes, quiet. After so many harsh months of cannons detonating and guns firing and men crying out in pain and fear, quiet was something Jason Farraday had believed he would never enjoy again.

He certainly had not found any at Farraday Hall. Upon his return to his family's estate, he had been the focus of great exuberance. He could understand why his sister and his mother were pleased to have him home after his time on the Peninsula. That he had arrived home in one piece and without any visible scars thrilled them even more. And that was all for the good, but why had they assumed that he would become quickly bored with the *quiet* of the countryside? They seemed determined to fill every *quiet* moment with events and guests, especially young women with an eye on matrimony. He had bit his tongue, keeping back the truth that would have turned his mother's smile into tears, until that dashed surprise party. Didn't anyone realize what shouts of "Surprise!" would do to a man who had learned that any sound could be a harbinger of death?

He grimaced when he reached for the glass on the table beside his chair. The borrowed shirt was too tight across the shoulders and so short that it threatened to lump at his waist with any motion. The breeches were even more uncomfortable, for the seams cut into him where a man never wished to be pressured by his own clothes.

Taking a deep drink of the wine, he tried to smile. He had no one but himself to blame for having to exchange his well-made clothes for these poorly fitting ones. His coachman had urged him to stay out of the way when the carriage became mired in the road a few miles from the inn. Not heeding the coachee, Jason had insisted on helping to loosen the wheels from the mud. It had taken little more than a moment for a splash to drench his clothing with the filth. He should be grateful that the proprietor of the inn, a hospitable woman named Mrs. Kettlewell, had been able to find him these things to wear while his own were being laundered.

The door opened with a muffled squeak of the hinges. When Jason looked over his shoulder, trying to keep the blanket around him from slipping, he saw his man Greene in the doorway. Greene's full belly and face beneath his graying hair bespoke the valet's appreciation of the best Farraday Hall had to offer. Jason knew his valet did not understand the desire to leave Farraday Hall so shortly after arriving home, but Greene had not spoken of that even when they left at dawn.

Something tried to scurry past Greene's feet. He halted the gray cat by blocking its way with the side of his shoe.

"Cats!" he grumbled in his deep voice. He bent to pick up another one and toss it gently back into the passage. "If this inn had as many patrons as it had cats, Mrs. Kettlewell would be as rich as Midas."

Jason set his glass on the table beside his chair. With a

smile, he said, "Greene, it is not like you to be unsettled by something as commonplace as a cat."

"Not *a* cat, my lord. I swear a full score of cats and their kits followed me up the stairs from the common room. It was like a dashed parade."

"Ah, that explains your dismay. We had quite enough of parading about on the Peninsula."

Greene opened his mouth, then closed it so hard that Jason could hear the snap of his jaw even across the small room.

"Stop trying to hold your tongue, man," Jason ordered. "What is amiss?"

His valet abruptly wore the expression of a naughty lad who had been caught at some misdeed. It was an amazing countenance for a man of his many years.

"I hope nothing is amiss, my lord. In my vexation with the cats coiling around my ankles, I mistakenly opened the door across the hall rather than this one."

"Did you intrude upon anyone?"

He shook his head. "There was nobody in the room." Leaning forward, he lowered his voice, even though there was nobody else to heed his words. "The young lady Mrs. Kettlewell told us was spending the night here must be using that room."

"An easy assumption, as there are but two rooms in the open wing of the inn." Settling back in his chair, he said, "As there was no one within the room, it appears as if your error went unnoticed."

"I will not be so unthinking in the future."

Jason sat straighter again. This time, the coverlet fell off his shoulders. As he pulled it back into place to keep the cold at bay, he asked, "By Jove, Greene, what is disturbing you? You did not walk in on the young woman when she was dressed only in her smallclothes, forcing me to accept a challenge by her watchdog to meet in a duel to remedy such a blemish on her reputation. Nor did you interrupt her while she was doing whatever a miss might do at an inn on a snowy evening."

Greene shuffled his feet, then stiffened his shoulders. "Thank you, my lord, for reminding me of that."

"Do not become as on edge as my sister whenever someone calls. One would think she was an aged spinster rather just having celebrated her first-and-twentieth birthday." He frowned as he recalled the ado surrounding the gathering to celebrate that anniversary.

His sister, Olivia, had disappeared before the evening was barely begun, and he had found her crying in her room. She had refused to tell him what had put her to tears. The sad sound of her weeping still resonated in his memory as he sought some quiet at a country inn only a day's drive from Farraday Hall.

"I do believe, my lord," Greene said, "she remains hopeful he will call."

"He? Who?"

Greene again looked at his feet. "I should not have spoken out of turn."

"But you did, so spit out the rest. Has my sister set her heart on someone?" He was torn between pleased amazement and irritation that Olivia had not confided in him. He rubbed his forehead. Or had she? She had been prattling on about several people she had met in London during the previous year's Season, but at the moment he could not think of one name she had mentioned more than the others.

"Lord Marlowe," Greene said without looking up.

Now there was a name he had not expected to hear linked to his sister's. Jason stared at the fire flinging itself toward the flue. As a child, Raymond Marlowe, eldest son of a neighboring marquess, had been as irritating as a May fly and had, in Jason's opinion at the time, as much use. Jason had known Marlowe since they both first attended school, where Marlowe had been a sly prankster whose target was always the younger boys. Jason had seldom been Marlowe's victim, for the older boy had quickly learned that Jason would not cry in humiliation as other youngsters did. Their dislike had become enmity when Jason had come to the rescue of a boy who limped and had not been able to outrun Marlowe's gang of bullies.

He stared at his left leg propped on the stool. If there were any true sense of equity in the world, he would not be the one who now walked with a rolling gait. Marlowe would. Then again, Marlowe would never be so want-witted as to buy a commission and make himself prey to Napoleon's guns.

But Marlowe would not take any amusement at how fate had twisted Jason's life, for he had become a decent chap in the years during which they set aside their youth. He was respected among the *ton,* and Jason should not wish him ill.

By Jove! The whole of it made sense with the information Greene had revealed. Since he had returned home, he had heard Marlowe's name mentioned frequently, but always in connection with the Valentine's Day ball being held at Marlowe Manor. Olivia had shown more interest in Jason's attending than in going herself. He frowned as he recalled his sister saying over and over that the ball might be the very place for him to find someone to give him an heir. Not once had she mentioned that she was eager to attend in order to gain Marlowe's attention.

The blasted ball! It had been the final straw which had sent him bolting from Farraday Hall to find a quiet haven far from flirtations and matchmaking mamas. His unsteady leg would not lessen the pursuit, for his family's title was old and respected. It would only slow him from evading the company of some ardent miss.

His hand clenched on his glass. He was letting his grim spirits overwhelm him. Better he should concentrate on his wine and the comfort of the fire. Otherwise, the loathing he had first felt for a young Marlowe would become self-loathing once more.

"If I said anything I should not have," Greene said, intruding on Jason's thoughts, "please forgive me."

"There is nothing to forgive." He frowned at the fire fighting back the wintry cold that had settled on the Pennines. "Mayhap I should speak to Marlowe about this matter."

"An excellent idea. However, Marlowe Manor is, with these barely passable roads, a journey of two to three days beyond Farraday Hall."

Jason glanced over his shoulder, but Greene was busy bustling around the room. He could not accuse his valet of doing Olivia's work in making Jason aware of her *tendre* for their neighbor. Not wanting to put his suspicions into words, for that would suggest he trusted neither his valet nor his sister, he decided the best tactic would be to change the subject. But to what?

"I suppose I should consider putting an end to this long day," he said.

Greene gasped. "Is your leg giving you pain, my lord?"

"No." Speaking of the injuries he had sustained during the war was another topic he wanted to avoid. "You are fretting like a governess watching over a royal heir. Do not fret about me, and do not feel guilty about entering the young woman's room. I trust," he continued when Greene remained silent, "that I shall be able to wish her a good rest of her journey on the morrow. It would not be seemly to interrupt her evening with an uninvited look-in." He pulled at the too short sleeve on his borrowed shirt. "Nor would it be appropriate to speak to her dressed as I am."

"Your riding clothes should be ready before we take our leave in the morning," Greene said, drawing back the covers on the bed. "If this accursed storm ever passes. I am sorry, my lord, that there is nothing better for you to wear until then."

"I am grateful to have a fire and a roof over our heads." He rocked the glass he held, watching the ruby wine catch the light from the flames. "Thank you, Greene, for your efforts in this matter. You should be seeking your own bed, for our start in the morning shall be early."

His valet turned away, but not quickly enough. Jason saw Greene's grimace. Did Greene pine for the years when Jason had kept town hours? Late to bed after a night of cards or flirtations and late to rise to begin the pursuit of pleasure again had been customary until he had learned that did not serve a man well while he was serving the king.

Jason leaned back against the worn cushions on the chair and balanced both of his bare feet on the stool. The heat from the hearth warmed his toes to toasty comfort, which he once had thought would never be anything but either icy or sweaty again.

Quiet.

It was so blessed quiet here. A man could even force his thoughts to be silent while he enjoyed a pleasant quaff of wine.

A woman screamed.

That wine splashed across his borrowed shirt as he jumped to his feet. What the deuce! Who was screaming like a pack of hounds at full cry?

He started for the door, then paused to set the glass on the table by the chair. He heard a door slam. Nearby. He scowled. That door was the one across the narrow passage from his room.

Throwing open his own door, he heard the woman scream again. A shadow fled toward the stairs. Even though every inch of him wanted to give pursuit to the person who must have caused the scream, he turned to the room across the cold hallway.

The door was ajar, and it came open farther when he rapped against it.

"Do you need help?" he called.

"Yes! Yes, come in!" came back a rather desperate reply from within.

Jason opened the door to discover the room was almost a

mirror image of his own. There were some differences, however. Instead of a single narrow bed, there were a pair pushed beneath the slanting roof, and a beam thicker than his upper arm cut the room in two, so anyone taller than a child of ten or twelve must duck to pass beneath it.

Other aspects of the room might be dissimilar, but he had no time to take note of that because his eyes focused on a young woman. She was almost his height, and black curls shimmered along her shoulders before dropping along the front of her dress, which was in shreds. Pulling the coverlet off his shoulders, he held it out to her.

"What good will covering up the damage do?" she asked, her voice raw with rage.

"I thought you would wish it to cover up *you.*"

"Me?" She began to lower the ruined dress slowly.

Jason knew a gentleman would look away or hold up the blanket between his eyes and the unquestionably feminine form in front of him. He did neither, vexed at himself for believing, as Greene must have, that the woman was of quality. Now she was acting like the lowest member of the *demimondaine*. He should have guessed such harlots would be glad for the opportunity to linger at inns in hopes of persuading lonely men to part with a coin or two. It would be best to put an end to the woman's ploy posthaste . . . before the ache along him, a most pleasurable sensation which he had almost forgotten, urged him to throw caution aside and enjoy being seduced by such a pretty lass.

"You are wasting your time," he said, not trying to conceal his irritation. She was lovely with the high color on her cheeks, but her screams had intruded on his *quiet.* "I have no interest in what you are suggesting."

That was not quite the truth, for she was a fair lass. Mayhap on another night when he had basked in all the tranquillity he longed for, he might have appreciated her attempts to seduce him. Again a half-truth, because his thoughts wandered from peace and quiet to hearing her soft breath against his ear as he drew her closer.

"What *I* am suggesting? Sir, I have no idea what you are speaking of." She flung the dress on the bed. "Look at that!"

He could not. He could only stare at the lovely sight before him. Now the woman's dark curls slowed along her simple gown's décolletage cut stylishly low across her breasts, but still far more demure than what a harlot would wear. The pink fabric, its shade almost identical to her cheeks, had a sheen that suggested it had cost her dear. As had the single strand of pearls at her throat, he suspected. By Jove, the whole situation was spiraling out of control.

"Well?" asked the young woman.

Only then did he notice a trio of kittens rolling about the bed as they engaged in mock battles with each other's tails and ears. A gray tiger squeezed out from beneath a ginger-colored kitten and pounced on the black one that had been chewing on its ear. The black kitten arched and hissed before scrambling away. Its claws caught in the rents in the gown's sleeve, and it struggled to escape.

As he heard the material rip farther, Jason scooped up the black kitten. The sleeve hung from its pin-sharp claws. He tried to loosen the dress without damaging it more, but the kitten was wiggling like a maddened creature. When it drilled its spiked milk teeth into his thumb, he yelped, dropping kitten and gown back onto the bed.

The woman muttered something reproachful, which might have been aimed at him or the kitten or both, as she disentangled the kitten from the gown. She motioned to the other two on the bed.

He gathered them up and went to the door. Opening it, he put them outside. They scampered away, eager to look for more adventure, or mayhap their mother. When he heard a plaintive mew behind him, he took the black kitten.

Shaking his head ruefully, Jason said to the little creature,

"You are only a few weeks old, and already you are bringing bad luck to those who cross your path."

"Do you always allow the cats to run tame through a guest's room?" asked the young woman.

"Do I . . ." He stared at her, uncertain what she meant.

She put her hands at her waist, emphasizing its narrow curves as well as the fuller ones above. In a tone he had last heard when he had been scolded by his governess, she said, "I do believe I told your mother upon our arrival that my abigail is afraid of black cats."

"My mother?"

"Is Mrs. Kettlewell your mother?" Her eyes widened as she appraised him from head to his bare feet. "Or your wife?"

"Neither." He understood her mistake. Seeing his rough clothes, she believed him to be the owner of the inn or a member of their hostess's family.

Before he could acquaint her with her mistake, she asked in the same uncompromising voice, "How could this have happened? I know neither Corette nor I left the door unlatched." Tears filled her dark eyes, making them glisten like a pair of stars on a moonless night, but she raised her chin, obviously determined not to let them fall when he was watching.

He had to admire her resolve, and he was grateful she was not collapsing in a swoon at the sight of her now bedraggled gown. "I am afraid your door was earlier opened by accident. At that time, the kittens must have darted in without being noticed."

"How could you be so careless?"

He locked his hands behind his back. He did not intend to point to Greene as the cause of this bumble-bath, nor did he plan to remain here to be dressed down by this young miss. She might be a delight for the eyes, but she was berating him like an old tough.

"I will endeavor," he said, his words icy, "not to allow this to happen again."

That chill timbre seemed to have no effect on her. He was

amazed the tears in her eyes did not boil away with the heat of her anger and frustration. "What does it matter?" She picked up the torn sleeve. "My dress is ruined."

"It can be repaired."

Again she eyed him as if he had no more wit than one of the kittens. "Mayhap you have not looked as closely as I requested. The fabric is shredded in several places."

"Any garment can be repaired."

"You must have a modiste nearby who can work miracles." She dropped the sleeve back onto the bed with a scowl. Then, she picked up the gown and shoved it into his arms. "Please take this to her. I will be delayed here for several days while my carriage is fixed, so if she can truly do such sorcery, tell her that Miss Woodward will be eternally grateful." Ducking beneath the low rafter, she did not look at him as she said, to give him his *congé,* "There will be nothing else for now. Good night."

"Miss Woodward," he began, wondering how he could do what she was asking. It was his obligation to correct the damage done to her gown. Folding the ripped dress over his arm, he wondered if there was a modiste in the small town not far from the inn. A modiste who could do magic, he had to own as he saw where the fabric had been snagged in dozens of places along one sleeve.

Before he could add more, the half-opened door bumped into his back. Mrs. Kettlewell, a blonde woman old enough to be his mother, exactly as the young woman had noted, peeked in. Her blue eyes grew round as she looked from him to the young miss.

"I was told—that is, I thought—" she faltered with a dismayed expression.

As the young miss launched into an explanation of what had happened, Jason decided it was his opportunity to retreat from the room. He would speak with Mrs. Kettlewell in the morning about having a seamstress repair the young woman's gown.

Greene was waiting in the room across the hall. He paused in his pacing when Jason entered.

"How bad is it?" the valet asked. "I never thought to check if a cat had followed me into the room."

"Not just one, but a trio of very destructive kittens who created havoc with Miss Woodward's gown." Jason started to hold up three fingers, then paused as he realized he still held Miss Woodward's dress.

"How badly was it torn?"

"See for yourself." He unfolded it and draped it over the foot of the bed.

Greene's forehead furrowed even more deeply. "Why do *you* have the dress, my lord?"

"The young lady believes me to be employed here, and she has given me the task of having her gown mended."

"You?" The valet swallowed so hard that Jason could hear his gulp. "My lord, I am so sorry for the trouble I compounded by offering to send for the inn's owner when I heard the young woman cry out in dismay."

"Just before I arrived to see what was wrong, I collect."

The valet nodded.

"No wonder she mistook me for Mrs. Kettlewell's son." He smiled wryly. "Or husband."

He hobbled back to his chair, then realized he had left his blanket in the other room. He glanced at the bed with only another thin cover on it and considered sending Greene to retrieve the blanket. When he heard a cry of dismay—in Mrs. Kettlewell's voice, if he were not mistaken—he suspected it would be better to be chilled than to subject his valet to the shocking mull on the far side of the passage.

When his valet reached for the latch, Jason called him back.

"But I must apologize to the young woman," Greene said. "It is my fault."

"You might prefer to apologize when she has had a chance to compose herself."

"I must tell her as well that you are Lord Farraday."

"On the morrow, *I* will tell her the truth, for *I* allowed her misconception to continue." He dropped into the chair and sighed. Such a discussion was guaranteed to disrupt his hope for peace, serenity, and quiet.

"In the morning? I thought we were leaving at dawn."

"It appears we will be staying here longer than I had planned." He looked at the dress on his bed. For a moment, his thoughts filled with the image of how Miss Woodward's soft curls would stream across his pillow. He shook those thoughts away. If he had wanted to let a woman clutter up his mind, he could have stayed at Farraday Hall, where his mother was hinting about several lasses who would appreciate a call from him. "But not a second longer than we must."

Chapter Two

"Thank you, Mrs. Kettlewell. I know you are very sorry," Amaris Woodward said as she shut the door behind the innkeeper.

Amaris leaned back against the door, closing her eyes. She had appreciated Mrs. Kettlewell's apologies . . . at least the first dozen times the innkeeper spoke them. After that, Amaris wondered if her head would forever echo with the repeated words.

She wondered what else could go wrong. Was the ruined dress a sign that her journey was going to continue to be wretched, or was it a warning she should put an end to it now that she had no fine dress to wear for the ball at Raymond Marlowe's manor house? The baron had very high expectations. Her mother had reiterated those very words to her over and over. Papa had insisted that Amaris go to the assembly at Marlowe Manor in spite of how he had taken too sick to journey with her.

"Your mother will remain here to tend to me," he had said each time she tried to protest that any calls on Lord Marlowe could wait until Papa was hale again. "You must go to the man who we hope will come to depend on you to tend to him. He is a marquess, you know."

She did know. Papa had been insistent that no one less than a marquess would be suitable for his daughter and the grandson he hoped she would bring him. That grandson would have what Papa lacked, in spite of the fortune amassed by the family. A highly placed title.

"He is a man of best character," Papa said. "Something I know well, for we have done business for many years."

She understood that, too. Papa was a skilled businessman, and he had worked with many belonging to the *ton.* Not only had he been made a partner in the investments made by those in the Polite World, but he had helped several peers save their families' fortunes with his shrewd business advice.

"And you will be able to come to depend on him to take care of you as you deserve to be taken care of," Papa had continued.

She knew that should inspire her heart to beat with greater affection for the man who Papa believed wanted to marry her. It might have if she could recall more about the single time she had been introduced to him. She had been very young, and, because he was five years older, he had seemed to be almost an adult. She did remember Lord Marlowe had the brightest red hair she had ever seen.

But is he as handsome as the man who came into my room tonight?

"Egad," she whispered, distressed at her own thought. She should not be comparing Lord Marlowe with a man who worked at an inn. She should not even be thinking of the man and his bothersome way of looking at her.

Mayhap bothersome was not the exact word she wanted. He had regarded her as if she were no better than a strumpet when she had confronted him with the damage done to her gown by those three kittens.

But, she had to own, he had drawn her own gaze time and again. His hair was the warm gold of thickened honey, and his eyes only a shade darker. She had never seen eyes of that color, and she had been fascinated by how they glowed in his bronzed face, which suggested he preferred to work outdoors. With too much ease, she could imagine his broad shoulders moving effortlessly as he tended to some chore. Only when he had turned to take his leave had she noticed his slight limp, and she was curious how he had hurt himself. She had had to bite her tongue to keep from posing that question to Mrs. Kettlewell.

Pushing away from the door, Amaris ducked beneath the low rafter. She turned as the door reopened. She tried to smile when she saw the woman who was close in age to Mrs. Kettlewell, but with silver hair. Almost short enough to walk beneath the beam without bending, she rushed to Amaris's side.

"Oh, dearest me, Miss Amaris! I heard about what happened to your gown. What are you going to do?"

"I have no idea, Corette," she replied to her abigail. Corette always saw the darkest side of any cloud, but, tonight, Amaris was tempted to agree with her.

"You cannot meet Lord Marlowe in tatters."

"Don't you think I realize that?" Knowing her voice sounded too sharp, as it had when she spoke with the man, she hurried to add, "Forgive me. I am all on end."

"Mayhap we should take the night to think of a solution."

"An excellent suggestion." She wondered what result there could be except throwing the dress away. In spite of the man's assertion, she doubted even the most skilled modiste would be able to repair the gown that Papa had been so proud to have made for her.

After she had prepared herself for bed and bid Corette, who was settling into the other bed, a good night, Amaris hunched down into the pillows and stared at the odd shadows cast by the low rafter onto the slanted ceiling. Mayhap she was being too gloomy. Any situation could be turned to the good. Papa had reminded her of that many times. Not with his words, but with his actions—because her father had been able to build a valuable shipping business from a single, leaky ship his uncle had bequeathed him.

Something vibrating brushed her right foot, and she almost screeched. She halted herself when she realized the quiver came from a purr too soft for her to hear.

Drawing back the covers, she saw the black kitten, which must have found a way to sneak back into the room, curled into a fuzzy ball against her foot. She pulled the covers carefully back over both of them and fell asleep, glad that another disaster was not awaiting her tonight.

The morrow would be soon enough to seek an answer to the questions taunting her. She should be able to find one for each of them, save for the most important.

Could she persuade herself to accept Lord Marlowe's offer of marriage?

The morning smelled of fresh snow and cool air and what was being baked in the inn's kitchen. As Amaris hurried to dress with her abigail's help, she hoped whatever was being served would taste as delicious as the aromas seeping up through the chinks in the floor.

Corette was oddly reserved while Amaris checked her appearance in the small glass over the water bowl. Each time Amaris's gaze settled on her abigail's reflection, Corette hurriedly looked elsewhere.

Amaris wanted to ask if Corette had expected her to find some sort of miracle during the night. Mayhap Corette had hoped to have some fairy tale elves sneak into the inn and make the dress as perfect as it had been before the kittens ruined it.

She could not continue to be vexed at the man who had come into her room last night. It was clear the gown had been destroyed by accident. He had not hesitated in explaining what had likely happened, not shifting the blame to someone else as the owner of the last inn had when confronted with the damage to her carriage. She needed to apologize to him for her sharp words last night.

Amaris had to own that the inn appeared far more welcoming in the daylight. When she went to look out the low window tucked into the gable, she saw lazy snowflakes drifting by on a gentle wind. The storm was passing, and they would be able to continue on their way once the carriage was fixed. Those repairs were sure to take several days, so she had that respite to discover a way to replace her damaged dress.

She drew her wool shawl more tightly around her shoulders as she descended the narrow stairs to the floor below. Voices came from outside the inn, but the breakfast room on her right was silent save for the crackle of flames on the wide hearth.

Beams ran the length of the ceiling, which was so low she could have touched it without stretching. The light from the large window was swallowed by the aged wood paneling on the walls. A long table held two place settings with two steaming cups of hot chocolate, so she guessed the gentleman who was staying in the other room had not yet eaten.

Amaris flinched when something moved in the shadows. When the man who had come into her room last night stepped into the light, holding a covered basket, she could not keep from staring. He now wore traveling clothes befitting a member of the Polite World. His dark jacket, without a hint of lint upon it, accented his broad shoulders and casually tied cravat. Buckskin breeches vanished into well-polished boots.

"Good morning, Miss Woodward," he said, smiling.

She had to say something. She could not simply gape at him, openmouthed, curious about who this man truly was. "Good morning . . ."

"Jason Farraday," he said, bowing before motioning toward a chair close to the open hearth. "I collect you would prefer a seat farthest from the cold air coming around the glass in the window."

"Thank you. Your thoughtfulness is appreciated." She spoke the words by habit as she struggled to make her mind work. She had never encountered an innkeeper who dressed like quality, but she had to own she had met only two innkeepers before she arrived at this inn. Who was this man? She wanted to ask that question. But how could she pose it without sounding like a widgeon?

He held out the covered basket as she sat. Drawing back the cloth atop it, he smiled. "I think you will enjoy one of these muffins," he said.

"Thank you." She set the muffin on her plate, trying to figure out what else to say while he placed the basket on the table by the place setting across from where she sat. "Your other guest is late abed."

"My other . . ."

"I heard his arrival last night. He was complaining bitterly of how the mud from the road had left him beau-nasty."

"You use town cant with ease, Miss Woodward. Before we go any further, I must tell you that—"

An older man rushed into the room, snow flying from the soles of his shoes. He paused when he saw her and drew himself up before he turned to Mr. Farraday.

"What is it, Greene?" Mr. Farraday asked.

"I spoke with the man who brought milk to the inn. The roads are impassible by carriage now. If you wish, I can have a message sent to Graystone Manor, so Lord Blackburn knows we have been delayed."

"Unnecessary. A single look from his window will be enough for him to understand why we have not arrived."

Greene bowed his head. "As you wish, my lord."

"My lord?" gasped Amaris. She clapped her hand over her mouth, then quickly lowered it when she realized how want-witted she must appear.

The two men exchanged a glance, and Greene, his face a fiery shade of red, hurried out of the breakfast parlor. He closed the door behind him, and silence filled the room, a smothering silence that Amaris knew she had to escape.

Coming to her feet, she mumbled, "Excuse me." She took a single step toward the door, then halted when Lord Farraday stepped in front of her. She focused her gaze on his chin. "Good morning, *my lord*."

"Allow me to explain."

"And what do you wish to explain?" She hoped her icy tone would cover her dismay at such a faux pas.

"Before Greene burst in," he said, his voice revealing his distress, "I was about to atone for my unthinkable behavior of storming into your room like a knight in search of a dragon."

"And for failing to introduce yourself?" She met his golden-brown eyes steadily and tried to ignore her fascination with them. "You should not have allowed me to continue with my misconception."

"If you recall, I had no chance to correct the notion last night."

Amaris opened her mouth to retort, then closed it. He was right. She had been in such a pelter that she had babbled like a prattle-box.

"Shall we begin anew?" He bowed toward her. "Allow me to introduce myself. I am Jason Farraday, fifth viscount." He took her hand as he asked, "And may I have your name, miss?"

"Am-Amaris Wood-Woodward," she stuttered while she watched him raise her hand to his lips. She held her breath, not even daring to release the one locked in her lungs, as he kissed her hand. His mouth threatened to sear her skin, and she wondered how long the heat would remain.

"I beg your indulgence, Miss Woodward, with my untoward behavior last night."

He released her hand, and she felt suddenly adrift. Too many thoughts were swirling through her head. Each one was focused on Lord Farraday. His rich baritone, the dramatic planes of his face and how they changed with every emotion, his firm yet gentle fingers, those arresting eyes. She should think of something else. She *must* think of something else.

She went to look out the window, hoping her motion would suggest more serenity than she felt. Snow was blowing about on the wind, blurring the view of the garden, and the mountains were lost within a fuzzy cloak of clouds.

"You shall be snowbound here for another day as well," Lord Farraday said from behind her.

"It is not the snow that has halted my journey." She did not face him as she stepped back from the chill beside the window. "We cannot continue until our carriage is repaired."

"You mentioned that last night."

"I doubt it will be enough time to . . ." Fire scored her face, and she whirled to face him. "You still have my gown!"

"Yes." A hint of a smile tipped one side of his mouth.

"If you will return it—"

"I said I would have the damage rectified, Miss Woodward. I did not make that vow lightly." He leaned back against one end of the table and folded his arms across his waistcoat, which she noticed for the first time was a sedate pale blue. "So trust me to do as I offered."

"Thank you." She was unsure how else to reply. She decided the truth would be best. "I would not be so all on end, my lord, if the occasion when I am to wear that dress was not so important."

"I assumed it was a grand occasion, for the dress was finely made. Where are you bound, Miss Woodward?"

"Marlowe Manor."

"Marlowe Manor?" His eyes narrowed slightly.

"It is several days north of here. There is to be a Valentine's Day ball hosted by Lord Marlowe, and I had planned to wear that gown. It will not matter, I suppose, as Valentine's Day is only a few days hence, and I may still be at this inn then."

"You are welcome to use my carriage." He stood. "As I am already doomed to be late for my own destination, another few days will not make much difference to me. They will, it would appear, to you."

"You are very kind."

"I owe you the duty of rectifying all my mistakes of yesterday." He started to reach for one of the cups of hot chocolate, then paused. Looking at her, he smiled. "I am sure your host will understand, but I fear your escort will be heartbroken that you are not in attendance."

"My escort is also my host."

"Marlowe?"

"Yes."

"I see." Without tasting the chocolate, he set the cup on the table. He bowed his head toward her as he walked to the door, murmuring something she was unsure if she was supposed to hear.

She stared in astonishment while he left the room. He had reacted oddly when she mentioned Lord Marlowe's name, but that did not explain why she thought he had said, "This is sure to complicate matters."

Chapter Three

"Is there a modiste close by?"

Mrs. Kettlewell exchanged a glance with the young woman working in the inn's kitchen. Jason could easily translate it. They were quite certain he had lost his mind somewhere before he reached the inn. The only aspect they remained uncertain about was how dangerous he might be in his befuddled state.

"Is there a modiste close by?" he asked again. "Miss Woodward needs more than a bit of mending on her dress that was ruined by those kittens."

The girl gasped, "But Mrs. Kettlewell cannot afford to pay for a lady's gown."

"Hush, May," said the innkeeper, squaring her shoulders. "I do not bilk my customers. Miss Woodward's dress was damaged because she stayed here. Therefore—"

"I shall pay for the new gown," Jason said, wondering how long it would take to get an answer to such a simple question.

"But it was not your fault that the kittens ripped her dress."

"One cannot be certain who is at fault, for it is simple to mistake one door for another in an unfamiliar inn."

Comprehension filled the innkeeper's eyes, and she sighed with obvious relief at the idea of not having to replace a gown which would have required much of her profits for the past year. "Mrs. Bingham in the village does some fine sewing, but I doubt she can repair a dress that has been torn as Miss Woodward described."

"Mayhap if you looked at it yourself, you might be able to judge better what can be done."

"I can ask Miss Woodward—"

"The dress is in my room."

"Your room?" squeaked the girl. She flushed as Mrs. Kettlewell glared at her.

"I understand your surprise," Jason said, hoping that he could complete the arrangements soon. He had a book waiting for him in his room, and he was looking forward to the chance to read it by the fire in the common room he had passed on his way to the kitchen. It would offer him an escape from the thoughts plaguing him.

If he had known Miss Woodward was bound for Marlowe Manor to act as Marlowe's most special guest, would he have offered his carriage to her? Truth be told, whatever answer he gave changed nothing. He could no more rescind his offer to Miss Woodward to use his carriage than he could forget about the damage his man had allowed to happen to her gown.

The innkeeper looked at her servant again. He could tell by their expressions that either woman would have been glad to say that she understood, too, but neither did.

"If you would come with me, Mrs. Kettlewell," he said, gesturing toward the door.

Mrs. Kettlewell wiped her hands on her apron and nodded. She waited for him to lead the way. Was she being polite or simply hoping that she would not encounter Miss Woodward on their way up the stairs?

His mouth tightened. Mayhap *he* should be the one eager to avoid meeting the pretty brunette. He had been beneath reproach for walking out of the breakfast parlor so abruptly, but he needed to get his thoughts composed before he said something wrong. If Greene had not been so certain last night that Olivia was pining for Marlowe's attentions, he would not have reacted with such witless amazement to Miss Woodward's comment that Marlowe had invited her to be his special guest at a Valentine's Day ball.

And he had offered the use of his carriage to enable Miss Woodward to break his sister's heart. He told himself it might be for the best, because he could see that Miss Woodward reached Marlowe Manor and hurry back to Farraday Hall to find some way to keep Olivia from attending the fête. His sister had believed her heart touched by other men, and each time she had discovered her mistake before she could accept an offer and lay waste to her life by marrying the wrong man. Mayhap the situation with Marlowe was no different.

Fortune must have taken a turn in his favor, because Jason did not see Miss Woodward or her servant before he opened his door. He noticed her door was ajar. Reminding himself that he could not be excused from overstepping the bounds of propriety a second time, he left it open as he motioned for Mrs. Kettlewell to step through his doorway.

"The dress is on the foot of the bed," he said, unable to keep from glancing back out toward Miss Woodward's door. If another kitten went in there, more damage might be done.

He forgot that when the innkeeper gave him a shocked look before going to check the dress. Clasping his hands behind his back, he bit back his retort at her silent suggestion that he had done something lascivious by placing the gown there. He did not owe her an explanation of how he had left it there because he had not wanted lace tickling him when he sat in the chair.

"You must be hoaxing me, my lord," Mrs. Kettlewell said.

"I assure you I have been quite straightforward about the whole of the matter of Miss Woodward's gown."

"Then how can you expect anyone to repair it?"

His brow lowered. "You have barely examined it."

"I have seen enough." She shook her head. "The gown is utterly ruined. Even Mrs. Bingham could not fix it, and she is the best seamstress in the parish."

"Thank you, Mrs. Kettlewell," he said quietly.

She must have taken his words as a dismissal because she hurried out of the room. He heard her close Miss Woodward's door before rushing down the steps.

He did not move. He had promised Miss Woodward he would have the dress repaired, and he had assured her that he did not break vows. Now he must. The very thought was as distasteful as knowing she might be about to break his sister's heart.

Amaris knocked on the door across the hall from her room. After speaking with Mrs. Kettlewell when she arranged for the afternoon tea, Amaris had discovered that Lord Farraday had no hopes of having the gown repaired.

The door swung open slightly. Was someone opening it or was the door ajar? She had come up to her room earlier to discover two older cats curled up on her bed. Mrs. Kettlewell had sent a maid to have them removed.

"Yes?" she heard from beyond the door. It was not Lord Farraday's voice, but his valet's, she realized when she saw the older man's stern face.

"I would like to speak with Lord Farraday."

"He does not wish to be disturbed. He came to this inn to enjoy the quiet." The valet started to close the door.

She grasped the edge. "It will take but a moment."

"It will take but a moment *later.*"

She jerked back her hand before he could shut her fingers in the door. Raising her hand to knock again, she lowered it. She would achieve nothing but bruising her knuckles, because the valet intended to keep her from bothering Lord Farraday.

Whirling to go to her room, she went down the stairs instead. She went into the common room and sat on a comfortable chair by the hearth. She did not want to return to her room. Corette's lamenting had continued without surcease the whole afternoon. The words still rang through her head.

How will you explain to Mr. Woodward that the dress he paid so dearly for has been ruined?

How will you explain to Mrs. Woodward that you have accepted the offer of a ride from a stranger?

How will you explain to Lord Marlowe that you have accepted a ride from a man who failed to tell you his real name the first time you met?

"I do not need to explain myself to anyone," she said to the fire.

"A wise attitude," came an answer from behind her.

She was astonished to hear Lord Farraday's voice. As he bent his head to enter through the low doorway into the common room, she said nothing. He carried a tray as he crossed the wide floorboards with a grace that matched his leonine coloring. He ducked again beneath the lamp hanging from the thick rafters before making himself comfortable on the settee only an arm's length from her across a low table.

He set the tray on the table. A teapot and a pair of cups were flanked by two plates topped with what smelled like apple tart.

"Our hostess sent this with the hopes that it would help warm a chilly day while she prepares our supper." He handed her one plate. "I find I owe you another apology, Miss Woodward."

"For what?" she asked as he reached for the other.

"I—" He yelped when two cats jumped up next to him, almost upsetting the second plate on his lap.

"Push them aside if they bother you," she said when both cats regarded him with curiosity.

"They are no bother."

"Mrs. Kettlewell's maid told me when they invaded my

room that the gold and black one is Tabby. The brown and gray is Mince." She smiled. "She also mentioned that they are quite interested in the inn's guests."

"So I see." He took a bite of the tart, then broke off a piece for each cat.

Tabby sniffed it, then slithered onto Lord Farraday's lap and curled up into a ball. Mince ate both pieces and jumped up onto the back of the settee to watch each bite he took.

"I owe you an apology, Miss Woodward," Lord Farraday said as if there had been no interruption, "because Greene was overly forceful in tending to his duties."

"He was only trying to do what he believed was best for you."

"As your abigail is when she scolds you?"

Heat seared her face. "You heard that?"

"The raised voice only, Miss Woodward. The reason for the scold remained in your room." He smiled, and she knew he had guessed exactly why Corette had been giving her a dressing-down. "But that is not the only apology I owe you. It seems I was not aware of the true expanse of destruction caused by three small kittens. I regret that I may be unable to fulfill my vow to have your gown repaired."

"Mrs. Kettlewell informed me of that."

He chuckled. "I should have guessed as much."

"I appreciate your attempting such an impossible task."

"I said I would."

She set her plate back on the tray as she poured two cups of tea. He placed his plate next to hers, trying not to wake the cat on his lap. Mince perched with its front paws on his shoulder as it stretched across the back of the settee and stared at the plate.

When she gave him one cup, Lord Farraday took it. He sipped it, then held it back out, being careful not to jostle the cats. "More cream if I may." He chuckled. "We might as well use it before our feline companions decide to make sure it does not go to waste."

Amaris relaxed at his jest. Sitting back against her chair, she asked, "Where were you bound, my lord, before you changed your plans on my behalf?"

"I was planning to call on an old friend, but he is a patient man. He learned to be so when he was a courier for the king."

"Really? How exciting!"

"In retrospect, I suspect. At the time, I would guess it was quite harrowing."

"Did you work with him?"

"No, I served the king on the Continent. I—" He sneezed once, then again.

"Bless you," she said as she poured cream into his cup.

He sneezed again . . . and again.

In dismay, she watched the cats get up and, giving him a irritated expression, walk out of the room. They vanished up the stairs. Not wanting to voice her suspicion, she had to ask, "Do cats make you sneeze?"

"Do you think I would have let them crawl all over me if they did?" A renewed detonation of sneezes swept out of him. "Not cats, but—have you seen any catnip around here? Will you look?"

In dismay, Amaris nodded. He did not notice, for he sneezed and sneezed. She motioned for him to stand, but he remained a captive to his sneezing. With his hand over his mouth, he leaned forward, his elbows propped on his knees.

She stood and went to the settee, knowing what she needed to look for. Corette had shown her catnip rolled into a square of cotton and sewn into a ball. Mrs. Kettlewell had given it to her abigail to use if the kittens invaded the room again. They would be drawn to it and away from anything they might damage. It had seemed sensible, for Amaris had done much the same for her cats at home. Her pair of cats adored torturing it and each other. When thoroughly intoxicated on the catnip, her Kit would hide the ball so Puss could not find it.

Amaris got down on her knees to look under the settee as Lord Farraday continued to sneeze. She saw a bone that a dog must have left there, but no catnip ball. Running her hand along the top of the settee, she found nothing.

"It would help if you would set yourself on your feet, my lord," she said as she dug her fingers down behind the cushions.

He glared at her with one watery eye, started to speak, then sneezed again.

"Stay where you are then," she murmured, realizing he could not move. She leaned forward to dip her fingers into the space between the cushion where he was sitting and the arm of the sofa. With a satisfied smile, she pulled out a clump of well-chewed cotton. She went out of the room and to the door on the other side of the entry. Opening it, she tossed the catnip ball in before she came back to the common room. "You should be fine now."

He answered her with another sneeze.

She took his arm and tugged him to his feet. He shuddered against her as he sneezed again. Turning her face, she steered him away from the settee. His other arm draped over her shoulder as she guided him from the room and to the front door. He leaned heavily on her, but she managed to lead him out onto the steps.

"The fresh air shall revive you quickly," she said, hoping it would.

As the snow swirled around them, Lord Farraday took several ragged breaths, wheezing like an old man. He lowered himself to sit on the step as he drew in one deep breath, then another.

Going back into the house, Amaris picked up the cup of tea she had poured for him. She rushed back outside.

"What is amiss?" asked Mrs. Kettlewell as she followed Amaris back out onto the steps.

"Catnip causes Lord Farraday to sneeze," Amaris said as, paying the snow no mind, she handed him the cup. "He was sitting very close to where one of the cats had hidden a catnip ball."

He wiped his eyes and gave them a weak smile. "Miss Woodward bravely saved me from the stupendous danger of a piece of cloth and some catnip."

"How are you faring now, my lord?" Mrs. Kettlewell was going to wring her hands right through her apron.

"I shall be fine."

"You will become chilled out here."

"I will return inside," Lord Farraday said, "once I have let this tea soothe my throat."

Amaris lingered by the door, unsure if she should follow the innkeeper back into the house. Darkness had swept aside the day while they had been speaking in the sitting room. She heard a whistling tune, which must be coming from the stables behind the inn.

"You need not watch me as if you fear I shall cock up my toes and be put to bed with a shovel." Lord Farraday's voice suggested his throat was still raw.

"It would not be *de rigueur* to have you die on the steps while I watched."

He chuckled, then winced as he rested one hand behind him. After taking another deep drink, he said, "I daresay such an event would cause quite a bit of chitchat to be bandied about."

Kneeling on the step beside him, she said, "If you had given warning, Mrs. Kettlewell would have made sure that neither Tabby nor Mince brought their toy near you."

"It is not something that I think to mention upon entering an inn. After all, how often am I assaulted by catnip concealed beneath the cushions?"

"There are many surprises while traveling," she said, hoping to lighten his tone. "Some of them are not so good."

He leaned toward her and smiled. "And some are."

"I . . ." Her answer faded as she realized the arc of his arm surrounded her. When his fingers rose to curve along her cheek, she gasped. Succulent sweetness flowed through her with the heat of the hot tea. His mouth moved closer to hers as he tilted her face. She raised her hands, but drew them back when they touched the firm muscles beneath his sedate waistcoat.

When his lips brushed her cheek, she gasped again and pulled away. She came to her feet. He did the same, and she stared at him in astonishment, not sure what to say.

He grinned as if he kissed her cheek every day. "Do not look so astonished. That was a thank you for rescuing me from my own foolishness."

"Foolishness?"

"I should realize where there are cats there is likely to be catnip. Thank you, as well, for being kind enough not to remind me of my rude behavior, Miss Woodward, of sneezing all over you." Without a pause, he asked, "How long have you known Marlowe?"

"I must say since I was a child, although I have met the marquess only once."

His eyes widened. "Is that so? But you are on your way to pay a call on him with only a maid to accompany you."

"My father is ill, and my mother is overseeing his care. Both were insistent that I not delay this call at Marlowe Manor." Heat clung to her cheeks as she added, "Lord Marlowe has spoken to my father about an arrangement."

"For marriage?"

She wished her voice could be as even as his. "Yes."

"I see."

She bent to pick up the cup and saucer on the step to hide her uneasiness. Even if he saw it, Lord Farraday would be unlikely to realize what was causing her distress. She was on her way to meet the man her parents hoped for her to marry. She should not be hoping another man would kiss her.

"Would there be, mayhap, another piece of that delicious apple tart?" His false lightness suggested he was eager to change the subject.

"I shall check." She straightened and froze as she discovered how he had stepped closer to her.

For a moment that seemed to be an eternity, he did not move. His smile created a fluttering sensation in her center. Then he stepped aside and opened the door to let her enter the inn. She went in without a backward glance. She was uncertain what she might see on his face if she looked back. And if he wore that same beguiling smile, she was even more uncertain how she might react. She did not dare to find out.

Chapter Four

The carriage took a bend on the twisting road, and Amaris peered through the snow. The faded silhouette showing through the storm must be a house, if she could call something so large a mere house. Once it might have been a castle, but any walls to repel invaders had vanished, save for the stone wall they had just passed through.

"Have we reached Marlowe Manor so soon?" she asked, astonished. She had been traveling with Lord Farraday and their servants since just after sunrise, and she had thought it would take longer to reach Lord Marlowe's estate.

"No." Lord Farraday's cloak was littered with the snowflakes pelting the carriage. "We are stopping at Farraday Hall. I told my coachee to halt here if the storm looked as if it were worsening. To go farther could mean sliding off the road and being stuck out in the snow and wind."

Amaris nodded. Even Corette, who customarily would have been distressed by such an unplanned delay, was silent. As the carriage had climbed the steep road over the ridge of the Pennines, clouds had closed around them and the chill air became icy cold. The higgledy-piggledy scattering of fields edged with hedgerows had vanished into the fog. She wondered how the coachman could even see the road in front of the horses' noses.

She waited for Lord Farraday to say something else. He had grown more silent with the passing of each mile, and she could not keep from pondering that he might regret the offer of his carriage. Now he was taking on the added burden of acting as her host until the snowstorm passed and she could continue with Corette to Marlowe Manor. She wanted to thank him as she had before, but he had seemed embarrassed by her gratitude.

As they neared the house, she saw dozens of windows were set into the façade of gray stone. On either side of the main section of the house, window bays that reached to the top of the third story were of a paler gray stone. They must have been added far more recently and had yet to weather. She doubted it would take long if the weather was often as inclement as the past two days had been.

The house curled away in both directions into the storm. The wings might be for servants or for guests or lead to outbuildings. On a clear day, every window must offer a glorious vista of the valley.

The carriage halted beneath a porte-cochere, and the door beside Lord Farraday was opened by a footman. The blue of the footman's livery was almost gray in the dim light.

"Welcome to Farraday Hall," he said with an aura of boredom that suggested he had repeated those words often. He stiffened, his shoulders straight as a soldier's, as he added, "My lord, we were not expecting you to return so soon."

"I had a change in plans." Lord Farraday motioned the young man aside and stepped out. "Miss Woodward?"

Amaris put her gloved hand on his while he handed her from the carriage. Before she could as much as thank him, he released her fingers, told her to hurry inside, and turned toward the back of the carriage. She heard him give orders for the bags to be removed from the boot and rooms to be made ready.

With her abigail, she walked up the pair of steps to the doors that were decorated with identical dull brasses. She could not guess if they were a family crest or meant to be something else, because snow swirled around them. She wondered why they had not been polished to impress guests. She almost laughed out loud. Everything about this estate was so magnificent that there was no need to dazzle anyone further.

A finger beneath her chin pushed her mouth, which she had not realized was agape, closed.

With a laugh, she looked at her abigail. "Thank you, Corette. I know I should not be put so much to the stare by this house."

"You must accustom yourself to such grandeur, Miss Woodward." Corette was glancing about with just a touch of avarice in her eyes. "Surely Lord Marlowe's estate must be far more resplendent, for it is the home of a marquess. This belongs to a mere viscount."

"Mere?"

Corette's face became as gray as the sky. "Miss Woodward, I meant no disrespect to Lord Farraday."

"Don't forget that, without his kind generosity, we would have been obliged to remain at the inn until my carriage was repaired." Amaris's next words were silenced when the double doors opened.

Another footman bowed them into the foyer. Several other servants edged past them, bound for the carriage to help retrieve the bags in the boot.

She turned to look around Farraday Hall's foyer. Her breath caught. The massive space was as quiet as a cathedral and almost as ornate, with its white marble floors and alabaster columns following the half-moon of the foyer. Her gaze went to the staircase that led up from the foyer. Each riser appeared to be nearly three yards wide. Life-sized statues were set in niches along the curve of the stairs. Draped in classic robes, the statues must represent Grecian gods.

Was Lord Farraday fascinated with ancient history? Or

was all the beauty a legacy from his ancestors? The entrance to the house was filled with art. Not only were there the incredible statues, but the friezes aligned along the ceiling and the upper galleries were scenes of fauns and nymphs cavorting in a meadow.

"This way," intoned a footman, motioning toward the stairs.

Amaris tried to keep her mind on the steps so she would not stumble while looking at each statue. Up close, they were even more amazing. No two faces were alike, and even each body shape was unique. Her fingers rose toward the perfectly carved hand of one, but she jerked them back before anyone could chance to see.

She was glad she had resisted the impulse to touch the statue when, just as they reached the top of the stairs and the gallery that curved around the upper edges of the foyer and into shadow, a woman appeared.

The woman could define the word beautiful. She was petite and stylishly blonde and each motion graceful. In a soft voice, as her dark brown eyes widened, she asked, "Who are you?"

Amaris was abruptly aware of her windblown appearance. Hours of sitting in the cramped carriage had left every inch of her wrinkled. Her shoes were damp, and she must look like a bedraggled urchin.

"I am Amaris Woodward, and this is my abigail." She tried to smile, but her face seemed abruptly as frozen as the falling snow. "Lord Farraday—"

"Jason!" the blonde called out, looking past them.

Amaris had barely enough time to step aside before the young woman brushed past her to fling her arms around Lord Farraday's neck. A twinge of something she could not explain tightened her stomach as she watched the two embrace.

"Don't look like that, Miss Woodward," hissed Corette.

"Like what?"

Her abigail did not have a chance to answer before Lord

Farraday untangled himself from the blonde's arms. He said, "Olivia, I see you have already met our guests."

"Guests?" asked Olivia. She turned to smile at Amaris and Corette. "Why didn't you let us know you were returning so quickly and with such an *unexpected* guest?"

Jason shifted his gaze to Miss Woodward as well. Olivia's emphasis on the single word announced that she believed he had brought Miss Woodward to Farraday Hall to make an announcement. He had, but he would not be making the announcement Olivia expected. By Jove, Miss Woodward's presence was about to cause a tumult.

"If you will restrain your questions for a moment, Olivia," he said quietly. "Miss Woodward, allow me to introduce Miss Olivia Farraday, my sister."

Something flashed through Miss Woodward's eyes, too rapidly for him to guess what the emotion might be. Her taut smile did not change as she greeted his sister. The usual pleasantries of discussing the unpleasant weather were exchanged.

When Olivia started to ask about Miss Woodward's destination, he jumped in to say, "I believe our guests would appreciate the chance to warm themselves in front of a good fire before we gather for dinner." He motioned to a footman. "Please take Miss Woodward to the blue guest room."

"Thank you," Miss Woodward replied.

The common words should have required only a nod or a simple response from him. Instead, they swirled around in his head, as exhilarating as Jamaica rum. In the carriage, he had avoided speaking with her, not wanting to become more caught up in the spell she cast upon him with no more than a smile. He had been certain when he returned to the familiar rooms of Farraday Hall he could shake off this intoxication.

He had been wrong.

As he watched her walk away with the footman, her abigail trotting behind, he let his breath sift past his tight lips.

When had he last taken a breath? Had he held it during the whole journey from the inn? He had heard the term breath-taking many times, but he suspected he was just coming to comprehend its true meaning.

"She *is* very pretty," murmured Olivia, lowly enough so her voice would not reach Miss Woodward. She linked her arm through his and drew him in the opposite direction along the gallery. Opening a door, she smiled. "I daresay Mama will be surprised you brought home such a bedraggled kitten."

He walked into the small parlor, where the family gathered to enjoy quiet winter evenings. "Please do not mention the word kitten."

As he explained, taking care not to mention Marlowe's name, his sister's eyes crinkled with amusement. She laughed even before he was finished and said, "Jason, such a to-do over three kittens' antics. Whatever were you thinking?"

"To make sure the damage done to her was repaired. You have spoken highly of the seamstress who made your dress for the last assembly of the Season."

Slipping her hand again within his arm, she walked with him to a chair beside the roaring fire. The room had a trio of windows, all now hidden behind gold draperies in hope of keeping out the winter's cold. Instead of a settee, several chairs were set near the hearth. The arrangement allowed for easy rearrangement for conversation or reading.

He sat when his sister gave him a gentle shove on the shoulders, but he almost came to his feet when Olivia replied, "Silly! That seamstress is in London."

"Is there one nearby?"

"Here?" She laughed and pulled a low stool with an embroidered cover closer to his chair. "Do not be want-witted, Jason. Do you have a tailor here in the country?"

"Your point is well taken."

"I am glad you are home, Jason," she said as she sat on

the stool. "And that you brought along a damsel in distress. Now you can escort Miss Woodward to Lord Marlowe's Valentine's Day ball."

His right hand closed into a fist. Postponing the truth would not make the telling any easier later. It would be better to be forthright now. "There are some things you need to know about Miss Woodward, Olivia."

Folding her hands on the chair's left arm, she leaned her chin on them and smiled up at him. "Very well. Tell me all about her. Please don't leave out the reasons why your eyes glow each time you look at her, even when you are trying to wear a stern expression."

"Glow? My eyes? You have lost your mind."

"Would you like a looking glass?" She giggled.

"Olivia, I would like to speak to you seriously about Miss Woodward."

"You were determined not to attend the ball at Marlowe Manor, but now you are back and you have brought with you a lovely young woman." She laughed again. "I wager you intend to ask her to marry you at the ball. How romantic of you, Jason. What can she say but yes?"

He shook his head, not only to disabuse her of her assumptions. He wanted to rid himself of the images Olivia's words created. Images of Miss Woodward standing within the circle of his arms on an otherwise empty balcony and of her eyes closing as she offered her mouth up for his kiss as they swayed to the music.

"Don't be silly," he said, as much to himself as to Olivia. He had not danced since he returned from the Continent, and he had no intentions of inflicting his uneven steps on Miss Woodward. To own the truth, he should have no intentions for anything in regard to Miss Woodward. He shifted in the chair, wanting to get to his feet, but that would mean pushing his sister aside. "I met her scarcely two days ago, and it appears that Miss Woodward will soon be promised to another."

"Oh, bother!" She sat up and waved her hand at him. "Now that she has met my brave, handsome brother, how can she accept an offer from someone else?"

"Because her parents wish it to be so."

"Mayhap she will be like Miss Ross and Mr. Cooney, who defied their parents and rode off to Gretna Green to be wed." She smiled. "Gretna Green is not very far from Farraday Hall, Jason."

Putting his hand on her shoulder, he said, "Olivia, Miss Woodward's parents hope for her to make a match with Raymond Marlowe."

She stared at him, her eyes flooding with tears as her smile fell away. Slowly she came to her feet. As he stood, she backed toward the door.

"Olivia—"

With a sob, she ran from the room. The door slammed back against the wall so hard that it almost swung closed again.

He rushed after her, but halted when he saw another form in the doorway. His mother was staring after Olivia. Turning, she looked up at him, for she was more than a head shorter than he. Her eyes, the same shade as his and just as direct, were filled with dismay.

"I did not think," Lady Farraday said as she motioned for him to step aside so she could enter the room, "that you would send your sister flying from your company when she has been so eager for you to return home in time for the Valentine's Day ball at Marlowe Manor."

He bent and gave her a kiss on the cheek. " 'Twas the tidings I brought with me."

"And what are they?"

He did not hesitate. His mother would wish to hear the truth without any sweetening of the facts. "Miss Woodward—"

"The young lady you brought here because her carriage was damaged?"

"Yes." For once, he was pleased how swiftly such tales

spread through the house because it saved him from having to explain at least *that* aspect of the muddle. "Miss Woodward is on her way to Marlowe Manor."

"I expected as much, if she was traveling in this direction in such inclement weather. I understand the marquess is having a very large gathering." She walked past him, the soft fabric of her dark green dress whispering against the floor. "But that fact would not send your sister into panicked flight."

"Miss Woodward is on her way to Marlowe Manor," he repeated before saying the repugnant words he must. "Her parents have high hopes of a match between her and Marlowe."

Lady Farraday's white brows lowered. "Now *that* is enough to upset Olivia. I told her she should have made her feelings known beyond these walls before now." Her right brow rose. "And it is enough to upset you, I would suspect, for you are not happy to have Miss Woodward intended for another man."

"Mother, I have but met the young woman. Don't be trying to make a match with her for me, too."

Now both brows were arched high, and he knew he had revealed something his mother had not expected. Going to a chair, she sat. "This is sure to complicate matters."

Hearing her echo his own words did nothing to ease Jason's consternation at the situation that he guessed was going to become even more confusing and complex before the Valentine's Day ball.

Chapter Five

Amaris paused, looking around herself. Was this the right passage? She climbed the stairs and walked along the corridor. When she did not reach her room, she knew she had made a wrong turn somewhere. That was no surprise, because she had been thinking of the strained meal in the breakfast parlor.

When she had come into the yellow room this morning, she could not have imagined what would happen. Lord Farraday had been helping himself from the covered platters on a mahogany sideboard. At the table, his mother had sat reading a newspaper.

"Come in, Miss Woodward," Lady Farraday had said with a smile as she lowered the newspaper. "I trust you slept well."

"Yes, and I wish to thank you again for your hospitality."

The older woman chuckled, the sound reminding Amaris of the viscount's laugh. "We are accustomed to inclement weather depositing unexpected guests here. Do help yourself to a hearty breakfast. It is a necessity during the winter, when the house's walls allow in every chilly draft."

Thanking the lady again, Amaris went toward the sideboard. She paused as she waited for Lord Farraday to complete his selection.

"We do not stand on ceremony at breakfast," he said as he handed her a plate. Lowering his voice, he added, "It would behoove you to try a bit of everything, so you do not insult Cook, who keeps an eye on all of us from yon door." He gestured with his left elbow.

Amaris glanced to her left and saw the door shift so she could not catch sight of the cook. "I believe most cooks consider such spying their prerogative," she whispered.

"Now you can understand why I was seeking a peaceful haven." He smiled and winked at her. She was taken aback at the bold action, but could not keep from smiling in return. Raising his voice to a normal volume, he said, "The chocolate pot is on the table. As I recall, you prefer that to coffee in the morning."

"Yes." She knew she should turn her attention to selecting her breakfast, but her gaze remained locked with his. Those golden eyes contained so many mysteries she would love to solve.

Love?

Amaris hastily looked away. She was letting her fanciful thoughts wander in the wrong direction. She hardly knew Lord Farraday. She was on her way to meet Lord Marlowe, who had her parents' approval. Lord Farraday wanted to be left alone to savor some quiet. She *knew* all that, so why were her thoughts going in dangerous directions?

She dug into the eggs, dropping more than she planned on her plate. She started to brush part of them back into the server, but, from the corner of her eye, saw the door to the kitchen open a bit wider. Turning so her body shielded the serving dish from the nosy cook, she put more than half of the scoop back. She hastily took a bit from each of the other dishes, wondering how she could manage to eat so much. Her plate was filled with meats and fish and mushrooms and bread. There was enough on it for several people.

Lady Farraday regarded the heaping plate without comment. She folded the newspaper and put it beside her own plate. To her son, she said, "It seems the storm has abated at long last."

"The cold should make the roads icy, but passable by midday," he replied as he poured a cup of steaming chocolate. Handing it to Amaris, he did not look at her. "At that time, Miss Woodward should be able to continue her interrupted journey."

"Not that you have been a burden," Lady Farraday hurried to say, with a reproving scowl at her son.

Before Amaris could reply, Lord Farraday chuckled. "Quite to the contrary. You have saved us the task of explaining to Cook yet again why we cannot consume all that she prepares each day."

"I don't usually . . ." Amaris paused, trying to gather her thoughts. "That is, I seldom eat this much. I did not realize how much . . . that is . . ."

"Eat what you wish," Lady Farraday said with a sympathetic smile.

Deciding doing as the lady suggested was the best course, Amaris bent to the task of taking a bite of each thing on the plate. The food was delicious, and she found she wanted more than a single bite of the sweet roll. She was reaching for her cup when she heard footsteps.

Lord Farraday and his mother exchanged a glance, one whose meaning she was not privy to. It must have to do with Miss Farraday, who was entering the room.

The viscount came to his feet and said, "Olivia, you are just in time. The food is still warm. Shall I pour you some chocolate?"

Olivia Farraday paused in the doorway and scowled at Amaris. "Excuse me," she said in a tone far icier than the wind beyond the walls. "I no longer have any appetite." She walked away.

Amaris stared, not sure what she had done to earn the

young woman's enmity. She started to push back her chair, but Lord Farraday motioned for her to stay where she was.

"I will speak with Olivia," he had said in a tone that matched his sister's. "Good morning, Mother, Miss Woodward." He walked out of the breakfast parlor.

Amaris had excused herself as quickly as she could, offering Lady Farraday some excuse about needing to tend to a matter in her room. Now she could not even find that room.

She went back to the top of the stairs she had climbed to on this floor and realized three corridors led off from it. All three were identical, with the same carpeting. A wide window at the far end of one told her it was not the corridor she sought, for she did not recall seeing the window before. She smiled wryly. She had been in so much awe of this house and its art yesterday that she would have failed to notice a pig lying in the middle of the floor.

Deciding to try the other corridor without a window, she walked along it. Only a few lamps were lit, and the passage grew duskier with each step. Most doors were open, and she looked in. If these were guest rooms, they appeared to be waiting for others to arrive.

She stopped when she reached the last door at the end of the corridor. Unlike the other doors, it was not solid wood. An etched glass panel with a design of a trio of ribbons was set into it. The room beyond was neither a sitting room nor a bedchamber. Tall windows at the far side of the generously sized room were covered with dark drapes. A white marble hearth glistened palely in the dim light.

She noticed all that before her gaze riveted on the pianoforte set in front of one window. It was a grand pianoforte made of burled maple. The painted side panels with the scene of a pair of cherubs could have been taken from the friezes downstairs. Gently curved legs matched the crescent of the main body.

She took a single step into the room, hesitating. Then she walked across the floor, drawn to the pianoforte as if a beam of light focused upon it. She pulled back the thick velvet drapes on one side of the closest window. Dust danced in the sunlight, but she paid it no mind as she drew out the bench.

Sitting, she stared at the closed lid. She was being bold—mayhap overly bold—to consider playing the pianoforte without permission. Yet the temptation to play was too great.

She jumped to her feet and went to the door, pulling it closed. If she played quietly, no one would be the wiser, and she would have a chance to exult in the music as she had not been able to let it enthrall her in more than a year. Not since her parents decided it was time for her to join the *ton* for the Season. She did not want to think about that now.

Slowly she sat and even more slowly she lifted the lid to see the black and white keys beneath it. The lid thudded against the front of the piano as she folded it back. She stiffened, but no one came storming into the room.

Her fingers trembled as she held them over the keys. She closed her eyes as they found the first notes of her favorite piece. When she missed a note, she laughed ruefully and began again, this time with her eyes open.

The music swirled around her like a living caress, each note as sweet as a beloved smile. Letting her fingers fly across the keys, finding the notes that had been imprisoned in her mind, she exulted in each bar.

As the piece came to an end, she barely paused before starting another, a Bach fugue as wild as the passion his music elicited within her. Into it she poured all her frustration. Her frustration with her parents, who were obsessed with doing what they believed was right for her; her frustration with the broken carriage and the ruined gown; her frustration with the events at breakfast. She did not understand why her life had had to change when she had been so happy. But she had been willing to do as her parents wished her to do . . . until she met Jason Farraday. What was it about the man that made her question everything she had assumed should be?

When she finished the last notes, her hands were not the only part of her trembling. The music echoed in the far corners of the room, and she knew her intention of playing softly had been for naught. Caught up in the music and the release of her captive emotions, she had let the piece thunder through the chamber as it was meant to do.

She reached to close the lid of the piano, but a broad hand halted her. With a gasp, she half turned on the bench as she exclaimed, "Lord Farraday! I did not hear you come in." She lowered her eyes, knowing she sounded foolish. How could she have heard his uneven steps when she had been pounding out the music? "How is your sister?"

"She is recovering from her temporary lapse in manners." He leaned toward her. "What were you playing?"

"I know I should have asked your permission to play, but I saw the pianoforte and I gave into the longing to play."

"What was that piece?"

Her gaze rose along the green-striped front of his waistcoat to his perfectly tied cravat and along his firm chin. Higher, it went past his lips and his strong nose to his eyes. Slowly and with little awkwardness, he knelt beside the bench, and her eyes remained locked with his.

"Amaris," he whispered, "what were you playing?"

"It was a Bach piece." She spoke as lowly as he, even as her heart thudded at the ease with which he spoke her name. As if he had practiced saying it often in his dreams.

"Which one?"

"Toccato and Fugue in D Minor. It is meant for an orchestra, but I love it even on the pianoforte."

"Piano."

She frowned. "Excuse me."

"Piano is the *à la modality* term among the Polite World now." He took her right hand in his, and a sensation as heady as the music surged through her. "It is amazing to think that these slim fingers can create such music."

Her frown became a smile. "I did not create it. Johann Sebastian Bach did. I simply attempted to play it."

"You play very well."

"I love to play the pianofor—the piano!"

"You must practice often to be so skilled."

She looked away, not wanting to share with him that her parents were so eager to connect the family's wealth with a revered title that they had decided finding a husband was a more suitable activity for her than music. Coming to her feet, she again reached for the lid. "I know I have ruined any attempts by you to enjoy some quiet. I am sorry if I disturbed you in whatever you were doing."

Once more, he halted her from lowering the top. "You did disturb me. You disturbed me so much that when I heard music being played with such fire, I had no choice but to come and see who was creating such music." Coming to his feet, he smiled. "Wait here."

He went to a music table that she had not noticed in front of the next window. Tossing back both sides of the draperies, he stood bathed in bright sunshine. She stared at his hair glistening with golden fire. The light cut through his lawn sleeves, revealing the muscles that she had felt pressed against her when she had helped him get away from the catnip at the inn.

He turned, and she hastily lowered her gaze to the keyboard. If he had seen her gawking at him, he showed no sign as he walked back to the piano. He excused himself for sitting while she was standing, then opened a piece of music and set it on the piano.

"This is something I heard only recently, Amaris. It is by Ludwig van Beethoven. Do you know anything about him?"

"I have heard of him," she said, wondering if she should speak to him as informally. It would be better to keep her focus on Beethoven. "But I have never heard his music. It is said to resemble angels singing."

"Angel song should be something that you experience for yourself." Jason stood and motioned for Amaris to take his place on the bench.

She regarded him as if he were mad. Mayhap he was, for he was using her given name right after attempting to calm his sister by reminding her that no announcement had come from Marlowe Manor about a match between Marlowe and Amaris. Yet speaking her given name was so effortless, while continuing to address her as "Miss Woodward" had become a task. Nothing was going as he planned. He had left Farraday Hall to seek quiet solitude. Instead of finding it, he had returned with a woman who upset his family even as she created powerful and loud music that suggested she possessed depths of passion he had not envisioned until he heard her play.

He watched as Amaris sat and picked up the music. Scanning it, her eyes widened. Her face was filled with joy and anticipation almost too private to share. He wondered if she would wear that expression in his arms.

She glanced at him again, then set the music in place. With hesitation at first, then more on tempo, her right hand played the repeating trio of notes as her left hand created a deep undercurrent to the melody. She paused at the bottom of the first page. He thought she might say something, but she started over, this time with the intensity he had heard when she had played the Bach piece.

The notes whirled around the room like two lovers caught in a wild waltz. Catching a motion from beyond the closed door, he saw others gathering on the far side of the door. He doubted if Amaris noticed the silhouettes as she lost herself in the melodies created by Beethoven's genius and her obviously instinctive understanding of his music.

When the last notes lingered for a breathless moment before fading into nothingness, Jason did not move or even dare to breathe. Amaris stared at the music before her, her fingers lowering to her lap. Her face was warm with color and her chest rose and fell with rapid breathing that suggested she had carried the piano by herself up the front stairs.

Curious and excited voices came from beyond the doors, and the soft pink on her cheeks became a fiery red. She jumped to her feet, reminding him of a frightened vixen when the hounds were giving chase.

He put his hand on her shoulder and said quietly, "Stay here while I send them on their way."

"Please forgive me if I disturbed Lady Farraday or Miss Farraday further—"

"Mother or Olivia would have come in to discover who was playing." He smiled. "I suspect you have given an impromptu concert for the household staff. Wait here."

Jason went to the door and opened it only wide enough to slip out. He closed it before anyone could see who else might be within. Waving aside questions, he dispersed the servants with the help of the housekeeper, who was arriving to discover where her staff had vanished.

"Don't scold them," he said when Mrs. Bowen frowned at the maids who had neglected their duties to listen. "They were lured here by a pied piper."

The lean woman looked puzzled, but nodded. As she walked away, herding the servants ahead of her, she glanced back more than once as if she expected him to explain more.

He went back into the music room and found Amaris running her fingers over the piano's lid as if she intended to pull music from the wood as well. With her skill, he would not have been surprised if she could.

She looked up, and his smile broadened. He said nothing when she stepped away from the piano with clear reluctance. As she crossed the room, he enjoyed the sight of her willowy motions. He would never be able to look at her again and not recall the fiery music. Drawing her hand within his arm, he placed his other hand atop hers.

"Does that piece have a name?" she asked as he led her out into the shadowed hall.

"It is called *Moonlight,* but I have heard it called *The Moonlight Sonata.*"

"Moonlight? It does sound like moonlight falling on a stream surging down a hill." The color returned to her cheeks, and he wondered why she was embarrassed to reveal that image to him. Before he could ask, she added, "The Bach piece is no longer my favorite. This one is. If you do not mind, I would like to play it again before I leave for Marlowe Manor."

He forced his smile to stay steady as she spoke with such ease of leaving. "Play it as often as you want, but on one condition."

"Condition?"

"Whenever you plan to play it, please let me know so I might listen."

Again her cheeks reddened, but this time with delight. "You flatter me, Lord—"

"Do call me Jason, for I have already overstepped the boundaries of propriety by calling you Amaris."

"As you wish."

"Are you always so compliant to others' wishes?"

She stopped in midstep and faced him. He said nothing, aware of the danger to any man who tried to delve the depths of those ebony eyes. Yet he was tempted as he had never been to take that risk.

He put his finger beneath her chin. Tipping it, he thought of his mouth on her skin, setting it and himself alight with ripples of pleasure. His fingers longed to brush against her hair, her skin, those incredible lips that were parting in an invitation to sample not only them but the smooth pleasures within her mouth. He longed to savor her slender curves through her gown and the beat of her heart pulsing like the yearning within him. To . . .

"Here you are!" called a deep voice.

Amaris pulled back, folding her arms in front of her, as she looked at two men striding toward them. The one at the rear was wearing the Farraday family livery, and he was doing his best to keep up with the other man, who was setting the pace. The man leading the way was shaking snow from a dark cloak that spread out behind him like a sail taking the full measure of the wind.

Beside her, Jason said something too low for her to hear past her pounding heart. She did not dare look at him because she doubted she could keep from putting her arms around his shoulders.

"I came as soon as I heard," the man in the cloak continued as he reached them. "I owe you a debt, Farraday, for seeing to Miss Woodward's welfare."

"Mine?" Her voice squeaked out in astonishment.

He stepped forward and took her hand, each motion as smooth and precise as a dancing master's. He threw back the hood of his cloak, revealing bright red hair and well-favored features. His dark blue eyes swept along her as he bowed over her hand. "Did you lose all your polish during your time on the Peninsula, Farraday? Do be a good host and introduce us."

Amaris looked at Jason, but he was watching the man who held her hand as he said, "Amaris, allow me to introduce you to your host for the upcoming Valentine's Day festivities. Raymond, Lord Marlowe."

Chapter Six

Amaris later was unsure what she said in reply to Jason's announcement. If she had not been so swept up in the fantasy of Jason kissing her, she would have recognized Lord Marlowe straightaway because of his bright red hair. He had not changed much from her childish memory, although he seemed much shorter. The top of his head was several inches below hers.

She was grateful that Jason filled her silence with conversation about the weather and Lord Marlowe's journey from Marlowe Manor. Trying to gather her thoughts and her composure, she had no chance before two more forms came toward them. This time both forms were female.

Corette rushed to Amaris's side, giving her a chiding frown. Tempted to tell her abigail that she had missed nothing about this first meeting with Lord Marlowe, Amaris kept her tongue between her teeth. Corette wrung her hands, but said nothing.

The second woman was Jason's sister. Her smile looked as forced as when she had come into the breakfast parlor earlier. Then she looked at the marquess, and Amaris could not miss how her expression softened.

Lord Marlowe returned Miss Farraday's warm smile. "Olivia, I had hoped to have a chance to hear for myself that you will be coming to the ball on St. Valentine's Day."

"I would not miss it." Miss Farraday held out her hand and, when he bowed over it, colored prettily.

That bright pink and her smile and the sparkle in her eyes were enough for Amaris to comprehend why Miss Farraday had looked daggers at her earlier. Miss Farraday had a *tendre* for Lord Marlowe.

Did her brother know? Glancing at Jason, she was not surprised to see him watching closely as Miss Farraday and the marquess laughed over some jest Amaris had not listened to. When he looked up at the ceiling, his mouth taut, she was certain he was aware of his sister's infatuation with Lord Marlowe. Had he invited Amaris here in an effort to put an end to that affection? She hoped not, for such an action would prove Jason was not the man she believed him to be. He *had* offered his carriage before he knew the marquess was acting as her escort to the ball. A gentleman, as always, he would not have reneged on that offer even after she revealed the truth.

"Miss Woodward, you were set upon by kittens?" asked Lord Marlowe, bringing her attention back to him. He was smiling broadly with an amusement that was not at her expense, but in commiseration.

She forced a smile, realizing that, while she was lost in her uneasy thoughts, Jason must have told the marquess how they met at the inn. "A trio of miscreants," she replied. Her voice was too flat, but nobody seemed to notice except Jason, who regarded her with a face devoid of any emotion. It could have been a mask worn to a masquerade, but even those possessed more feeling.

"But your misfortune became good fortune when you were able to continue on your journey with Farraday's help," the marquess said. "Now you will not miss the Valentine's Day ball."

"I am afraid I cannot attend."

"Not attend?" His green eyes almost popped from his skull. "But why not? We are not far from Marlowe Manor, and if the pleasant weather continues, the roads will soon be passable by carriage."

"The gown the kittens ruined was the one I had made for the ball." She held up her hands. "I have nothing else with me appropriate to wear to such a grand assembly."

Lord Marlowe smiled at Miss Farraday. "You must have something you can lend to her for the evening, Olivia, for you told me when I called last week that you were intending to go to Town for the upcoming Season."

"Me?" choked Miss Farraday.

Amaris could read Jason's sister's thoughts easily. She wanted to say that she had nothing for Amaris to wear, which would keep Amaris from attending the ball. At the same time, Miss Farraday yearned to win the marquess's good will . . . and much more.

"I am sure there is something here at Farraday Hall that can be redone for Miss Woodward," Jason said, adding when his sister scowled at him, "and Olivia will be glad to help in any way she can so the Valentine Day's ball does not start off on the wrong foot. Won't you, Olivia?"

"Yes," she said in the same clogged voice. Clearing her throat, she smiled. "Yes, of course I will be glad to help in any way I can." Her smile grew crisp as she looked at Amaris. "In every way."

Jason wondered how Marlowe could be such a widgeon that he had missed the anger Olivia aimed at Amaris. As he watched his sister lead Amaris along the corridor, he considered giving chase. Olivia seldom became so vexed, but when she did, anyone who had infuriated her would be wise to remain as far from her as possible. Poor Amaris might have no escape, and she would bear the brunt of Olivia's fury.

Or was avoiding that fury why Marlowe had made his suggestion? If he had been calling at Farraday Hall frequently enough so he addressed Olivia by her given name, Marlowe might be well-acquainted with her temper. Jason almost laughed at that thought. *He* was using Amaris's given name, and he had known her a short time.

"How about something to take the chill off the day?" Marlowe asked, rubbing his hands together. To warm them or in anticipation?

Jason frowned. Anticipating trouble that he had brewed himself was something Marlowe would have relished as a youngster. Mayhap the marquess had not changed as much as Jason had been led to believe.

Realizing he owed Marlowe an answer, he said, "There is some brandy in the small parlor."

"That should be exactly the thing to slice the chill from my bones."

"This way." He motioned toward the far end of the passage.

Marlowe prattled like a young miss as they walked to the gallery and the small parlor on its far side. He spoke about the weather and other such commonplaces as if they were of the greatest interest. Not once did he mention Amaris or the fact that he had discovered his prospective bride alone with another man.

"Do you mind?" Marlowe asked as he closed the door behind them.

"Not at all." Pouring two glasses of brandy from the decanter set on a table not far from the hearth, he handed one to Marlowe before sitting in his favorite chair. He gestured for Marlowe to take the one opposite.

The marquess stayed on his feet. He rocked the brandy, then took a deep drink. Wiping his mouth with the back of his hand, he said, "She is nothing as I expected."

"Amaris?" He saw no reason for the hypocrisy of returning to calling her Miss Woodward. "She explained she has not seen you since she was just a child. I would think you had expected some change in her."

"She seems quite withdrawn, nothing like her exuberant father."

Jason almost laughed at Marlowe's appraisal, for if the marquess had heard her play the piano or seen her high huffs when the kittens shredded her dress, he would have had to own how wrong his estimation was.

"I am certain she was overwhelmed with meeting you," he said, glad to fall back on cliches.

No need, he discovered, when Marlowe mused between sips of brandy, "I hope Olivia can find it in her kind heart to help Miss Woodward. Don't think that I am oblivious to the breadth of generosity I am asking of her. No young woman wishes to share an unworn gown with another in the weeks leading up to the Season." He tilted back the glass to empty it. "I would not ask it of any other woman, but Olivia is unlike other women."

Setting himself on his feet, Jason went to get the brandy. He refilled Marlowe's glass and set the remaining brandy on the table between his chair and where Marlowe still stood.

"In what way?" Jason asked.

"Pardon?" Marlowe's eyes were struggling to focus on him, and Jason wondered if his neighbor had been drinking before he rode out to Farraday Hall. A beef-headed thing to do on a cold day, but Marlowe may have believed he needed to bolster his courage before meeting Amaris.

"In what way is my sister unlike other women?"

Marlowe's smile returned. "You should be able to see that for yourself. She is lovely and spirited and intelligent. Unlike other young misses, she never changes her mind to avoid an argument."

"That is true." He set his glass on the table. "Marlowe, you sound like a man who has been struck by Cupid's arrow."

"I know." He started to drink. Then, sitting facing Jason,

he placed his glass next to the other one. "I was unaware of the impact until very recently."

"When you invited Amaris to the Valentine's Day ball?"

Marlowe scowled. "Any answer to that question would be to insult one lady or the other."

That lack of answer told Jason all he needed to know about the state of the marquess's heart, but there were other aspects of the situation that continued to puzzle him. "You could have avoided this quandary by not extending an invitation to Amaris."

"That was not an option."

"What do you mean?"

Marlowe rubbed the furrows between his brow and closed his eyes. He did not open them as he began to explain. It did not take Jason long to understand why.

Chapter Seven

Amaris pulled her cloak closer to her chin as she went out the nearest door and down into the wintry gardens. She needed to escape from the tension in the house. Lord Marlowe had thought he was handling a difficult situation by asking Miss Farraday to help Amaris find something to wear to the ball, but he had instead created a greater problem.

In Miss Farraday's lovely pale pink bedchamber, Jason's sister had sent her abigail for a selection of gowns. The young woman's icy voice had persuaded Amaris to accept the offer of the first dress she was shown, even though the style was one of the least flattering for her, especially with a wide ruffle added to the hem—anything to be done with the assistance Miss Farraday did not want to give.

She had found her way back to her own rooms, but only to face Corette, who was all on end about the tangled situation.

"You should have been happier to see Lord Marlowe. He rode through the cold to learn how you fared," Corette said as soon as Amaris entered and closed the door behind her.

"I appreciated his effort." She tossed the gown on the

bed. "He must have come as soon as he received word that I was here. I must remember to thank Ja—Lord Farraday."

Corette bent to straighten the dress. "You call our host by his given name?"

"He asked me to. I saw no reason to disoblige him on the matter." She turned away so her abigail could not see how her heart soared as she recalled how easy it was to speak that name.

Stepping around her so Amaris could not avoid her, the abigail wagged a finger at her. "Miss Woodward, you know what your father's wishes are for your future."

"I must wed at least a marquess."

"Lord Farraday is a viscount."

Amaris sat on the white brocade chaise longue and stared down at her clasped hands. "If you wish only to repeat facts I am well familiar with, then there is no need to continue this conversation. I know why I was invited to Lord Marlowe's ball."

"What opinion do you have of the marquess?"

"He is very kind."

"Is kindness all you want from a husband?"

She looked up, astonished. "Corette, what are you saying?"

"What you are thinking."

She came slowly to her feet. "That I want to be with someone who can touch my heart? Corette, I have spoken barely a score of words to Lord Marlowe."

"But you needed no more words than that with Lord Farraday, did you?"

"Which side of this argument are you taking?"

Corette put one hand on Amaris's shoulder. "Your parents sent me with you to watch out for your welfare during our journey. I have never wavered from fulfilling that task. You are facing a danger greater than any other. Four hearts are at risk, and, to own the truth, you must have the courage to do what is right."

"I know."

The tears that had filled her eyes then—tears of gratitude for Corette's understanding mixed with tears of sadness at the choice she knew she must make to do as her parents wished—blinded her now as Amaris trudged through the snow and slush.

Hearing voices from the direction of what she guessed was the kitchen, she went in the opposite direction. She reached some steps and hurried down into the water garden, swerving around the trees and the shrubs. She jumped over green stems that were poking bravely through the snow and slowed only when she reached a weathered boathouse by an ice-shrouded pool. Reaching out a tentative hand, she tried the latch on the door. It rose easily. No one was near. Here she could think in peace. She hoped she could devise a way to ease the strain in the house.

Opening the door, which protested loudly, she slipped inside. A narrow walkway edged the wall. Small boats rocked in the water, lapping the ice along the edge of the boards. Light seeped through a single window and the space between the double doors that opened onto the pond, but it could not reach far into the water. She took a deep breath of the thick air with its scents of mud.

Carefully she picked away across the warped boards, which were slippery in spots. When one creaked threateningly, she hurried to the next. It was the only sound other than her breathing. She sat on a bench beneath the window and stared at the sluggish waters.

She clasped her fingers in her lap and sighed. She had made a muddle of this. Now her mind was jammed with images of Jason's face as he laughed, as he frowned, as he had bent to kiss her cheek. Her skin recalled the brush of his breath and his fingers against it. She wanted more than just these few memories. She wanted to sample more of his tightly reined passion.

That was impossible. Her father had arranged for her to

come here to meet Lord Marlowe in the hopes of a match. *My daughter deserves to marry a duke or a marquess.* How many times had she heard him say that? She had never protested, because she wanted to make her father happy by giving him a connection to that title he longed for. Would a viscount's title satisfy him?

Her laugh was laced with sorrow. Why was she worrying about such a thing? Although she had seen the heat in his eyes when he looked at her, Jason had offered friendship, nothing more. His chaste salute at the inn was proof of that.

But he was going to kiss me in the music room! Her heart was sure of that, but she could not be sure of her heart now.

The bright sunshine dimmed, and Amaris glanced up at the multipaned window. It rose with a squeak.

"Jason, what are you doing here?" she gasped, glad that she had not voiced her concerns aloud as she was wont to do when she was distressed.

"Are you all right, Amaris?" Honest concern filled his voice. "I saw you taking off as if the devil was at your skirts."

"I am fine. I just came here to be alone."

She thought he was willing to grant her that privacy he had gone to the inn to find, because he moved away from the window. Instantly she wanted to call him back. He truly wanted to be alone. She truly did not. Then, as if he had heard her thoughts, the door opened. He walked in, closing the door behind him. The boards creaked beneath him, too.

"These really need to be replaced," he said as if to himself. "One of these days, someone is going to fall right in and—"

A sharp crack echoed against the low ceiling, and the water-worn plank gave way beneath him. She called a warning as he fought for balance. His arms windmilled wildly. She leaped toward him, but her fingers caught only air.

With a splash that sprayed her and the floor, he fell into the icy water. He was on his feet before the ripples had spread beyond the boats, spitting out muddy water and wiping it from his eyes and face. Groaning with disgust, he looked at his soaked and filthy clothes. He vented a furious curse, then raised his eyes to meet Amaris's.

She stood beside the broken board. She ignored how her dress was speckled from the water he had splashed. When he glowered at her, she pressed one hand over her mouth to restrain her laugh. He shook his hands and splattered mud on his own face. That was too funny. She could not keep from laughing.

"You think me being soaked by icy water is amusing?" he demanded as he affixed her with a fearsome scowl.

Amaris put her hands on her waist and surveyed him from the top of his dripping hair down over his cravat, which had become a dreary shade. She looked along his coat clinging to his waistcoat and down to where his legs disappeared into the swirling, brown water.

She laughed again. "To own the truth, yes, I find your predicament very amusing!"

Jason's hands covered hers on her waist. When her eyes widened and her mouth became round with astonishment, he tilted her toward him.

"What are you doing?" she cried.

"How about a swim for you?"

"No, Jason, no!" she pleaded as laughs still shook her. "You cannot do that!"

"I cannot?" His eyebrows arched as he began to pull her toward the water.

Her imagination offered up beguiling visions of being pressed to the muscles outlined by his soaked clothes. Even the chilled water within the boathouse would not be able to cool the heat that exploded through her at that thought. She had to put an end to his teasing while her reeling mind still could help her resist the temptation in his smile.

She wiggled, trying to escape him, then froze as she saw his eyes light with gold fire. Each motion was an enticement neither of them needed. She should not have allowed him to kiss even her cheek, for now she wanted to taste his skin.

"Please, don't," she whispered, not trusting her trembling voice further. "The water will ruin my dress!"

"I have already been the cause of one of your gowns being ruined. Why not another?" With a wicked chuckle, he jerked her forward. Her scream echoed in the low rafters and sent the birds there flapping out through openings in the roof. He caught her before she could fall into the water. When he cradled her in his arms, she wrapped her own around his neck.

Her eyes grew even wider when he said nothing. As his fingers stroked her leg, she quivered. She felt his breath catch in his chest, directly beneath her pounding heart. Her lips were in the perfect position to meet his. She could no longer refuse her longings. Reaching up, she brought his mouth down over hers.

She savored the warmth which burst from deep within her. Her conscience shouted that this kiss was wrong, so very wrong, when they could share no more than a flirtation. Her parents wanted her to wed Lord Marlowe. Yet she wanted this man to kiss her with sweet fervor. When his lips moved to explore her neck, she gasped as sensations she had never imagined, not even in her most daring fantasy, flooded her.

With a regretful sigh as he raised his mouth from hers, he carefully placed her back onto the unbroken floor and heaved himself out of the water. She paid no attention to his filthy breeches as he slipped his arm around her waist and tugged her to him again. If she was to be a fool, why not enjoy every bit of witlessness before she had to face the consequences? When her lips softened beneath his, his tongue learned the secrets of her warm mouth. At her gentle moan of delight, his arms tightened around her.

"Isn't this better than being alone?" he whispered against her ear.

"You are making it impossible to think as I had intended."

"There are times for thinking and times for not thinking." He tilted her face back and teased her lips with the tip of his tongue. "You are even more luscious than Mrs. Kettlewell's apple tart."

Amaris stepped back. How could she have surrendered to her craving for his spellbinding kisses? She had been sitting in the chilly boathouse considering the very complications such a kiss would create, and then she had quite literally tumbled into his arms.

"What is it?" he asked, bafflement stealing his smile.

"This has been a mistake. A terrible mistake."

Something flickered in his eyes. Agreement, or anger that she would speak so? She wished she could take back the words, but it was too late now.

As she saw him reach out to her again, she took another step away. The back of her slippers slipped on the edge of the icy flooring. She shrieked.

Jason caught her flailing hands, but he did not pull her back up to where she could stand. "Are you sure you do not want to go for a swim, Amaris?"

"Jason!" She struggled to stand upright, but he refused to let her recover her balance. Her eyes widened as her right shoe slid off the slick rim. She scrambled to set it back onto the board.

With a broad grin, he drawled, "Seems to me you need some help, Amaris. A white knight to come to your rescue."

"A truly chivalrous knight would not let me fall in!"

"Shall we strike a deal?" His eyes twinkled with merriment as he loosened his grip on her. When she gasped, he said, "If a man rescues a lovely lady from a horrible fate, she should be suitably grateful. What would you do to stay out of the water?"

She did not hesitate. "Anything, Jason. Just don't let me fall in."

His golden eyes filled with a fiery glow once more. In a

tone abruptly unlike his humorous one, he said, "Anything, Amaris? I do not think you truly mean that."

"Are you suggesting that I trade my virtue to you in exchange for being rescued?" She yelped as her slipper inched off the board again. "A true knight in shining armor would not tease me so. He would rescue me."

"Then I shall." He pulled her from the edge and into his arms.

Before she could thank him, he captured her mouth. His hand on her back kept his wet strength close to her as he leaned her back against his arm. Her fingers came up to tangle in his hair. The simple touch magnified her yearning into a torment that demanded to be eased.

But she must not!

Amaris put her hands against his wet waistcoat. For a moment, she doubted he would release her. For a moment, she hoped he would not.

Then he stepped back. His breath was ragged as hers was as he said, "We should not stay here."

"No." She did not move.

"Are you feeling better?"

"I believe so." She struggled to smile as she went to the door. "I do believe my equilibrium has returned. Thank you, Jason."

"Thank you? Are you suggesting I fell into the water to lighten your spirits?" He laughed, and she glanced back at where he stood. Somehow, even with mud freezing on his clothes, he possessed an allure she could not deny any longer. Yet somehow she must.

"Did you?" she asked, because she had to say something.

"My dear Miss Woodward, if I was going to fall for you, it would not be into that slimy pond." He twisted her to face him, his hands stroking her shoulders in a silent invitation to edge closer to him once more. "If I were to fall for you, Amaris, it would be in a totally different way."

For a second, her heart thudded within her, then she told herself not to be foolish. Nothing had changed, save for how much she longed for his kisses. She lowered her eyes.

"Amaris . . ."

She looked up at him, and his lips found her willing ones once more. She could not fight her own traitorous feelings, which stirred so deeply when he held her close. When he stepped closer, pressing her back against the wall, she savored the touch of him all along her. Her eyes closed and her lips turned up in a smile. His breath warmed her ear as his mouth sought to learn every curve.

His fingers touched her cheek softly. "Open your eyes, Amaris," he ordered in a muted whisper.

"No, I want to stay in this fantasy," she said as softly. "Let me believe this is truly possible."

He took her hands and held them up against his chest, drawing her to him once again. "Do you want to stay here longer?" Her heart soared again at the idea of staying with him at Farraday Hall, then crashed once more when he added, "Do you have more you need to think about?"

She opened her eyes, but stared past him. "Yes . . . no."

"Which is it?"

She met his eyes, falling into their brilliant fire. "I know what decision I must make, but it is a difficult one."

"Most decisions are."

"Was it difficult for you to decide to go into the army?"

He smiled, surprising her because he had not spoken of his experiences. "That decision was easy, which is why it should have been suspect. Making a decision based purely on emotion and with a complete disregard for logic seldom proves to lead one in the best direction."

The unwanted tears welled up in her eyes, and she blinked them away. He was correct. She knew it, but, even so, hearing him speak so threatened to shatter her heart.

"What has been difficult, Amaris, is deciding how to live with the consequences of that decision." He glanced down at his weakened leg. "It would be easy to stay away from everyone and pretend that quiet is all I want."

"Which is what you had hoped to find at the inn."

"Yes, but instead I found a lovely woman who made me begin to question if I was being a coward for not embracing life once more." He released her left hand and stroked her cheek with the back of his right one. "As I wanted to embrace her."

"Jason—"

He put his finger to her lips. "Let me finish."

She nodded.

"I can stay within the walls of my solitude, or I can be brave and dare to bell the cat."

"The cat?" She laughed in spite of the gravity of his words. "Must there always be cats and kittens as part of our conversations?"

"I suspect so." His finger traced warmth across her cheek. "And you must decide the same thing."

"I don't understand."

"Yes, you do." He cupped her chin and tilted her face toward him. "You must decide if you are going to do what you are told, just as you have always done, or if you are going to be brave enough to choose what you want. Are you willing to defy your parents' wishes?"

"About Lord Marlowe?" She lifted her chin off his hand and went to the door. Leaning her head against it, she ignored the drafts coming between the boards. "Your sister loves him, Jason."

"I know. I would say young Cupid has been busy in this parish."

She turned to face him. "Yes, because I love you."

"Which is very inconvenient for you."

"Yes." The tears bubbled at the edge of her eyes. "I had hoped for a different response from you."

"As I had hoped to have a response to the question I just posed to you."

"Am I willing to defy my parents' wish to have me marry the marquess?" So easily she could tell him yes, but she owed her parents a duty, too. They wished for her to be happy and well-settled. "They could not have known of your sister's state of heart when they arranged for me to come to Marlowe Manor." Her eyes widened, and two tears escaped. "But Lord Marlowe must have. How could he acquiesce when he knows of your sister's *tendre* for him?"

He wiped both tears away with a gentle fingertip. "He acquiesced because he was thinking of the business deal he wishes to arrange with your father. Only when you arrived, and he realized how difficult his swift decision was about to make the whole situation, did he think more clearly."

"I thought you said emotional decisions were the easy ones. That logic serves one well."

"In all but matters of love." He curved his hand along her cheek. "There is no logic in love, just as there is no quiet. The heart clamors for what it wants." He brushed his lips across hers. "And mine wants yours, so tell me, Amaris, will you defy your parents' wishes and wed a viscount?"

Chapter Eight

Flitting about the elegantly decorated room like a child on holiday, Corette warned Amaris not to forget her gloves, her fan, the necklace that she had brought to Marlowe Manor yesterday to wear for the ball. She readjusted the hastily tailored borrowed gown and made sure the wide ruffle at the bottom revealed no more than was proper. Amaris must look perfect for the Valentine's Day ball tonight.

"You have to smile tonight," Corette scolded as she had before. "Everyone will be expecting to see a delighted smile on your face when you enter the ballroom on Lord Marlowe's arm as his special guest."

Amaris heard a knock on the door. Already she could hear music from the ballroom on the floor below, and a steady procession of carriages and sleighs had been arriving at the manor since shortly after the first silvery fingers of daylight. While Corette had believed she was napping in order to be wide awake for the late festivities tonight, she had stood at the window for most of the afternoon. She had watched for the carriage from Farraday Hall, but she had not seen it.

Corette motioned for her to stay where she was. The abigail believed a guest of honor should not be seen before she made an entrance into the ballroom.

Hearing astonishment in her abigail's voice, Amaris went to the door.

"There must be a mistake," Corette was saying.

"This basket is to be delivered to Miss Woodward at exactly eight o'clock," replied a woman who wore a maid's dress. The chiming of a clock brought a satisfied smile to her face. "It is exactly eight o'clock." She held out a covered basket that shifted in her hands.

Amaris caught the basket before it could fall to the floor. Lifting off one side of the wooden cover, she gasped as a trio of kittens poked their heads out and mewed in exasperation at having been closed into the basket.

Three kittens. A gray tiger, a ginger-colored one, and a black kitten.

With a cry of dismay, Corette backed away. "Black cats bring bad luck."

"I don't agree," said Amaris as she cradled the basket close, sure the happiness she was feeling now was what her parents had always wanted for her. Even now, she could not believe that her father had made his next business deal with Lord Marlowe contingent on a marriage announcement. Dear Papa! He had been so certain that the man he admired so deeply would make her the very best husband. He had been wrong, something he had owned to in the letter that had arrived early this morning by an exhausted messenger. She sensed her mother's handiwork in the background because it was not Papa's way to say he had made a mistake.

She must not let herself be blinded as her father had been. She stepped past the smiling maid as a shadow moved in the dim corridor. Jason walked toward her. Every bit of her was focused on his smile as he held his hands out.

She placed the basket in them. "Our three miscreants?" she asked.

"The same ones." He closed the lid of the basket, bringing a new chorus of mewing. "I don't want them to wander off and get lost before they return to their new home at Farraday Hall."

"With them, you shall never have quiet again."

"A chance I am willing to take, although I shall forbid catnip being used within the Hall."

She laughed. "A rule I think your household will find easy to follow."

"I did not think it would take as long as it did to return to the inn." He set the basket on the floor and folded her hands between his. "Missing the ball was not something I would consider doing, so I brought them directly here. I left instructions to have them returned to Farraday Hall after they paid a call on you."

"Mayhap it was meant that they should be here. They were with us when we began this unexpected journey."

"So they should be with us if we announce our betrothal tonight?"

She gasped, "If? You have changed your mind?" Her senses spun with dismay. When she had accepted his offer of marriage in the boathouse, she had not guessed that he would reconsider.

"Never." He drew her into his arms and whispered against her hair, "But on my way up here, I saw Olivia. She reminded me of something she mentioned the night you arrived at Farraday Hall."

"And what is that?"

"That Gretna Green is not far from here."

A shiver of uncontrollable joy rippled through her. "Are you suggesting that we elope?"

"Some decisions should be made without considering anything but emotion." He chuckled. "The carriage is waiting. What do you say?"

"Lord Marlowe—"

"Is already in the carriage with Olivia. They want to be gone before anyone notices our host is missing. Decide quickly, Amaris, for I doubt they will wait much longer for us."

Saying yes was the easiest—and best—decision she ever would make.

A Tangle of Kittens

Valerie King

Chapter One

Bath, 1818

"My darling, my darling! You have come to me just as I asked!"

Anne Cassington stared at the handsome stranger, not understanding in the least why he was calling to her in such a romantic, familiar fashion. She even looked behind her to see if perhaps someone else was nearby, but the shrubberies along the lane were empty save for the flitting and chattering of several lively sparrows.

"I beg your pardon?" she queried politely.

The gentleman dismounted his horse in the easy manner of one who has ridden since childhood. Anne caught her breath, for when he did so she was nearly overcome by his presence, by the sheer athletic beauty of his person, let alone the striking appearance of his face. He was, she believed, the most handsome man she had ever seen.

Tying his horse to the nearby hedge, he then removed his hat and quite strangely flung it onto the ground. His hair, she could now see, was a glossy black and quite wavy in a very pleasing manner. His eyes were a cool gray, but there was nothing of coldness in his gaze. His jaw line angled strongly, giving him a powerful appearance that in turn was softened by the warm smile he bestowed upon her. His nose was quite perfection, being rather straight, and his lips seemed . . . kissable. Oh, dear, where had such an errant thought come from—except, of course, that he was bearing down on her with such intent in every feature.

"But, sir!" she cried, as he suddenly untied the ribbons of her bonnet.

"And to be shy of me as well and to call me 'sir'! You are the dearest girl! My darling, this is the very sweetest Valentine gift you could have given me, to meet me in the lane when you knew it was what I wished. I begin to think you are not so reserved as you seem."

Her bonnet flew back, his arms slipped tightly about her waist, and before she could protest again, his lips were on hers in a passionate kiss.

For a moment, Anne froze, unable to credit or understand in the least why the stranger was kissing her. Not that it was unpleasant, for indeed something inside her began to thrum with excitement. However, a brief moment's consideration set her to forcing her hands against his shoulders and drawing back.

"But, sir, I fear you do not . . . I mean you *should* not be kissing me. Indeed, you should not! I cannot understand . . ." she broke off as a look of deep hurt and disappointment slid into his eyes. She finished her statement with a sad little, "Oh."

She did not comprehend what was happening in the least or why she felt so sympathetic as she looked into the stranger's eyes, except that she *was* sympathetic. She felt she understood quite to perfection just how this gentleman was feeling.

"Then I was mistaken in you?" he asked quietly, his hold on her gentling.

Anne felt so odd of a sudden. She clasped his arms tightly. "So you desire to kiss me more than anything on earth?" she queried. "Is that what you are feeling?"

He searched her eyes. "You must know that I am. You must know how very much I love you. Have I not told you a thousand times?" The smile on his face grew so tender, so very sweet that her heart seemed to melt in her breast and tears touched her eyes.

She smiled faintly in return. "No, not a thousand," she returned. Of course, she was not speaking about the man still holding her in his arms, but of Freddy, her betrothed.

The stranger drew in a deep breath, "Perhaps not, but then you cannot have been listening to the desires of my heart, for I have wished to do so a thousand times, but there never seemed to be a proper occasion. But now that you have come to me, I am free to begin."

"So you are," she responded. Good God, she must have gone mad to be pretending to be whoever it was the stranger believed her to be. Yet to do otherwise when his eyes were full of such affection, such adoration was unthinkable.

She allowed him to kiss her again, only this time Anne gave herself completely to his embrace, slipping her arms about his neck and letting him have his way, if but for a brief few minutes. How warmly he assaulted her tender lips, how tightly he held her, how fully he gave expression to the love he felt, if not for her, then for the woman who had so completely won his heart. How much she wished she were that very woman!

He drew back and laughed suddenly, swung her in circles and kissed her a little more. She laughed with him, yet at the same time a very deep pain rose within her. This gentleman was not hers to engage in this manner. She was taking something precious that clearly belonged to another young woman. Besides, she was being wholly unfaithful to her dearest Freddy.

"Will you come to me tomorrow?" he asked. "You are very

different away from your house, just as I knew you would be."

Only then did Anne draw from his arms. "Sir, as I tried to explain before—but you seemed so very sad—I cannot be who you think I am. Although I must say for you to have been so mistaken in me, you might wish to be fitted with a pair of spectacles, for how you came to think I was—"

"My darling, what are you saying? I do not understand you in the least."

She felt he was so very confused that she ought to make a proper introduction. "You are under no small misapprehension, sir. My name is Anne Cassington. I am but recently arrived in Bath from Sussex and am presently residing in the Royal Crescent with my two sisters, my mother, and five very sweet little kittens. I am not, however, *your darling,* though I feel very wretched in telling you so when you have been so . . . so passionate with me."

He stood staring at her in utter astonishment. He frowned, he grimaced. He even stomped away from her for a moment before returning. "Mercy, what the devil is wrong with you? Why do you torment me in this reprehensible manner? Are you . . . that is . . . are you perchance . . . unwell?"

Anne laughed. Indeed, the whole circumstance was so bizarre that she suddenly wondered if she was mad or at the least perhaps dreaming. "No," she responded simply. "I am not in the smallest sense 'unwell.' I fear I am too sensible a creature to be insane, but my name is not Mercy. 'Tis Anne. Pray, will you not look very closely and determine for yourself just how you have mistaken me for your Mercy?" She turned her profile for him to view first one side of her face, then another. "Although it is clear I must resemble someone you love very much, and for that reason I think I also must beg your pardon for having allowed you to kiss me. I took sore advantage of you, I fear."

For the longest moment he continued to stare. "There is a

profound likeness," he said at last, awestruck, "but I see the difference now. You have the faintest cleft in your chin, and Mercy does not. Also, she has never worn her blond curls in such a sweet array on her forehead, but in all other respects, madame, you are the spitting image of my betrothed."

"Indeed?" she queried. "Do you know that yesterday, when I was walking in Brock Street, I had several persons greet me as though they had been long acquainted with me. Do I, indeed, resemble this lady so very much?"

"Enough to prompt me to accost you—only, Good God, Miss . . . er . . ." he groped for her name.

"Cassington. Anne Cassington," she supplied helpfully.

"Only, Miss Cassington, why on earth did you permit me to kiss you? I am completely astounded that you did so."

She leaned down and picked up her bonnet. "I cannot say precisely, except that I found myself understanding far more than I wished to why you appeared so sad when I was about to refuse your advances. And yet, there is something more. I cannot explain it, but I feel as though I know you, that I have known you for years. How is that possible?"

"I have known Miss Hencott—my betrothed—for several years." These words he spoke as if from a distance. He then gave himself a mental shake. "I shall importune you no further, Miss Cassington. Please, accept my apologies." He picked up his hat and brushed it off.

"Of course," she responded.

With that, he mounted his horse, wheeled about, and began trotting down the hill.

Anne was left for several minutes to try to comprehend what precisely had just happened.

Lord Marecham could not bring himself to pay his usual daily call upon his betrothed, Mercy Hencott. The encounter with Miss Anne Cassington had so affected him that he did not believe he could greet his bride-to-be with the smallest equanimity. He was persuaded that the passionate encounter with Miss Cassington might prompt him to do the unthinkable with Mercy—to accost her and kiss her senseless, something he knew quite well she would dislike immensely.

He sighed very deeply. The day before, he had begged Mercy to meet him in the lane just at this hour that he might have an opportunity to be with her in private. She was always in the company of her doting mother, a circumstance that was well in its way, but hardly one that allowed for a warmer exchange of affection and endearments than he was generally permitted. He had spoken to her at length of his need to be with her privately and, after blushing adorably at his hint, she had said she would make an effort to be the sort of lady he desired her to be. Such words had not given him great hope, but he had ventured forth this morning determined to encourage Mercy to be more natural and open with him.

What intervention of fate had occurred, therefore, to bring Miss Cassington to him at the appointed hour, a lady who resembled his betrothed so nearly that he had not hesitated in accosting her? Of course, when he had first seen her in the lane, he had been a little surprised that his bride-to-be had actually walked two miles out of her way, for she was not a very great walker. Regardless, he had experienced a profound flood of hope that his dearest Mercy was as anxious as he to be kissed, embraced, and loved.

Now, however, his hopes were dashed anew. He realized he had been deceiving himself about Mercy Hencott. She would no more meet him in the lane and allow him to kiss her than she would tie her garter in public.

There was nothing for it. He must face the inevitable and accept the truth—that he had been completely and utterly mistaken in his bride-to-be, that she would never be truly comfortable in his arms.

* * *

When Anne returned from her lengthy walk to Lansdown Hill, her mind was still sunk in a deep mist. Once inside the entrance of the elegant town house in the Royal Crescent, she untied her bonnet and without thinking dropped it on the black and white tiles. Her gloves followed.

She saw through the long hall leading to the back garden that her sisters were playing with the family's kittens. She began walking in their direction. The housekeeper, having arrived in the entrance hall, called after her. "Miss, is there something wrong with your bonnet?"

She turned and saw that her bonnet and gloves were lying in a heap on the floor. Had she left them there? How odd. She offered a shake of her head in response, but she could not see her precisely. No, her mind was still full of but one thing—the stranger's kiss.

As she turned to continue down the hall, she realized she had been dogged the entire distance down the hill and all the way to the Royal Crescent with the feel of the gentleman's lips upon hers. At first, when he had departed, she had been entirely stoic about the event, understanding that this was just a kiss that had occurred by mischance—he had mistaken her for someone else, a lady with whom he was deeply in love.

However, she had not completed a quarter of a mile of her return jaunt when her thoughts shifted to her betrothed, Lord Frederick Wooton. Though they had been attached to one another for several months, and had been betrothed for nearly three weeks now, Freddy had never kissed her, not even once. He believed, quite rightly so, she supposed, that all such displays should be reserved for the wedding night. He had said that anything else would be a serious blight on the perfection of their forthcoming union.

Oh, dear, what would he think had he known that she had given herself to the rather wild kisses of a perfect stranger?

Worse still, that she had been able to think of nothing else for the entire hour following?

As she opened the French door to the garden, she saw that the kittens had become tangled in a great deal of green yarn. At the sight of them, and of her sisters laughing nearly hysterically at their antics, the strange fog began to clear.

"Do but look, Anne!" Meg cried, lifting the orange-striped kitten, the only one of the litter of that color. The kitten's ears were flattened by several loops of yarn.

Anne could not keep from laughing as well, but she added quickly, "My dear, I do most strongly suggest you release them lest any begin to suffer unwittingly."

"Of course," Meg agreed readily and, cuddling the kitten in hand, she slowly unwrapped the yarn from about its head. She was ten years old, intelligent and quite mature for her age. She wore her long blond hair dangling nearly to her waist. She would one day be a beauty.

Kate, seventeen, began untangling the kittens as well. "We have been having so much fun with them," she cried, "you can have no notion!"

"But why are you out here when it is so cold?" she asked. The February sky above had grown cloudy and dark. "I do believe it may begin to rain soon. Are you not freezing, either of you?"

"Not by half!" Meg cried out gaily. She had untangled the orange kitten and placed him in the wooden crate that had been the litter's home since leaving Sussex a sennight past.

Mrs. Cassington had permitted the animals to attend the journey with the strict understanding that once arrived in Bath all three sisters would make an effort to see them placed, the sooner the better. Because a good mouser was always in demand, the task of securing good homes for the kittens did not seem an insurmountable problem for any of the ladies.

When the yarn had been removed safely from all the kittens, the ladies moved inside. Pelisses were shed and given to one of the maids. The kittens were taken to the drawing room, where a coal fire was keeping the chill off the room.

"Where should we begin in finding them homes?" Meg asked.

"We could go from door to door," Anne said, "although I must say I am not partial to the idea, since we are completely unknown in Bath."

"I know it may seem scandalous," Kate said, an impish smile on her face. "But I have been pondering the notion of taking the gray kitten in my muff to the Pump Room. It is one thing to say we have kittens available but quite another when a kitten purrs against one's shoulder."

"You are very right," Anne cried. "But I do not think it in the least proper to take a kitten into the Pump Room. Indeed, I would not be surprised were there a regulation against it."

"But the gray kitten is always so quiet," she returned, her blue eyes glittering with mischief. "I should not think it would be the smallest bother to anyone."

"I think not," Anne said quietly but firmly. She was eight years her sister's senior and more than once found it necessary to curb Kate's habitually high spirits. She was a lovely young lady with light brown hair, a heart-shaped face, and a perfect bow of a smile. In a year or more, when she entered Society more fully, she would undoubtedly break a great many hearts, an object Kate viewed with great pleasure.

When Mrs. Cassington descended the stairs and bid the girls prepare for their trip to the dressmaker's in Milsom Street, the kittens were given to one of the scullery maids and the subject was let drop.

Later that afternoon, Anne was seated before her writing table in her bedchamber when Kate scratched on the door begging entrance. Anne bid her enter and laughed outright. "Whatever are you doing with three ostrich feathers in your hair?"

"I thought I might wear these to your betrothal ball."

"Mama will never permit you to do so," she cried, even though she knew Kate was not in the least serious.

"There was another reason why I wore them just now, however," she said, closing the door behind her and venturing into the chamber.

"What would that be?" Anne asked, curious. She draped her elbow over the back of the chair upon which she was seated so that she could look at her sister.

Kate threw herself on the bed, reclining on her stomach and propping up her chin with her elbows. "Well," she said, blowing at one of the feathers that had fallen across her face, "I hoped to make you laugh."

"What ever do you mean?" Anne asked, surprised.

"Only that while we were at the dressmaker's, which I know to be one of your most favorite places in the entire world, you seemed out of spirits nearly the whole time. I wanted to say something then, but I did not wish to cause even the smallest reason for Mama to be concerned."

Anne was reminded that however feisty her sister's disposition, she was also quite perceptive.

"So what is ailing you?" Kate continued. "Are you ill?" She was smiling as she asked these questions.

"No,"Anne responded. "You can see that I am not."

"Then what is troubling you—and pray do not attempt to humbug me, for I can see that something is amiss. I promise I will say nothing to our sister or our mother."

"I know that I can always rely on your discretion, Kate, but I do not think I can speak of what is distressing me."

Kate blew the feather a second time then pushed it away with her hand. "Nonsense. You know you may say anything to me."

She regarded her sister pensively. "I have always thought it remarkably strange that you are so much younger than I. Somehow I feel as if scarcely a handful of months separates us in age."

"That is simple to explain," Kate returned. "I have followed your example in everything, or at least tried to."

"I never once put ink in the vicar's tea!" Anne cried.

Kate trilled her laughter and rolled onto her back. "Oh, dear me! That was one of my happiest days, for he gave the worst sermons in the world and we had relief that Sunday, for he would not preach with his teeth blackened as they were." She gave herself a shake and turned back on her stomach. "You might as well tell me what is troubling you. Otherwise, as you very well know, I shall plague the life out of you until you do."

Anne rolled her eyes. She settled her chin on her arm and, without giving it too much thought, told her sister what had happened to her earlier that morning when she had walked up Lansdown Hill.

Kate listened attentively, her eyes wide. She even gasped several times and at some point in the recounting, Anne heard her sister sigh deeply.

"He was very polite in the end. He mounted his horse and rode away."

"You are in love with him!" Kate exclaimed sitting up suddenly. "There can be no two opinions on that score!"

"No, no, indeed you are mistaken," she protested.

"Then how do you account for your having kissed him as you did?"

"I do not know."

"Then why do you think you are so incredibly saddened by the event?"

Anne shook her head. She did, indeed, feel very sad, but she simply did not understand why.

Kate continued, "I for one am grateful that this stranger has come to disrupt your life."

Anne sat up. "Why ever would you say such a thing?"

"Because now you will not marry Freddy."

"What?" Anne cried, greatly shocked.

"Surely you will not wed him now that you are in love with another man."

"I am not in love with him," Anne cried, aggravated.

"But are you in love with Freddy?" she asked.

"I do not see how you can ask me such a wretched question," Anne retorted. "Of course I am. I never should have accepted of his hand in marriage otherwise."

"No, I suppose you would not have, for that is not your character in the least. If you love Freddy, then why are you distressed? Are you feeling horribly guilty? Is that what is troubling you?"

Anne thought for a very long moment. Finally, she said, "Guilt does not have me in its grip in this moment. No, the larger question is, how could I profess to love Freddy yet take such sweet delight in the embraces of another man, even a stranger? I begin to think there is something terribly wrong with me. Now, why do you look like that? What are you thinking?"

"You have confided in me and I am honored, but I feel I must say this though you may be very angry with me—I do not believe Freddy can make you happy. I never have. Pray, do not protest. 'Tis not necessary and I shan't broach the subject again, I promise you, only I felt I must have my say. However, should you still choose to wed Frederick, you will never hear a single word of reproach from me."

With that, Kate rolled off the bed and landed on her feet. Offering a sad little smile, she quit the bedchamber.

Anne was left feeling so stunned that she remained draped over her chair for a very long time, indeed. The single question repeated itself through her head again and again. Could Freddy make her happy?

On the following morning, Lord and Lady Lankhurst as well as Lord Frederick came to call. Mrs. Cassington entertained the earl and his wife, asking them a great many questions about the house they had recently purchased near Bath and how the renovations were progressing. Lady Lankhurst spoke enthusiastically about Withyham Hall, in particular about all the decorations she had planned for the ballroom on Valentine's Eve. "We are sparing no expense for our son's betrothal ball, and a number of our friends are traveling great distances for the event."

Anne, desirous of having some of her present anxieties relieved concerning her forthcoming marriage to their son, soon drew him to the opposite end of the drawing room. She longed to speak with him privately, to engage him in a serious conversation in order to discover, if she could, what had so prompted her to give herself to another man in a kiss she could only describe as exceedingly passionate. However, he refused to discuss anything with her so long as his parents were nearby. She therefore waited impatiently for them to leave, for Freddy meant to stay behind, but the minutes passed like centuries.

Finally, the earl and his wife rose to take their leave and Anne found she had to struggle to restrain her enthusiasm at their departure.

At the same time, Mrs. Cassington and Kate suggested a trip to the Pump Room. Though she could see Freddy was about to agree and, that quite enthusiastically, she quickly intervened. "I fear I must decline, Mama. I . . . that is, I have the headache and wish only for Freddy's society this morning. I hope you are not too disappointed."

Mrs. Cassington shook her head, "Of course not, so long as you assure me you are otherwise perfectly well." She drew on her gloves as she spoke.

"I am."

Her mother drew close, kissed her cheek, and smiled warmly. She whispered, "I can recall having just such headaches when I was betrothed to your father."

The ladies left, though Kate cast Anne a penetrating glance just before quitting the house. Anne soon found herself quite purposefully alone with her betrothed. She sat down and patted the seat beside her. "Will you not join me?"

Freddy lifted a brow and intentionally took up a seat opposite her.

"Come," she called to him gaily, "will you not sit beside me? There is much I would say to you."

Freddy frowned. "I do not think it wise in the least." He then smiled softly. "I am far too tempted when I am so close to you."

For the next several minutes, Anne argued the point. She wanted desperately to have him near, perhaps even seduce him into a kiss. She had only one desire, to feel safe again in her affections for him, but Freddy was not to be moved. He even changed the subject and began pontificating on the state of the late mid-winter weather and did Anne think it would rain again today?

Sighing deeply, Anne finally gave up the fight. Even a desire for conversation deserted her. She rang for tea and was consoled only by the arrival of Margaret with her crate of kittens. She was glad for the diversion, since her thoughts had grown rather gloomy.

"I say," Freddy called out warmly. "Bring them to me. I told Mama of them and meant for her to have a look before she took her leave. Her favorite cat has disappeared and she was saying she might have one of yours, Meg, perhaps the gray one."

Margaret brought him the box. "I should be happy for Lady Lankhurst to have a kitten. I know she likes cats very much and would make a good home for one of them."

Frederick looked into the crate. Anne took up her seat once more, staring at the man she loved and feeling horribly desperate that Kate might be right. What if she was making a dreadful mistake in wedding him? If only she had been able to cull a kiss from him, perhaps then she could be more at ease. Perhaps then she could be assured that she loved him and he loved her.

"Where is the gray kitten?" Freddy asked.

A blush climbed Margaret's cheeks, and she glanced guiltily at Anne. "Oh, I forgot!" she cried.

Anne gasped. "Meg, tell me at once! Kate did not—" she exclaimed.

"Yes, she did, but all will be well!" Margaret cried.

"What did Kate do?" Freddy asked.

Anne shook her head and rolled her eyes. "She took the gray kitten to the Pump Room hoping to find a home for it."

Freddy appeared quite disappointed. "But I wanted the gray kitten for my mother," he said. "She is partial to gray."

Anne said, "I am certain we can sort this out when Kate returns, for I have very little expectation that she will find a home for it at the Pump Room."

In this, Anne proved correct. Within the hour, her mother and sister returned, with the kitten peering from Kate's muff.

Freddy immediately moved forward and took the kitten. "There you are! You will be happy to know, Miss Kate, that I have a home for this one."

"I am sorry," Kate said, appearing amazingly distressed, "but I have already promised this kitten to another—to a young lady in fact."

Anne realized by the tone of her sister's voice that something was amiss. Glancing from her mother to her sister and back again, she now knew something of some significance had happened at the Pump Room. "Have you been forbidden to return because you dared take a cat within?" she inquired.

Kate shook her head and stared at her. "Nothing so simple," she said.

Anne wondered if she had heard her correctly. "Whatever do you mean? And why does Mama appear as though she might swoon? Indeed, Mother, you should sit down. You look very unwell, indeed!"

At that she guided her parent to a chair.

Kate drew near and said, "Anne, you must prepare yourself, but the lady who desires to have this kitten is . . . your twin!"

Chapter Two

Anne stared at her sister and recalled how completely the stranger had mistaken her for his betrothed. "Then you have met Miss Hencott?"

"You know her name?" Mrs. Cassington asked, greatly shocked.

Anne instantly regretted having said as much, for she could hardly reveal to her mother and certainly not to Freddy the circumstances by which she had learned of Miss Hencott's existence.

"Er, yes," she replied hastily. "More than once I have been mistaken for her, and I finally asked the last person who erred in this way the name of the lady whom I resemble so very much."

"Yet you said nothing to me?" her mother asked.

Anne shrugged. "It seemed an unusual circumstance but, indeed, Mama, she cannot be my twin."

"Oh, but she is," Mrs. Cassington returned, her complexion growing paler still. "At least, there is a strong possibility she is."

Anne was stunned. She wanted to know precisely what her mother meant, but she could see that she was greatly overset. Instead of pelting her with all the questions that rose within her mind, she took her hand. "Mama, I can see that you are unwell. Shall I fetch you a glass of sherry?"

"Yes, if you please."

Anne brought her the sherry, then drew her chair close. As her mother sipped the fortified wine, she began to ponder for the first time that Miss Hencott might indeed be her sister, yet it seemed entirely incredible.

"Mama," she inquired softly when her mother's color had returned if but a trifle. "I beg you to tell me how it is possible I may have a twin. You have never mentioned before that I had a sister."

At that her mother's face grew pinched with pain. "Yes. But your sister was stolen from us, you see. I had you both in a basket at the bottom of the garden where there is a row of apricot trees. I fell asleep on a chaise longue nearby, but when I awoke, your sister was gone. You were both but a month old, so she could not have slipped unawares from the basket." Tears trickled down her cheeks and she laughed, if too brightly. "It was all so long ago yet these memories feel as though they occurred a half hour past. I never thought to see my daughter again, yet there she was today in the Pump Room. I was never more astounded in my life. I nearly embraced her, I was so excited. But to think . . . Elizabeth . . . alive!"

"Her name was Elizabeth?"

"We called her Beth." Her voice was so quiet.

"Mama, do have another sip of sherry."

Mrs. Cassington obeyed. "If only Henry were here. He was as devastated as I."

"Do I really have another sister?" Meg called out suddenly.

Kate turned to her. "So it would seem."

Freddy, holding the gray kitten now, said, "And there is another lady in England as beautiful as my Anne?"

Mrs. Cassington smiled. "Dear Frederick. How you warm my heart in saying so. The answer must be yes."

The next hour was spent in discussing the matter in depth, all the means which their father had employed in trying to discover the missing child, the pursuit of gypsies that had been encamped nearby but who had disappeared the same day, the fruitless appeals from market squares and church pulpits in a twenty mile radius of their home in Sussex.

"Only after six months," Mrs. Cassington said, "was the search relinquished. I broke my heart that day. I still cannot credit that it is true, or at least possible, that Miss Hencott may be my dear sweet little Beth."

She looked into Anne's eyes, the pain so deep that Anne immediately embraced her. After a moment, she drew back and asked, "But why did I never know of Beth?"

Mrs. Cassington said, "I could not bear the grief. I felt as though I were dying, very slowly. There was only one means by which I could continue—I refused to hear her name spoken aloud by anyone. I forbade the servants to speak of her, and to my great relief my friends and neighbors accommodated my suffering in the same way."

"And to think," Anne marveled, "that all these years I never once heard the smallest reference to her. I believe I may be more amazed at that than anything else, that gossip about Beth never reached my ears."

After the initial recollection of grief had been expressed, felt, and released anew, a different sensation began to permeate the drawing room, of renewal and hope.

Where Mrs. Cassington had been lethargic and depressed she now took to pacing the carpet. "If this is my Beth, my darling Beth, what shall I do? How do I approach her or the family? How do I learn the means by which they acquired my child?" Agitation and excitement replaced her prior sadness.

Anne began to smile. She had a sister, a twin! A new thought struck her so hard that she was suddenly, deeply ashamed. She had kissed her sister's betrothed! How horrible!

"We must make the acquaintance of the Hencott family as soon as possible," Mrs. Cassington said. "I must, I will write a letter even now!"

She quit the chamber on a run and left the sisters and Freddy to stare at one another in complete astonishment. They gathered about the crate of kittens, each expressing wonder at this extraordinary turn of events.

In the midst of the lively discussion that followed, Freddy suddenly announced, "I shall take the gray kitten. She is as sweet as anything and will suit Mama to perfection."

Kate laughed aloud. "Do think, Freddy, I already promised her to Anne's twin."

Freddy appeared affronted. "Do you not wish me to have her?"

Kate shook her head and laughed a little more. "But I have already promised Miss Hencott. You would not wish me to go back on my word, would you?"

"No, of course not."

The next two days were spent exclusively in an exchange of letters between Mrs. Hencott and Mrs. Cassington. Each letter both coming and going was read aloud to the family so that Anne knew precisely what was going forward at each stage of the correspondence.

At first, Mrs. Hencott expressed only complete disbelief and dismay but admitted that the date and times of the arrival of Mercy in her life were too coincidental to be ignored. She was adopted from an orphanage in Bristol, which had told her the baby was a foundling, left on the doorstep. She also revealed that over the past several days, Mercy had been experiencing strange encounters with friends and acquaintances who were very offended by having been ignored by her on recent previous occasions. She therefore understood that the likeness between the girls must be very great, indeed.

The very last letter was an invitation for the Cassington ladies to take tea at the Hencott home of Watersfield Lodge, located but two miles from Lansdown Hill. The day was set for Thursday and the hour for two o'clock. Freddy had been included in the invitation, since in a previous correspondence he had been introduced as Anne's betrothed. It had also been decided that Meg would bring the gray kitten to Miss Hencott.

The drive to the Hencott home some three miles in a northwesterly direction from Bath was a very quiet one. Scarcely any of the ladies were inclined to engage in conversation and even the gray kitten, snuggled deep within a basket that had been lined with a blue velvet cloth, was fast asleep. Anne was completely lost in thought, besides spending much of her time trying to settle her nerves. She had a sister, a twin, and she would meet her this very day.

Freddy was the only one who spoke, perhaps understandably so since he was not in any manner connected to Anne's twin. "I wonder if I could persuade Miss Hencott to exchange this gray one for another," he said, peeking into the basket that Meg held on her lap. "I do so wish for Mama to have this kitten. I know it would please her immensely."

All the ladies turned to look at him and his expression grew conscious. "I do beg your pardon," he murmured. "Was not thinking! Of course your concerns are far greater than my mother's loss of her gray cat." He seemed quite overset.

Anne patted his hand and would have held it in a light clasp had he not withdrawn with a disapproving shake of his head.

Anne withheld a sigh. Given the excitement of visiting 'Beth,' or at least the hopes that Miss Hencott would prove to be her sister, she had forgotten all about the stranger who had kissed her four days ago. Somehow Freddy's reluctance even to hold her hand brought the tall dark gentleman, Mercy's betrothed, strongly to mind.

She glanced at Freddy and tried very hard to recall just how it was she had tumbled in love with him. He was not in the usual style. His hair was a light brown and so very curly that he could manage it only by keeping it cropped short. His complexion was freckled, his nose straight, while his blue eyes were always in possession of a kind expression save for those moments when he was reproving her. He was a handsome man but in a very youthful way, quite different from the stranger whose dark looks and piercing gray eyes had seemed filled with power and something more that even in recollection seemed to rob Anne of her breath.

She supposed there could be no comparison between the men, yet she knew she loved Freddy. She valued his kind disposition. Though at times he might prove to be a trifle insensitive, still he never failed to apologize when he was in the wrong and certainly expressed a proper amount of remorse. He was highly attentive and called every day. He was intelligent, he was welcome in the drawing room of even the most fastidious hostesses, and in every proper respect was a gentleman.

With so many qualities of which Anne heartily approved, she could only wonder now that she had somehow grown disenchanted with him. Was it truly because he refused to caress her hand or embrace her or kiss her? She simply did not know.

At last arriving at Watersfield Lodge, Anne walked with her family to the drawing room situated down a long hall at the back of the house. Meg trailed behind, carrying the basket carefully lest the kitten be disturbed and awakened. The manor was rather small, but a large window revealed an expansive and beautifully tended garden that included a maze.

A moment more, and with her heart beating strongly in her breast, Anne saw her twin for the first time in five and twenty years. She gasped, for indeed, save for the faint cleft in her own chin and the lack of curls on the lady's forehead, she was gazing into a looking glass.

"Oh, my," Miss Hencott murmured, fingers pressed to her lips.

Mrs. Hencott moved forward at once, walking briskly toward Anne. She took both her hands in hers and squeezed them. "I vow I am looking at my daughter. Indeed, I am."

"There can be no mistake," Mr. Hencott called across the chamber, staring at Anne. "You are twins."

Anne glanced his direction. She saw a tall, somber gentleman whose expression was anxious. "How do you do, sir?"

His smile was faint as he bowed and murmured, "Very well, Miss Cassington."

"Of course, of course! Permit me to make the introductions," Mrs. Hencott cried. She proceeded with grace though her voice trembled at times and she appeared as one who could scarcely breathe. She moved to stand by her husband, who supported her with a hand beneath her elbow.

Mercy addressed Mrs. Cassington. There were tears in her eyes. "I was told I was an orphan. I often pretended my parents were still living and searching for me even though I had the best of homes. I believe it is not uncommon with those who do not know their ancestry. But here you are."

"My Beth," Mrs. Cassington whispered. She could not restrain herself a moment longer but gathered up the young woman in her arms. "I gave up hope so long ago, and now here you are."

Anne glanced at Mrs. Hencott and saw that she had turned and buried her face in her husband's shoulder. She thought she understood. She joined her mother and said, "But her name is no longer Beth, is it, mama? How do you do, Mercy? I am your sister, as is quite evident."

Mrs. Cassington released her lost daughter and, swiping at her tears, said, "Oh, yes, of course! You were my Beth for only a month. Now you are Mercy, and I am so happy to make your acquaintance. I hope you will forgive my excessive display of emotion."

Mercy, however was also weeping. "But it is like a dream,"

she said sweetly. "I have sisters. Mama, look! I have three sisters!" Mrs. Hencott, however, had begun to sob. Mercy crossed to her and embraced her fully. "Pray do not cry, Mama! You have not lost a daughter. Indeed, you have not! You will always be my mother. Always." By this time, even Frederick was dabbing at his eyes.

Several minutes were required for everyone to regain their composure, at which time Anne took her seat along with the rest of the company. Tea arrived and with it a calming spirit that gentled every overwrought nerve.

Mercy took up a seat beside Anne and, perhaps because they were twins, a quick and easy conversation ensued about preferences and dislikes, about fashion and music, about the city versus the country. Their tastes were very similar, a circumstance that brought laughter between them more than once. In only one aspect did Anne feel she differed from Mercy. She felt in her sister a restraint, a withholding that Anne did not generally engage in. She was open but not confiding, she smiled but not too broadly, she laughed but not too loudly. In most other respects they were so similar in thought and feeling to cause her to stare at Mercy in awe.

After a few minutes, Margaret moved to stand before Mercy. "You resemble Anne exactly save for your chin."

Mercy laughed softly. "So I apprehend. But come, sit beside me and tell me of yourself. I cannot credit I have a sister, beside my twin. Two sisters." She glanced at Kate as well, who smiled shyly at Mercy.

Meg then offered the basket. "I have brought the kitten. She has been sleeping for hours now, but when she awakes she will need a bowl of cream."

Mercy gave a small squeal and looked into the basket. "How very precious!" she cried. "And yes, she is still sleeping. Perhaps we should leave her in the basket until she awakes?"

Margaret agreed readily and took up a seat on Anne's left.

For the next hour, tea was enjoyed until the pot had been refilled twice. Conversation flowed and flowed again. Laughter reigned, accompanied more than once by a spate of tears, each time from someone different as the strange but wonderful reunion progressed.

The front knocker was heard. Mercy glanced at her mother. "That must be Marecham," she said.

By now, Anne was familiar with the name: Marecham, Mercy's betrothed, the dark stranger who had kissed her. However, hearing of him was one thing, but his presence was quite another. Her heart would not be still, but beat so strongly in her breast that she had to take deep breaths to remain calm.

She was seated in the corner adjacent to the entrance so that she would most certainly see him before he saw her. For that, she was grateful.

A moment more and his firm tread could be heard approaching the drawing room. A second more and he was there, the maid introducing him, "Lord Marecham, ma'am." The servant was gone and the stranger, though no longer so, entered the chamber.

How exceedingly grateful Anne was that he did not meet her gaze immediately. Instead, he made his bows as everyone rose to be introduced and to offer civil bows and curtsies in return.

She had remembered him, yet she had not. She had not thought he was so very tall, and next to Freddy his shoulders were twice the breadth of her betrothed's. His eyes were darker in the chamber than they had been in the dull February light of the lane leading to Lansdown Hill.

Suddenly, her name was being made known to him and he looked at her. His gaze met and held. She tried to draw in a deep breath but it was as though the air had been stolen from her chest. She dropped her small curtsy and bowed her head, but she felt as though she might faint.

"Incredible," he said from across the room. "The very likeness, indeed. There can be no two opinions that you are twins."

"No, my lord," she said, wondering from whence she had found the ability to speak.

He smiled, his eyes warming immeasurably. "I am very happy to make your acquaintance, Miss Cassington."

Anne saw the knowing look and felt her heart give way in the strangest manner as though, again, she had known him for years instead of a handful of days.

His gaze moved past her, as Kate, Meg, and Freddy were introduced to him as well.

After a few polite exchanges occurred, Kate addressed Mrs. Hencott. "I see that you have a beautiful garden. I wonder if we might explore it a little. I do so love a garden. Even in February it is a sight to behold. I only hope I may see it in midsummer, when I can only imagine that it must be exquisite."

Mrs. Hencott's eyes brightened, though they were still a little red-rimmed. "I should like nothing better." She rose to her feet and turned and pointed toward the windows. "You can see there, Miss Kate, through the arch at the bottom of the garden a rather extensive maze. However, what cannot be seen is that beyond the maze is a meandering walkway leading through several garden rooms, all of which I believe you will enjoy very much."

Kate waited for no further encouragement. Meg was on her feet as well, but handed the basket to Mercy. For the first time, the kitten began to mew. "Will you come, Mercy?" she asked.

Mercy smiled but shook her head. "You can see that my new little charge has just awakened and, as you said before, she will be wanting her cream."

Kate turned to Anne. "And will you come?"

"I should like nothing better," she responded, rising to her feet. "Freddy, will you join us? For I, too, am unable to resist such a lovely garden."

Freddy winked at her. "I believe I shall remain indoors, if you do not object." He inclined his head slightly to Mercy, and Anne understood that he meant to negotiate for the kitten. Only with the barest restraint did she keep from rolling her eyes. She felt his timing was perfectly wretched.

Glancing at Lord Marecham, she felt obligated by a sense of propriety to extend the invitation to him. "And would you care to join us, my lord? You are undoubtedly quite familiar with Mrs. Hencott's maze, and if we become lost I daresay you will be able to provide us with the key."

He rose to his feet. "I should be delighted." He turned to his betrothed. "Unless, of course, you have need of me, my dear?"

Mercy glanced briefly at him. "No, not in the least. Pray, do show my new sisters the maze." Since her attention reverted instantly to Freddy, who had already begun to explain about his mother's recent loss, Lord Marecham was free to join the ladies.

Once warm pelisses and bonnets had been donned against the chilly February weather, the small party ventured into Mrs. Hencott's backyard.

Before long, Kate and Meg were running in the direction of the maze, each of them intent on solving the puzzle first. Anne found herself quite alone with the man who had kissed her four days past.

"So you are Marecham," she said, her hands slung behind her back as they walked in the direction of the maze.

"Precisely so. I hardly know what to say to you except perhaps to offer another apology for having importuned you on Monday."

"As to that, if we are to offer apologies, then I must beg you to forgive me for having entered into the kiss so . . . obligingly."

He chuckled. "A very mild word, *obligingly*. I think I should have described the experience a great deal differently."

"I try not to think on it overly much."

"I find myself thinking of scarcely anything else."

She glanced up at him and felt her cheeks grow warm. She wondered if he knew her thoughts, which equaled his precisely. She also had pondered the shared kiss times out of mind, wondering what to make of it, if anything. This, however, she did not say to him.

By now they had reached the bare rose arbor leading to the maze and passed through. Anne fell silent, as much lost in thought as not knowing precisely what to say to the stranger walking beside her. From somewhere in the maze, she could hear her sisters laughing and calling to one another.

"Mrs. Hencott mentioned several garden rooms beyond. I should like to see them."

"They are delightful even at this time of year. In mid summer, when the trees and hedges are fully leafed and the flowers in blossom, I must say there is a certain enchantment to the arrangement as a whole."

The rooms led from one to the next in a horseshoe shape, from archway to archway, where benches were found for seating, and with a different theme for each room.

"Thus far, this is my favorite," Anne said, glancing about her. "The third room, correct?"

"I believe so."

A shallow pool sat in the center of the room, a birdbath emerging from the middle, though iced over in February. "I imagine a dozen birds cluster here at once in the summer, all vying for the best perch."

"They do," he answered cheerfully, "particularly the sparrows. A very noisy bird, especially in the mating season."

Anne laughed. "So they are."

Passing into the next room, where there was a bench that faced the west and the descending sun, Marecham asked if she wished to sit down.

"I do," she answered and seated herself readily.

He did not join her but rather moved several feet away and turned to look at her. "The resemblance is perfect," he said, then smiled. "Except for the chin."

She touched her chin. "I was never more shocked when I saw Miss Hencott, that is, Mercy, for the first time. Truly, I thought I was regarding myself in a mirror. I can certainly understand now how you mistook me for her."

"I should have known better," he said, chuckling. "My betrothed would neither have walked so far nor would she have permitted such a . . . *familiarity.*"

"But you are betrothed," Anne countered. "Surely—" She broke off. The subject was quite improper. "Forgive me. I have no right nor ought I to say a word on the subject."

He regarded her with a soft smile. "You are just as I imagined you would be, as ready to speak of kissing as you were willing to engage in it."

"My lord, if you mean to make me blush, I vow you will very soon succeed!"

"It is not my intention to make you uncomfortable. However, let me say that I find this aspect of your disposition quite refreshing."

"What? My undecorous and even improper conversation and conduct?"

His smile broadened. "Precisely so."

"You are being ridiculous. Mercy is far more proper than I. She has a reticence that I do not, though perhaps I should. Perhaps I ought to be more guarded generally, in my thoughts, ideas and feelings."

"No," he responded firmly, moving back to her and this time sitting down beside her. "No, you should be just as you are. In truth, though I admire Mercy very much, I confess I would like it a great deal more were she less reserved—at least with me." He shook his head. "But I should not be saying this to you."

"No, indeed you should not. You should be saying as

much to your bride-to-be. I am persuaded were you to make your sentiments known, she would make an effort to speak her mind and feelings more readily."

"Do you think so, indeed?" he inquired, meeting her gaze rather forcefully.

Anne wished he would look anywhere but at her, for there was something about the expression in his gray eyes that tended to pierce her heart in the most pleasing manner. She didn't answer for a very long moment but continued to look at him. Her thoughts quite naturally flew back to being held in his arms and kissed by him earlier that week. She felt as though she were back in the lane with him, her bonnet on the ground, his arms tightly about her.

But this would not do! She gave herself a mental shake and queried, "What was it you were asking?"

He smiled again. "Whether or not my speaking with Mercy about her reticence would be of the smallest use."

She shrugged. "I once spoke to Frederick about . . . well, about a matter of significance to me and I received a rather strong lecture for my efforts. That is not to say that Mercy would give you a dressing-down. Oh, never mind. I do not know my twin at all to be able to advise you."

"Anne," he said softly.

Her heart leaped again. "Yes?"

He had turned toward her and she shifted to better see him as well. A breeze blew through the garden room, and a wisp of her blond hair crossed her cheek. He caught it with his finger and slid it away from her face. "What was it you asked of your betrothed?"

She felt very weak, indeed, and most certainly believed she should not reveal something so personal, yet the words tumbled out. "I asked him to kiss me, but he felt he should not, that to do so would be to cast a pall over the wedding night. Are you of a similar mind?"

There was something so gentle in the flow between them in this moment, so sweet and yet sensual, that Anne was caught, wholly and completely. She waited for his answer.

"You must already know that I am not," he murmured softly. "Not by half, though I have been made to feel that I was in the wrong. Tell me, is that why you allowed me to kiss you?"

She shook her head. "Only in part. You seemed so sad that day, but now I believe I understand."

"I was very sad," he confessed. His gaze fell to her lips and very slowly he leaned toward her.

She felt very odd suddenly, excited and fearful all at the same time. Oh, dear, was it possible he meant to kiss her again?

Chapter Three

His lips were suddenly on hers again, as though he was taking once more what Mercy would not give him. This time there was less passion and in its stead a tenderness that worked horridly at her heartstrings. At the same time, it seemed to her the most natural occurrence in the world that he would kiss her.

After a moment, he drew back. "Thank you," he said, a slight frown between his brows.

She blinked several times. "You have bewitched me," she said, laughing. "Twice now, merely with a few words and a stare, you kiss me without the smallest protestation falling from my lips. How is that possible, particularly when it is so very wrong?"

"You shall not make me regret what I just did, though you reproach me for an hour, so do not waste a single breath in such an effort. I shall not do so again, however. I merely wanted . . . but that hardly signifies. Instead, will you tell me of yourself and your family?"

Anne was surprised by the question. After such a kiss, she had supposed awkwardness would follow. Instead, he seemed more relaxed than ever.

"You truly wish to know more of myself and my family?"

"Very much so," he responded sincerely.

"Let us walk, then," she said, gaining her feet. Once in motion, she gave an account of her life in Sussex as a Cassington, how much she treasured her mother and missed her father, who had died the twelvemonth prior, how she played the pianoforte tolerably but the harp quite ill, how she preferred the French language to German, and how besides having come to Bath for a betrothal party on Valentine's Eve, she and her sisters also needed to place five lovely kittens in good homes.

"Ah, yes, and Mercy has bespoken the gray one."

"Indeed, she has, but Frederick desires the same kitten for his mother, so I have every confidence he has spent this half hour past attempting to cajole your bride-to-be into exchanging the gray one for another. This leads me to ask whether or not you have need of a cat, a good mouser to keep down the population of rodents in your town house?" She had learned from the exchange of letters between her mother and Mrs. Cassington that Lord Marecham had taken a town house in the Circus for the winter months in order to be near Mercy.

"A kitten, you say? I shall have to consult with my housekeeper. I am only leasing the house at present, so I tend to think not."

"Do you like cats?" she asked.

He smiled. "I have a great fondness for them." He glanced at her. "But now I see I have surprised you. Why would that be?"

"It has been my experience that most gentlemen do not favor them in the slightest, having a strong preference for their horses and dogs."

He seemed to consider the subject for a moment. "As to that," he began, "I do believe you may be right. However, I had a cat once that actually loved my two best dogs. He was a large gray old thing, as tough as leather. He even played with them, grabbing hold of their ears with his paws but never sinking his claws too deep."

"And did your dogs ever tire of him?"

He laughed. "I do believe the affection was mutual. All three would curl up on the hearth together."

"And it was a large gray cat, you say?"

"Yes," he said.

"Much like the one that Freddy and Mercy are vying for. Do you still have any of these pets?"

He shook his head. "No, not one, for that was many years ago, indeed. When I was a boy."

She could see he thought of them with fondness.

"This is a good beginning, I think," she said cheerfully. "For if we continue in this manner we can be easy in one another's company. Pray tell me of your youth, of your interests and your present concerns. I have spoken openly and expect nothing less from you."

The next half hour was whiled away as they walked through the remainder of the garden rooms. Lord Marecham 'opened his budget,' as her father was used to say. He spoke easily about his past. He had lost his father and mother in recent years, but enjoyed an excellent rapport with his five siblings, three of whom were wed with growing families and all of whom lived in relatively close proximity to his home county of Derbyshire.

"My youngest sister still resides at Challow Park and will be enjoying her first Season this spring."

"Always an exciting event for a young lady." She noted his frown. "Would you not agree, or is it possible your sister is not as enthusiastic about going to London as you would wish her to be?"

"On the contrary," he said, his smile affectionate. "Georgianna's enthusiasm can hardly be contained. If I seemed concerned, it was for the reason that I recalled something Mercy had said to me but recently, that she did not see the need for young ladies to be much in London and that a fortnight would suffice. In truth, since we shall be married within the month, I foresee a conflict. But then, perhaps I am being too anxious about the future."

"As to that, I cannot say," she responded. "I tend to fret a great deal more than I should, so it would seem we share the same malady."

He chuckled.

By now they had exited the garden rooms and were met by Meg, who came running up. "I reached the center first!" she exclaimed.

"Well done!" Anne said.

Kate, looking a great deal younger than her seventeen years, was very near to pouting. "So she did, but I returned through the maze more quickly."

"Then you are both to be congratulated," Lord Marecham said tactfully.

With that the younger siblings merely pulled faces at one another.

Anne suggested they return to the house. "For it is very likely Mama will be desirous of taking her leave."

With that, the party turned in the direction of the house.

Only as Anne actually entered the drawing room and saw her betrothed did she suddenly become painfully aware of the fact that she had again kissed Lord Marecham. Even though this last expression was quite friendly in its way and had not been nearly so passionate as their first encounter, she could not help but think how horrified her quite proper husband-to-be would feel should he know her perfidy.

Worse still, she had betrayed her new sister in having permitted the kiss. Rather than let these thoughts bring a fiery blush to her cheeks, however, she repressed them with a promise to herself that she would never allow Lord Marecham to kiss her again. Not that he ever intended to, just as he said, but she would be on her guard nevertheless.

She forced a smile and entered the chamber saying, "Your garden is quite charming, Mrs. Hencott. I only hope I might see it in full bloom this summer."

"I see no reason why you will not, since it has been agreed upon"—and here she regarded Anne's mother warmly—"that your family will enjoy a sennight's visit this July."

Anne glanced at both Mercy and her mother and felt her heart swell. "What an excellent notion," she cried. "I could think of nothing better."

"Nor I," Mercy said. She rose suddenly to her feet and for some reason appeared a little conscious. "You must forgive me, sister," she added smiling, "for I believe I have commanded the attention of Lord Frederick this hour and more. I do beg your pardon."

"What nonsense is this?" she cried. "I am only glad you had the opportunity to come to know him better. Only tell me, has it been agreed upon who shall get the gray kitten?"

At that, Mr. Hencott laughed loudly. "Of course not! I fear these two"—he threw an arm toward Lord Frederick and his daughter—"are both of such compliant dispositions that neither is willing to accept the cat now."

"Indeed, is this true?" Anne asked, laughing as she turned back to her betrothed.

"I fear it is so," Freddy said, wrinkling his nose. "I believe there is only one thing that can be done—Miss Hencott must see the rest of the kittens for herself."

"You will love them all!" Meg cried. "Perhaps you will want more than one!"

"No," Mercy's parents cried in unison.

"Are you free to visit us tomorrow?" Anne asked. "Then we might have a chance to converse a little more."

Mercy turned to Freddy. "Will you be there as well?" she queried. "I should like to know your opinions about each of them."

"Of course, for I know the kittens as well as anyone."

"Then you may guide my selection," she said. Turning to

Marecham, she smiled sweetly upon him. "Will you be so obliging as to accompany me, Marecham?"

Anne's heart did a small leap in waiting for his response. Though a vile wave of guilt passed over her for even thinking the thought, she believed nothing would please her more than to see him again.

"Yes, of course, if it gives you pleasure."

He chanced for the barest moment to meet Anne's gaze, and a shiver raced down her side. Did she see interest in his eyes as well, this man who had now kissed her twice?

The next morning, Anne sat beside Lord Marecham.

"So you are to be married in a month's time?" he asked.

Anne glanced at Mercy, who was presently looking over all the kittens, holding each one under the close supervision and instruction of Freddy and Margaret. Rain had pelted Bath the entire morning and she had not expected her sister, let alone Marecham, to make the journey when the weather was being so difficult. Yet here they were, and she did not know whether to be overjoyed or distressed. Her feelings seemed to move between the two extremes.

"We are to be wed the first Sunday in March, in Sussex," she replied.

"And your betrothal ball is on Valentine's Eve?"

"Yes."

"That is very romantic," he said, a soft smile on his lips.

A crack of thunder split the air above the Royal Crescent and she jumped in her seat, nearly spilling her tea—not for the first time. "I cannot believe the severity of this storm. And to think you ventured forth even when it had already begun to rain." Anne had several reasons to be on edge this morning, but the violence of the storm overhead made everything worse. For one thing she had thought of little more than the kiss she had shared with Marecham on the day before. For another, the guilt she was experiencing where her twin and Freddy were concerned nearly gave her the headache.

"Mercy was intent on coming," he said, also sipping his tea. "However, I am rarely bothered by such a display as this." In proof, another loud charge of thunder merely caused him to smile and continue sipping his tea.

"Regardless, I certainly hope you will both stay to nuncheon." She turned slightly in the direction of the kittens. "Would that be agreeable to you, Mercy? Will you join us for nuncheon?"

At that moment, Mrs. Cassington entered the chamber with Kate in tow. "Indeed, we should like it above all things, and I certainly could not countenance your leaving until the storm has abated a little."

Another flash of lightning and quick snap of thunder caused more than one of the ladies to squeal and jump.

"I have nearly spilled my tea three times now!" Anne cried, settling cup and saucer on the table at her elbow.

Mercy, cuddling the orange-striped kitten, addressed Mrs. Cassington. "I should like it above all things. To own the truth, even though we have been here above two hours now, I was dreading taking my leave and not because of the storm. I cannot remember when I have spent such an enjoyable morning."

"Nor can I," Freddy returned, meeting Mercy's gaze quite sweetly.

Meg held the black and white kitten aloft. "Try this one, Anne—I mean, *Mercy!*" She giggled at her mistake. "He is my second favorite. The moment you put him on your shoulder, he begins to purr."

Mercy obligingly traded kittens with Meg. "So he does," she cried. "Imagine that."

Meg beamed.

Anne turned back to Marecham. "It is settled then? You will dine with us?"

"Aye, nuncheon it shall be."

Anne did not know what to think about her odd relationship with Lord Marecham. From the time of his arrival, she had been engaged in a conversation with him that had begun yesterday in the various garden rooms at Watersfield Lodge and which seemed capable of continuing forever. There did not seem to be a lack of subject, and once even Freddy left his post beside Mercy and the kittens to inquire of what they were speaking so enthusiastically.

Anne had been laughing and with a broad smile, said, "I was telling Marecham of some of the smuggler's tales I knew from having been in Brighton summer last. You remember, Freddy, that at Mrs. Wittenham's fete, the very grand lady living on The Steyne, we were told the champagne was from French contraband."

At that, Freddy lifted a brow. "And if you remember, dearest, I was not pleased to hear of it."

Anne had forgotten about his views on the matter entirely and quickly begged pardon. "I suppose we should not be laughing."

"No, I think not."

Mercy had called to him, asking his opinion about the disposition of the black kitten, and he resumed his place by the wooden crate and Meg. Anne had felt relieved not to be required to show a proper amount of remorse to her betrothed and was afraid to meet Marecham's gaze for fear he would set her to laughing again.

He had leaned close and whispered, "You are very bad, indeed, to be speaking so about smugglers!"

She had pinched her lips together tightly to keep from laughing and had glared at him in response. Finally, when she had command of herself, she said, "Lord Frederick has very fixed opinions on a variety of subjects."

"All of which I suppose you are required to treat with the utmost respect."

She did not know what had prompted her to do so, but she had sighed and said, "Precisely so." She had tried to recover from revealing to Marecham one of the trials of her relationship with Freddy, but he would not allow it.

Instead, he had regarded her quite sympathetically. "Pray do not attempt to dissemble with me," he said in a low voice, "or to pretend it is otherwise with you and Lord Frederick. You have shown me your heart, and no words now can possibly alter that."

As they walked in to nuncheon together, still talking as though they had been great friends separated for years, Anne forgot all about Freddy and Mercy. Only as they arrived at the table did she become aware of what she was doing, and then only because her mother had given her a rather piercing stare.

She immediately said, "Mercy, I do beg your pardon. I am being uncivil."

Mercy, however, had been entirely engrossed by something Freddy was saying to her. At being addressed she turned to Anne. "I beg your pardon?" she queried. "I fear I was not listening."

Anne was a little surprised. She glanced at Freddy, but he was bringing Meg forward. She wondered what it was her betrothed had been saying to Mercy to have so captivated her attention. When everyone was seated, her twin enlightened the entire table.

"Freddy was just telling me the most interesting news, that there is to be a canal built across the northernmost reaches of Withyham Hall."

Anne nearly yawned at the introduction of the subject. Freddy loved to speak of the canal and any like project so much so that she often found her mind wandering the moment a word like bridge or road or canal was brought forth.

Mercy, however, was apparently of a different mind and continued, "I find I am most fascinated with such marvels of engineering. I believe the canals represent a strong view to the future of England." She addressed Freddy suddenly. "I forgot to tell you, but I once heard Sir Humphry Davy speak on the chemical aspects of electricity. I was never more enthralled."

"Indeed!" he exclaimed. "And how did you find him?"

Mercy beamed. "His mind is utterly brilliant, I cannot begin to say just how much. I could have listened for hours and was only saddened when the lecture came to an end."

"Have you been to the shipyards on the Thames?" Freddy asked.

"No, but I have heard it is a marvel to see everything loaded and unloaded. But what I should really like to see is one of these enormous ships being built."

"Anne," Freddy said, his complexion high so that his freckles were particularly bright, "once we are wed, why do we not take your sister to the London docks and perhaps later to Portsmouth to see the Navy ships of the line?"

Anne regarded Mercy for a long moment. Even her twin's expression was most enthusiastic. She loved that Freddy had said, *your sister.* "I should be delighted," she responded, smiling at Mercy.

Mercy's expression broadened to a grin. "How happy I am to have a new family." She glanced about the table, her expression warm and affectionate. "I feel as if I have known you always."

"I only hope," Meg cried, "that I will soon stop addressing you as *Anne.*"

With that, everyone laughed.

By the time nuncheon was finished, the storm had passed over the seven hills of Bath and a proper leave-taking began.

"Which kitten do you want?" Meg asked as Mercy was putting on her pelisse.

Mercy glanced askance at Freddy, then addressed Meg. A faint blush was on her cheeks as she said, "As to that, Lord Frederick will be bringing two of the kittens to Watersfield Lodge tomorrow. I should like my mother to know them and to help me choose. I would take the kittens now, but I wanted to prepare my mother first. You may come as well, if you like. Indeed, I hope you will."

"I shall!" Meg cried. She then turned to her mother. "If I am permitted to go, that is."

"Of course."

The invitation was extended to Anne as well, but a prior engagement with her dressmaker in Milsom Street prevented her from accepting. She was being fitted for her bride clothes.

So it was that on the following day Anne left the dressmakers and nearly collided with Marecham.

"You are precisely where I was told you would be," he said.

"Then your appearing here is not by coincidence?" she asked.

"No, I was just in the Royal Crescent inquiring after you and was informed of the location of your dressmaker."

Anne's heart took a strong leap. He had sought her out purposely. She realized she was much happier to see him than she had any right to be. "And to what purpose have you come to fetch me?" she asked.

He offered his arm. "Why, I need your help in choosing a kitten. May I escort you home?"

She looked at his arm and once more her heart seemed to jump in her breast. She felt very strongly that she should not take it, knowing full well she would like wrapping her arm about his more than she ought. However, he was wearing a thick greatcoat, so it would not be wholly dangerous to be so nearly connected to him all the way back to the Royal Crescent. As a rain-laden wind buffeted her bonnet of blue calico, she therefore daringly took his arm. The moment she did, her heart began pounding anew. "But I had thought you had no need of a cat," she said as they began to move in a northerly direction.

"As to that, we had a very serious commotion in the buttery this morning. At least two of the lower maids were screaming hysterically."

"A mouse."

"And never to be found, the poor creature. A circumstance, however, that has the entire female population of my home peering into every corner, under every table, and beneath every sofa and chair. Besides, you know what is said of a mouse."

"No, what would that be?"

"If there is one there is likely to be a hundred."

Anne laughed. "Then a kitten you must have!"

By the time they reached the Gravel Walks, she had laughed so much that her cheeks ached from smiling. A cold, damp wind blew down from the north, swinging along the curve of the walks.

"Oh, dear," Anne said. "I feared it would set on to rain and I did not bring my umbrella."

"There is only one thing for it," he hinted.

She knew precisely what he meant.

Just as the first drop struck the top of her bonnet, they began to run, as did all the others who had been out enjoying a little exercise. By the time they arrived at the Royal Crescent, which was not far from the Gravel Walks, Anne's bonnet was soaked. The maid took both her bonnet and his hat and with a curtsy said she would tend to them as well as their outer gear.

Kate came down the stairs in that moment and greeted Lord Marecham.

Anne addressed her sister. "Will you be so good as to fetch the crate of kittens? It would seem an emergency in his lordship's home has sent him to inquire if we have any remaining."

"You are fortunate," Kate said, "for we have not placed any yet. Although I am certain Mercy means to have one. Freddy and Meg left with the black and white kitten and the gray one shortly after you left for the dressmaker's. I shall only be a moment. I left the kittens sleeping." She turned and walked quickly up the stairs.

Anne led Marecham into the drawing room where a pleasant fire had kept the chill from the room. She offered him a glass of sherry, which he took gratefully.

"It is still so odd to look at you," he said smiling. "I sometimes wonder if—" He broke off, appearing suddenly uncomfortable.

"What is it?" she asked. "I feel as though we are old friends now and I hope you know you may say anything to me."

"I suppose that is the difficulty," he said. "I think I feel far more comfortable with you than I ought."

"Ah," she murmured, taking up a seat near the fireplace. He chose one adjacent to her. "I believe I understand you perfectly."

"Then I shall tell you what it was I wished to say. I wonder if I am grown so easy in your company because you are my betrothed's twin."

"As to that, I cannot say. I suppose it may be true. I, on the other hand, have no such excuse, for though I feel so at ease with you, there is not a single soul of my acquaintance who you resemble."

At that, he laughed heartily. "No, I suppose not." He appeared as though he wished to say more, but at that moment, Kate arrived on the threshold, the crate in her arms.

"What is the joke," she asked, "for I could hear you laughing when I was on the stairs?"

"It would seem," Anne said, pretending to be serious, "that I put Lord Marecham in mind of someone he already knows."

Kate frowned for the barest second, trying to comprehend her meaning, then suddenly burst out laughing. "You are referring to Mercy, of course."

She brought the crate to Marecham, which he took on his lap.

"They are all jumbled up on top of one another," he observed.

"That is how they are in their slumbers," Kate explained.

He looked them over. "I see a tabby, an orange and white striped kitten and a black one. Which do you recommend?"

"I believe Brutus would do well for you," Kate said, pointing to the tabby.

"Brutus!" Anne and Marecham cried in unison.

Anne continued, "However did such a small, sweet little creature receive such an enormous name?"

"Pray, not so loud or you will awaken them," Kate returned, but she was smiling. "As to that, you have Meg to blame, I fear."

"And what was her reasoning?" Marecham asked.

"I believe it is because when Brutus plays with the other kittens he ends up chasing them and jumping on them and he always seems to win. Meg thinks he will be a good mouser."

Marecham said, "I have been instructed to bring the selected kitten to my housekeeper for inspection. I am only letting the house in the Circus, so I believe she must have approval." He then whispered, "She is a horrible tryant, and I am deathly afraid of her."

The ladies laughed, for he was being absurd. Anne took him in at a glance, at the strength of his person, at the commanding way he held himself even with a crate of kittens on his lap, at his confident manner generally, and thought there was nothing less likely than Marecham being overborn by his present housekeeper. Still, she liked that he pretended it was so.

"So you think I ought to have Brutus, Miss Katherine?"

"Yes, I have said so. Although I believe Miss Muffy would also serve you well."

"Miss Muffy?" Anne queried. "Have all the kittens therefore acquired names? And was this one Meg's choice as well?"

Kate smiled. "Only two of the kittens have names and I

fear *Miss Muffy* was my choice for an appellation. Do you see how delicate she is, such a little lady? I thought Miss Muffy a perfect name for her."

"I suppose so," Anne said, "but if she is so delicate, then how can she compete with Brutus in skills as a mouser?"

"As to that, Miss Muffy is delicate only in appearance. She pounces on anything that comes to her notice, and I have seen Brutus win a battle with her only once. I believe she has sufficient spirit to manage a household of mice. So, my lord, which will it be?"

"I fear I cannot possibly say. I must rely on your advice. Tell me which I should offer first to my housekeeper, Brutus or Miss Muffy."

"Since I am highly partial to Miss Muffy, and still hope to persuade Mama to allow me to keep her, I will recommend Brutus."

"Brutus it shall be."

Kate glanced from Anne to Marecham and back. She seemed quite pensive of a sudden and said, "I have just realized, Anne, that your betrothal ball is in but a sennight."

"So it is," Anne said, "but why should that give you the smallest qualm? I can see that you are distressed. May I know the reason?"

"Y-yes," she murmured, but did not immediately respond. Instead, she regarded Lord Marecham for a long moment. Finally, she took a deep breath and asked, "Do you waltz, my lord?"

The question was so unexpected that he smiled suddenly. "Yes, of course."

"Forgive me," Kate said. "I should not have asked you." She seemed deeply perplexed.

Anne thought she understood. "Are you worried about how you will fare at the ball?"

Kate nodded. "I know all the dances quite well save for

the waltz, and Lady Lankhurst was saying that we shall certainly be performing the waltz at your ball."

"Ah," Marecham said. "Do you require a little practice with a partner other than your dancing master?"

She smiled at being so readily understood. "Yes, I do. I would ask Lord Frederick, but he has made his dislike of the waltz so well known that I have every reason to believe he would refuse a request for help because of his principles."

"He sounds a little like my Mercy." A sigh followed. "However, even if I were to disapprove—which I most certainly do not—I would not wish for any young lady of my acquaintance to feel uncomfortable at what must be one of her first balls."

"Indeed, Anne's betrothal ball is one of my first, though I have attended the assemblies in Sussex several times—but nothing so grand as a ball given at Withyham. Will you help me, then? It is not as though I value the waltz above any of the other dances, I merely do not wish to miss my steps."

He turned to Anne. "Are you able to play a waltz?" His expression was teasing, yet wholly challenging.

"As to that," she responded, placing her hands on her hips and narrowing her gaze at him, "your task will be to prove to me just how well you *perform* the waltz, *my lord!*"

He merely laughed.

A minute or two spent rearranging a few pieces of furniture permitted sufficient room for Marecham to guide Kate down the dance. Anne sat at the very fine rosewood pianoforte at the far end of the chamber and was able to watch her sister and Marecham proceed.

She began playing and Marecham cast an approving nod, accompanied by a smile and a laugh, after which he began guiding Kate about the chamber, his arm placed skillfully about her waist.

More than once, Kate stumbled and begged pardon. Anne watched Marecham closely to see how he would manage her sister and was pleased to find that he was always kind and very encouraging.

With a third stumble, Kate said, "Perhaps if I could see it performed properly. Anne, will you not dance with Lord Marecham for a turn or two about the room?"

Marecham addressed Anne, his brow arched quite provokingly. "Can you waltz?" he asked.

"What a beast you are," Anne retorted, rising from the instrument, "to tease me so. Of course I can."

Kate laughed at them both as she took up her place at the pianoforte.

Anne stood before Marecham and had the strongest sensation that the last thing she should be doing with him was the waltz. Her instincts warned her that she should not allow him to take her in his arms again, even in so innocent a diversion as a dance, yet she could not bring herself to refuse.

Oh, dear, she thought, *I believe I am in the basket!*

Chapter Four

Anne drew in a deep breath, preparing to waltz with Marecham. Of course, they were practicing the dance in a perfectly harmless setting, in her drawing room with Kate playing the requisite tune on the pianoforte, but that did not seem to diminish the strange nervousness that came over her.

Regardless, she strove to still the erratic beatings of her heart as she whispered a soft *thank you* for all his efforts. She was very grateful that he had responded so kindly to Kate's request for assistance.

"My pleasure," he murmured in response.

The music began and Marecham took her in his arms. Anne gasped faintly and was lost from that moment. She could not help but wonder what it was about his touch that somehow forced her to leave the confines of this world and enter the magic of another in which the only thing she could see or even wanted to see was his face.

He guided her expertly around the room, turning her well, drawing her up and back in the motion of the dance, always in command. She had never enjoyed the waltz so much as she did in this moment, with just Kate's fingers creating the tune on the pianoforte and Lord Marecham holding her.

Her gaze never once retreated from his face. "You dance beautifully," she said.

He smiled. "I should have said that of you, particularly since I have been thinking it from the moment we made our first turn."

"Anne, I think I have it," Kate called, but she continued to play. A giggling ensued.

Had Kate spoken? The words struck her ears but they made no sense. She realized she was having some difficulty hearing.

"Once more around the chamber?" he queried.

"If you please."

He drew her a little more tightly to him. She wondered what he was thinking.

Marecham looked into her face and thought how different she was from Mercy even in her features. He knew the ladies to be mirror images, but something about Anne set her apart from her sister, more than even the faint cleft in her chin.

She was certainly livelier than Mercy. His betrothed was rather reserved and even stoic on most occasions. Anne, he already knew, was not. He had never experienced a more open temper than hers. He supposed that growing up in a household of three sisters might have accounted for it, yet he could not be certain.

He realized he was enjoying himself immensely and found that he was highly grateful that a little brown mouse had chosen to invade his town house. The paltry excuse he had used to seek her out—that he needed a cat—was about the only one that would have sufficed. What other justification could there have been for him to call in the Royal Crescent and even to pursue her in Milsom Street? None, his mind answered sharply. He wondered if any of the family had seen through him. His intention, his hope, his desire had been only for being with Anne again.

Even now, as he twirled her round and round, steadfastly ignoring Kate each time she called out that she was ready to begin again, he knew he should not have agreed to dance with Anne. He had teased her, asking her if she knew how to waltz, when he would have wagered his fortune that she did. She was an extremely accomplished young woman and confident in ways he believed Mercy was not. Perhaps that was what affected him now. He knew Kate was ready to resume her lesson, but he was so unwilling to let Anne go. He wanted to continue holding her in his arms in this completely wondrous manner for as long as he could.

At last, he realized Kate had stopped playing altogether and there was no alternative for him but to bring the dance to an end.

"I believe this is rather hopeless," she whispered now, standing before him.

"You are to be married in a month's time," he returned.

"As are you."

"So I am."

Kate called out, "Are you ready for me, Lord Marecham?"

"Yes, of course," he said politely. Turning to Miss Katherine, he saw that she was smiling broadly. He knew then that at least one of the intimates of the town house understood his heart. "Come then," he said, extending his hand to her.

As Anne moved away from him, he heard her sigh very deeply.

She began another waltz, and he again guided Kate about the chamber. This time, she danced perfectly without the smallest mistake—indeed, without the slightest hesitation in movement or manner.

He became suspicious. "You have not stumbled even once," he commented.

She shrugged as he moved her up and back, round and round. "It was very helpful to have observed Anne dancing with you," she responded with great sincerity.

Too much sincerity, he thought.

He narrowed his eyes at her. "Indeed?"

"Yes, *indeed!*"

"I begin to think you a rather mischievous creature."

"I am," she responded. "But not one without wisdom, I hope."

He narrowed his eyes anew, desiring that she be more explicit. "And to what purpose do you invoke your mischief?"

"To the purpose," she whispered, "of ending two betrothals that should not be." She drew from his arms immediately after and said aloud, "I believe I have it now. Thank you so much, Lord Marecham. And since it has stopped raining, I shall fetch Brutus for you. He will be difficult to manage, so I shall fetch another crate as well. I shan't be above five minutes or so."

With that, she quit the chamber rather quickly.

He turned to regard Anne and felt a longing so deep that he did not hesitate but moved toward the pianoforte in long, purposeful strides.

"What was my sister whispering to you?" she asked, rising from the instrument.

"Only this." When he reached her and before she had a chance to protest, he took her forcefully in his arms and kissed her.

There was only the smallest struggle, and then she leaned into him as she had that first day. Good God, he had fallen in love with his betrothed's twin in but a handful of days. Yes, he loved her. He could not explain how it had happened or even what it was about Anne that so pleased him, but so she did. Only, what were Anne's thoughts? Was she as lost as he?

Anne received his embrace as in a lovely mist, just as on the first occasion. She knew she should not be permitting such an assault, but she felt powerless to repulse him. For the first time since having met him, she began to wonder if she was in love with him. But that was impossible. She loved Freddy. She was betrothed to Freddy. She was to marry him in four weeks. All the while that these thoughts plagued her, however, she continued kissing Marecham!

In the space of a few days, he seemed to have become as necessary to her happiness as sunshine and blue sky. She had but to catch a glimpse of him, let alone tumble into his arms, and her whole being trembled with delight. He was the embodiment of every girlish dream, and yet he was more, for there was tenderness in him, kindness, and an easiness of discourse that kept her arms locked about his shoulders. Did she love him?

Yes, her mind cried! *A thousand times, yes!*

How had this happened, this truly marvelous accident? Worse, however, how was she to relinquish her dear Freddy, who so depended upon her?

Not until the knocker sounded harshly on the front door did she fly away from Marecham as one burned by a hot flame.

"Oh, dear," she murmured.

"Exactly so," he responded, his eyes full of longing.

A moment more and Meg burst into the entrance hall and then the drawing room. "We struck the knocker!" she cried. "We thought it would be a great joke to make you think company had arrived, but 'tis only us!" A moment more and she was running upstairs. "I must see the kittens!"

Freddy appeared in the doorway next. Anne moved toward him and forced a smile to her lips. "How did your afternoon fare?" she asked. "Did Mercy make her selection?"

He removed his hat and ran a hand through his hair. "As to that, Mrs. Hencott favored the black and white kitten and Mercy still desires the gray one. So the kittens are to remain at Watersfield Lodge in order that the ladies might determine the disposition of each. Apparently, Mrs. Hencott had a very difficult experience with a kitten that could not be trained from climbing her silk draperies. She vows she will not have such a cat running about her house again."

"Most understandable," Anne said, but she was scarcely listening.

"I must go," he stated abruptly.

Anne was surprised, and only then did she realize he was quite agitated. He kept running his hand through his cropped hair, even scratching at it.

She felt panicky of a sudden. She was afraid to be left alone again with Marecham. "Must you go?" she asked. "For I have not seen you yet today."

He smiled falteringly. "I fear I must. I . . . I have the headache quite fiercely, as it happens. I do not like to complain, but there it is."

"I am so sorry," she said. "Allow me to walk with you to your carriage."

"No, pray do not trouble yourself. I believe it shall rain again very soon, and I would not want you to take sick."

Anne could see that he was determined. She therefore walked with him only to the door. He turned to her before leaving, swiftly caught up her hand, and placed a hasty kiss on her fingers. "I shall try to call tomorrow."

"Yes, please do," she said.

"No, pray do not frown or worry. All will be well. All will be well." He bowed and quit the house.

Anne remained staring at the door for a long moment. She did not want to face Marecham, not just yet, not when she had just bid good-bye to her betrothed, not when she was still reeling from the viscount's kiss.

Fortunately, Kate descended the stairs. "Was that Freddy? I thought I heard his voice." She carried a small crate in her arms. The tabby kitten was mewing.

"Yes," Anne said, "but he had the headache and felt obliged to take his leave."

"As must I," Marecham said, appearing suddenly in the doorway to the entrance hall. He was looking at her.

Anne glanced at him and felt as though she might burst into tears, for in his expression she saw into her own heart, her longings, her desire, her despair.

Kate handed him the crate. "He will be wanting a little cream when you reach your house."

"Brutus will be well cared for, I have no doubt whatsoever."

There was nothing left to do or say but to open the door and bid him adieu.

The next moment, he was gone.

Anne remained in the entrance hall, grateful that Meg called Kate away. She was now alone and did not try to stop the tears that began trickling unbidden down her cheeks. "Whatever am I to do?" she murmured softly, one hand touching the door lightly, the other swiping at her face.

The next day, Anne decided to call on Mercy alone. She included neither her mother and sisters nor Freddy. After having so betrayed Mercy by kissing her betrothed—*again*—she felt the surest way to begin a much needed process of separating from Marecham was to cultivate her relationship with her new sister.

Mercy received her with joy, even shedding a tear or two. "I am so glad you have come and that without an invitation. I hope you never feel it necessary to wait for one."

This was an excellent beginning, Anne thought. The visit progressed as she had hoped, with a sharing of interests and opinions on a variety of topics. If her sister tended to pontificate on those subjects nearest to her heart, such as the regulation of new buildings in Bath and the proper mode of conduct at the Upper Assembly Rooms, Anne allowed her such preferences. In these ways, Anne could see she was very different from her twin.

However, the mere mention of having been fitted the day prior for her bride clothes brought forward a subject that the ladies shared in common—an absolute passion for the current modes.

A lengthy conversation ensued of dimity, gauze, Irish linen, jaconet muslin, Persian silk, poplin, velvet, and even stuff, which had its uses on occasion. Close on its heels followed a lively discussion of all the different types of lace, trim, edging, and decoration for spencers, bonnets, pelisses, handkerchiefs, and slippers.

So well did the visit conclude that when Anne rose and Lord Marecham was announced, she felt quite protected against the spell he had seemed to cast over her. She bid him a friendly if indifferent good day and without once succumbing to his gaze, she quit the house.

The entire journey back to the Royal Crescent was one of great peace for Anne. She felt she had been very wise in her conduct and had laid an excellent foundation for a much needed stronghold against Marecham. A growing loyalty to Mercy would in every way help her to do what was good and proper.

The next two days were of a similar nature. She made certain she visited Mercy, once in company with her mother, who shed new tears in seeing her lost daughter again, and the next visit with Meg and Freddy in attendance.

On this visit, Freddy had come for the strict purpose of determining if a decision had been made as to which of the two kittens Mercy preferred. Freddy, Meg, and Mercy began discussing at length the merits of each of the kittens while Anne sat down with Mrs. Hencott.

She was taking tea and conversing with that lady when she noticed that her hostess had grown very quiet. She followed the line of her gaze and saw that Mercy was engaged quite deeply in a discussion with Freddy. Each held a kitten, but whatever the nature of the subject, both Freddy and Mercy appeared rather spellbound.

Anne once more glanced at Mrs. Hencott and saw her troubled look. She turned her gaze again to her twin and her betrothed and watched them as well for a very long moment. The deepest gratitude and appreciation for Freddy swelled in her heart. What a good man, indeed what a very fine gentleman he was to be engaging her sister so purposefully in conversation.

She knew quite well that many of the things Mercy said could be interpreted as prosaic, even boring. She therefore began to look upon Freddy with new, more generous eyes. He was a good man, which his attentiveness to her sister made quite evident. She was a very fortunate lady to be betrothed to him.

Mercy in turn spoke with great vivacity and enthusiasm.

"Freddy seems quite taken with my sister's society," Anne ventured politely.

"I suppose he does, but I have been wondering this half hour and more whether he has forgotten he is conversing with Mercy and believes he is speaking with you."

Anne chuckled. "I suppose that would be a natural mistake. I, for one, am delighted that they get on well. I would hope that my twin would be comfortable with my chosen spouse."

For some reason, Mrs. Hencott appeared to grow uneasy. She cleared her throat several times then finally queried, "Would you care for another cup of tea?"

"Yes, I would. Thank you."

"Well, I must say," she began, pouring the tea in first Anne's cup and then her own, "that we are all looking forward to the betrothal ball on Valentine's Eve. You must be quite excited."

"Very much so, ma'am."

"And will you tell me about your gown? Mercy said that by your description it must be quite elegant. We are much addicted to fabrics and trims, as you must know by now, and I should dearly love to hear the details by your own account."

Thus the visit was whiled away, Anne speaking almost exclusively with Mrs. Hencott while Freddy entertained Mercy.

In the end, however, Freddy became very attentive to Anne just before they were to depart. He seemed as agitated as he had been upon returning from his last visit to Watersfield Lodge. She wondered if he was getting another headache.

The dilemma with the kittens, however, was still unresolved. Mrs. Hencott, upon discovering that there was an orange striped kitten, pronounced her interest in seeing it. "I have always preferred them, having had three cats of a similar color when I was a child. They have the sweetest dispositions."

"Very good, ma'am," Freddy said, offering his bow. "Meg and I shall return on Wednesday. You may keep the black and white one until then."

"Freddy," Mercy began, though breaking off and correcting her form of address, "that is, Lord Frederick. I have made up my mind on one score. I do wish your mother to have the gray kitten. No, I will not hear a word of argument. The gray kitten must be your mother's. Nothing would give me greater pleasure."

Much to Anne's astonishment, Freddy then spent the next several minutes exclaiming over her sacrifice, a circumstance that did not cease even when they boarded Freddy's traveling coach. Instead, though the coach had long drawn away from the front door, he continued, "I am so struck by her sacrifice. I vow she is the most generous young lady I have ever known."

Meg, sitting beside him, began to scowl. "More generous than even Anne?" she asked, her chin set mulishly.

Freddy came up stammering. "Yes . . . that is no, of course not! They are twins and share the same exemplary temper. I never meant to imply—"

Anne only laughed at him. "You are safe with me if you choose to extol the virtues of my new sister. I shan't complain in the least, I promise you."

Freddy relaxed visibly. "I just would not want you to think . . . that is, I have known her such a short time, hardly long enough to truly comprehend all that her character is." He fell silent, but only for a moment. "Although, I must say I have always had an ability to form proper judgments about the characters of others even within a few hours of making an acquaintance. And Mercy . . . that is, Miss Hencott seems to me to be the sort of young woman about whom novels are written."

At that, Anne's brows rose and she exchanged a glance with Meg. Her young sister was soon scowling again and even crossed her arms over her chest. "You sound as though you have tumbled in love with her!" Meg cried angrily.

"Meg!" Anne exclaimed.

" 'Tis no such thing!" Freddy cried, a hand pressed suddenly to his wounded chest. "I am devoted to your sister, to Anne. How you could think otherwise—oh, dear, oh, dear. My dearest Meg, if I have said anything to give you cause to think something so horrid, I do beg your pardon even now."

"If I should write novels," Meg retorted hotly, "I should write them about Anne!"

"I did not mean . . . that is . . . oh, the devil take it!" He was now so flustered that he, too, crossed his arms over his chest and stared out the window the remainder of the journey back to the Royal Crescent.

Once arrived, Anne was not surprised to find that Freddy had another headache. She did not press him to stay, but the moment he was gone, Meg became indignant all over again.

"How could he have spoken so warmly of Mercy when you were sitting across from him and could hear every word?"

Anne put an arm about Meg's shoulder. "You do not need to feel so offended for my sake. Indeed, I was deeply gratified. You must realize, Meg, that Mercy is my sister, my twin. And it is almost as though when she is praised, I am praised."

"But . . . but he speaks as though he loves her."

"For some reason, that does not distress me."

"Because she is your twin?"

"Yes, precisely so."

"Very well, then I shall try hard not to be angry with Freddy, but I think he behaved abominably!"

* * *

On Wednesday, Anne had just returned from the Gravel Walks during a brief break in the February weather, and met Lord Marecham nearly on her doorstep. He bore Brutus in hand.

"I had to come," he said, smiling. "The housekeeper says Brutus will not do because *she*—yes, you heard correctly—will bear a litter of kittens before the year is out and then the house will be at sixes and sevens trying to place them all. I am willing to have the housekeeper take a look at Miss Muffy, if there is a chance Muffy is not a female."

Anne shook her head and clucked her tongue. "As to that, I could not say, but I fear in any case you are too late, my lord."

"Has Miss Muffy already found a home?" he asked, as she led him into the house.

"Perhaps. Freddy and Meg drove Miss Muffy to Watersfield for Mrs. Hencott to see. She has a preference for orange-striped cats and would have expressed it earlier had she known the litter included such a one."

"I see." He removed his hat, settling it on the table by the wall and held Brutus up at eye level. "Why did you have to be a female? I was actually growing fond of you."

"We certainly seem to have a tangle of kittens here," she said. "Although I believe it is finally settled that the gray one shall go to Lady Lankhurst."

"Yes, I know. I called yesterday at Watersfield and found Mercy quite talkative on the subject. I must confess I was a little surprised. I knew her to have a generous nature, but she spoke of your future mother-in-law as though she had some great interest in her. If I do not much mistake the matter, she cannot have as yet made the acquaintance of Lady Lankhurst."

"No, she has not, at least not to my knowledge. However, she and Freddy seem to be taking great pains, for my sake I believe, to become well acquainted. When Freddy expressed to her that he thought his mother would prefer the gray kitten, Mercy was unwilling to see the kitten placed elsewhere."

She watched him frown slightly. "What is it?" she asked.

"I confess I am a little surprised."

"By what?"

"Well, do you recall my having related to you my own happy experience with a gray cat when I was young?"

"Indeed. I remember it now with some fondness."

"Well, it seems odd to me that when I related the same thing to Mercy—oh, I suppose it is nothing."

Anne regarded him closely. "I believe I can guess. She did not seem to notice that you might have an interest in the cat yourself?"

"Yes, that is it. Quite ridiculous!"

Anne laughed. "Perhaps it is. In truth, I believe all our lives have been a bit jumbled of late, what with the discovery of Mercy's existence and her learning in turn to embrace a new family. For the present, I daresay nothing is as it ought to be precisely."

He nodded. "I believe you to be very wise in this moment."

She saw the light in his eye and the soft smile on his lips. She knew what he was thinking and she could not help but smile in return, though she added, "And some things are best forgotten entirely."

He nodded. "So they are."

Kate appeared at the landing and began descending the stairs. "I thought I heard your voice. Oh, dear, I see you have Brutus in hand. Your housekeeper did not like him?"

"My housekeeper did not like *her.*"

Kate trilled her laughter. "Oh, no, a *her,* indeed?"

"So it would seem. I am myself not sufficiently skilled to determine the difference, although I can see I have put a blush on your cheeks in saying so, Miss Kate. Do forgive me. I fear such plain speaking is the wretched tragedy of having been brought up with three brothers."

Anne, seeing that her younger sister was about to succumb to her blushes, invited Lord Marecham to stay for a little refreshment. "For we generally take tea at this hour."

He agreed readily. Anne was grateful that the entire family was at home so that she did not have to find herself alone with him again. Not that she anticipated a problem any longer. She had taken steps to steel her heart against him in part by developing her relationship with Mercy and in part by lecturing herself severely about her former conduct.

She had come to believe that her previous reprehensible conduct in permitting the viscount to take liberties with her had been a result of experiencing a sudden fright of the married state. Now that she had such fears under her command, she found she could bear being in Marecham's company much more easily.

A few minutes later, the knocker sounded and Kate, moving to the window to see who had called, announced that Freddy had returned early from Watersfield Lodge. "He has brought back Miss Muffy," she said happily.

"I wonder then if Mercy has finally decided on the black and white cat."

"We shall soon know," Mrs. Cassington said.

"Where then is the gray cat?" Anne asked.

Kate frowned. "I believe Freddy already took her to his mother, but I am not certain."

A moment more, and Freddy entered the chamber. He quickly relinquished Miss Muffy to Kate, who embraced the kitten as though she had been gone for an eternity instead of a day or so. "Did Mrs. Hencott favor still the black and white kitten?"

"Yes, very much," Freddy responded. "You may consider that kitten as having found a permanent home."

"That is good news," Kate said.

Freddy advanced into the chamber and greeted everyone in turn until at last he reached Anne. He leaned down and placed a surprising kiss on her cheek. In her ear, he whispered, "I mean to do better."

She slipped her hand in his and smiled up into his face. "Do have some tea."

"Tea would be perfect," he said.

Marecham watched the tender exchange and began to grow disheartened. He did not stay long after Freddy's arrival. Indeed, how could he when the sight of Anne smiling so sweetly up into her betrothed's face was like a knife to his heart?

Of course she could not know that his arrival today had not been because of Brutus. He could easily have sent the kitten back by way of one of his servants. No, he had come this afternoon to discover if her heart had been in the smallest way touched by their previous encounters.

Naturally, the presence of the family had made any sort of intimate discussion impossible, but he felt certain that had she felt anything for him, he would be able to determine as much even with others around them.

Though he had arrived with a strong belief that Anne Cassington was not indifferent to him, he was now no longer so certain. Earlier, in the entrance hall, she had seemed particularly detached and now, having witnessed for himself the obvious affection she most certainly felt for Lord Frederick, his confidence failed him entirely. Anne was in love with Lord Frederick Wooton.

Just before he left, Mrs. Cassington addressed him. "I believe you desired to take the orange-striped cat," she said, inclining her head in Kate's direction.

Lord Marecham saw the instant disappointment in Kate's eyes and interjected quickly. "Actually, I was wondering if I might take the black kitten to my housekeeper. I believe she is partial to black cats."

Kate cast him so grateful a glance that he felt utterly rewarded in this small piece of consideration, even if Mrs. Cassington did quickly assure her second daughter that Miss Muffy would be sent to another home regardless of her preference for the little creature. Kate nodded her head meekly, but it seemed to Marecham that she was intent on having the cat. One glance at the affectionate expression in Mrs. Cassington's eye told him what the outcome was likely to be.

For that reason, he was even more desirous of leaving the Royal Crescent. He loved Anne. He had admitted as much to himself. But he also adored being with her family. Knowing that very soon he would be obliged to part from them forever, save for a visit now and again with Mercy when they were husband and wife, he could not bear the sadness that had taken hold of his heart.

With the black kitten settled in Brutus's crate, he quit the town house and headed east toward the Circus. He could only laugh at his own stupidity. He looked down at the kitten and said aloud, "I was a fool."

The kitten returned so soft an expression, gentling his eyes, that he felt his sadness deepen. He had been precipitous in offering his proposals to Mercy Hencott before knowing of her reserve and the strangeness of her scientific interests. How odd to think that but three weeks before he was to marry, Fate should have sent a woman so perfect for him, a woman who turned out to be his betrothed's twin. He felt the gods at work, but not in a happy way. He had no doubt they were laughing at his wretched misfortune.

"Well, there is nothing for it, little one. I have made my promises. I will honor my word. I will wed Mercy Hencott."

Chapter Five

The day of Anne's betrothal ball arrived at last, Valentine's Eve, in which her forthcoming marriage to Lord Frederick would be announced and celebrated. Anne ought to have been deliriously happy. Instead, she was suffering dreadfully from a fit of the nerves, an ailment that rarely afflicted her. Generally, she was in complete command of her senses, even upon grand occasions. Now she felt as though every nerve was on fire.

She could not account for these sensations at all, since she had been able at last to distance herself from Lord Marecham and the quite wicked flirtation in which they had both been shamefully engaged. She understood now that her experience with the viscount had been a result of experiencing a momentary fright of the married state, and so she had allowed herself to be swept away by Marecham's dalliance.

Only . . .

No, she would not permit herself to think in terms of *only.* There was no such thing. All that existed was her promise to wed Freddy, and she would keep her promise.

He had been so sweet of late, ever since Wednesday when he had returned early from his visit to Watersfield Lodge. He had been kind and attentive, even affectionate. He had even told her he meant to do better. Once he had actually held her hand, something he had never done before. Perhaps he would prove to be an exemplary husband after all.

All was in order, just as it should be. Both betrothals were moving forward, she was coming to know her twin sister better, and nearly all the kittens now had homes. Marecham had sent her a polite note saying he was keeping the black kitten as a mouser. Mrs. Hencott was allowing the black and white one to remain at Watersfield Lodge. Lady Lankhurst was in possession of the gray kitten and even Miss Muffy was being allowed a permanent home with Kate and Meg. The only kitten remaining to be placed was Brutus.

Yes, everything was finally in order.

Without warning, as her maid was dressing her blond curls with artificial white flowers, Anne burst into tears.

"Miss Anne!" her abigail exclaimed. "Have I hurt you?"

"No," she cried, between sobs. "Not in the least. Pr-pray, continue."

"How can I when you are crying your eyes out? Whatever is the matter? Should I summon your mother?"

At that, Anne whirled on her maid. "On no account, do you hear me? She is not to be troubled by my excessive display of sensibility this evening. As it happens, I am merely . . . merely . . ." She could not complete her thought, but spent the next quarter of an hour dissolved into tears.

Her maid rubbed her back gently and spoke soothing words to her. "There now, have your cry. 'Twill be better in a moment or two, you will see."

If only Anne could see. She did not comprehend in the least why she was so completely overset. Looking in the mirror, she cried, "Now my nose is swollen and my eyes are red."

With that her maid expressed her intention of fetching a cold damp cloth. "And while I'm gone, stretch yourself out on your bed and try to relax. There is sufficient time to recover. Never fear."

Anne took her servant's suggestion to heart and reclined on her bed. She grew calmer as the minutes passed, more resigned.

She had made her promise to Freddy and she would marry him.

Yes, indeed, she had.

With that, she felt her tears cease for good.

At the appointed hour, Anne waited with Freddy in the antechamber of Lady Lankhurst's ballroom. From the doors opposite, guests streamed into the large chamber ready to hear the formal betrothal announcement. Freddy held her hand, but she could see that he was deeply troubled.

"What is it, Freddy?" she asked quietly. They were alone, and she hoped for an answer.

He shook his head. " 'Tis nothing. Nerves, I suppose."

Anne chuckled softly. So she was not the only one suffering this evening. She gave his hand a squeeze, but suddenly he pulled away from her and began pacing the room.

"Freddy," she called again, this time exceedingly concerned, for he never behaved in this manner. "What is wrong? Have I offended you?"

"You?" he returned, his expression panicky. "You could never offend me. Never. You are goodness itself. You are patient, kind, forebearing." Guilt descended on every feature and he dropped into a chair by the window.

Anne, realizing that something serious was afoot, closed the draperies separating the antechamber from the ballroom. She drew close to Freddy. "I sense there is something you wish to tell me," she said, though she could not imagine what that might be.

He gulped, but would not meet her gaze. "I kissed Miss Hencott."

Anne could not have heard him correctly. "You . . . you kissed my sister?" When he did not respond, she continued,

"Let me understand you precisely. You are telling me that you kissed my sister? You kissed Mercy? *You,* Freddy?" She could not have been more shocked.

"I have said so," he stated quietly. Only then did he finally meet her gaze. "I did kiss her, but only once and I regret it infinitely. I cannot think what came over me, but we were discussing one of Davy's inventions having to do with coal mines and suddenly I could not help myself. I took her in my arms and kissed her."

Anne was incredulous. "You kissed Mercy," she stated again in an idiotic manner.

"Yes. Your twin." He frowned. "Are you not comprehending what I am saying to you?"

Anne had never been more stunned in her entire existence. "You, Freddy? When you would hardly touch me?"

"Yes, I know. It is so unlike me. I do not believe in such displays of affection. But that is not to the point." He took her hand in a tight grip. "I merely wish to assure you with all my heart that it will never happen again. I vow before God, I will never kiss another woman so long as I live. Once we are married, you may rely on my loyalty, my fidelity for as long as I live."

Anne stared at him and began to understand what had really happened to Freddy. She thought back to the day he had come with her to Watersfield Lodge in order to discover if a decision had been made about which kitten Mercy was to take. She recalled watching Freddy and Mercy conversing with great vivacity, and the only thing she had thought at the time was that Freddy was being so very generous in his attentiveness to Mercy. She had thought his attentions a respectful tribute to his betrothal to her!

Instead, something quite different had been occurring in that moment. When she finally understood the truth, she dropped down on her knees beside his chair and cried, "Oh, my dearest, dearest Freddy! I see what it is now. You are in love with my sister!"

"No!" he exclaimed, rising abruptly to his feet as though he had been shot from a cannon. "That is not possible. I love you. I offered for you, and I intend to marry you."

Anne ignored these fierce protestations as she gained her feet as well. "Do you have even the smallest sense that Mercy returns your regard?"

"What does that matter? My obligation is to you."

She drew close and took up both his hands forcing him to look at her. "Freddy, you must answer me and as truthfully as you are able. Does Mercy love you?"

He met her gaze as one who was being sent to Tyburn Tree. "I believe, that is, I think she might have formed an attachment to me, but she has not said so."

"Well, let me ask you this," she began.

"Must we discuss this horrid subject?" he retorted, shaking off her hands. He was deeply agitated. "I have professed my guilt, I have affirmed my duty to you as the woman I love and there is nothing more to be said."

Anne knew it was a pure form of devilry that made her continue, but she feigned an austerity she was far from feeling. "I believe that since you kissed my sister, you are under a tremendous obligation to answer any question I desire to ask. What have you to say to that?"

He seemed surprised, but once more guilt appeared to flood him and he nodded several times briskly. "Of course you are right. You may demand anything of me when I have been so vile, when I have treated you so abysmally."

Anne would have laughed had she not known he was completely serious. "Then you must tell me whether or not my sister, my dearest Mercy, took delight in your, er, *display of affection.*"

His jaw worked strongly and she could see he was completely disinclined to answer her. However, he had said he would respond to any question she put to him, so he straightened his shoulders. "Though I know it will give you pain, I believe she did."

"Freddy, there is only one thing to be done now."

He turned to her. "For you to forgive me and then for us to be married," he stated, as one preparing to be executed.

From the adjoining chamber, Anne could hear Lord Lankhurst beginning their introduction. Though his voice was muffled by the drawn draperies between the ballroom and the antechamber she heard the earl say, "On the eve of St. Valentine's Day, I welcome you all to my son's betrothal ball. Let me just say a few words. When I first became acquainted with Miss Anne Cassington—"

Freddy offered his arm. " 'Tis nearly time."

Anne smiled warmly upon him. "I cannot take your arm, my dear, dear Freddy."

"Whyever not?" he cried, scowling.

"For the simple reason that I cannot marry you."

The expression that dropped over his face was one of the deepest chagrin. "But I have expressed my remorse! Do you not believe me? Do you not trust that as a man of honor—"

"I do not give a fig for that!" she cried. "Do not you see that you are desperately in love with Mercy?"

He lifted his chin nobly. "Even if I were, which I do not admit in the least, it is a hopeless business."

"It would only be hopeless if we were already married, but we are not. I hereby break my engagement with you. I will brook no argument."

Lady Lankhurst peeked her head between the draperies. "Dearests, is something amiss? Your father is done with his speech and has called your names thrice."

Freddy, his complexion white, addressed Anne. "But are you certain?"

Anne smiled. "I believe it is for the best. We do not suit, not by half. There was a time when I was so certain of my regard for you and yours for me, but of late—"

"Then you have had your doubts as well?"

"More than I can say."

He drew near and much of the distress left his face. "If you are quite certain."

"Yes," she stated firmly. "I will not marry you." She turned to Lady Lankhurst. "I most humbly beg your pardon, ma'am, but I cannot marry your son."

"So it would seem," she said as she stepped through the break in the draperies taking care to close them behind her. Contrary to the expectation that the countess of Lankhurst would take a pelter, she heaved a great sigh of relief. "Is this, indeed, so?"

Anne smiled, since it was very clear to her that Lady Lankhurst had not been entirely in support of the engagement. "It is so," she responded simply. "Of course, you must know by now that your son is in love with another lady."

The countess grinned, and in this moment Anne had never liked her better. "I knew it!" the countess cried, shaking her head at her son. "Oh, dear, what a muddle! Indeed, a terrible muddle, and all so very odd."

"Then you have guessed it, Mama?"

"Freddy, you have spoken of no one else but Mercy this and Mercy that for these several days past. I do not think you spoke of Anne once within my hearing. I vow I should have grown fatigued of her name had it not become perfectly clear that you had tumbled violently in love with her."

Lord Lankhurst, his face crimson, appeared between the two lengths of fabric just as his wife had earlier with just his head showing. "What the devil is going forward? Have any of you the slightest notion that we are keeping two hundred of our dearest friends and family in the rudest suspense?"

"Calm yourself, William," his sensible wife said. "There is not to be a wedding after all, at least not this one." She waved a gracious hand toward her son and Anne.

"What?" he thundered, moving swiftly through the draperies and throwing them closed behind him.

Anne intervened quickly, but addressed Lady Lankhurst. "Would it be a trifle more convenient, given all the circumstances, were I to suddenly take quite ill and faint?"

Lady Lankhurst, a woman of the world, pinched her lips together, but after taking command of her amusement said, "I believe it would, very much so. I commend your foresight." She turned to her husband. "William, pray throw the curtain wide, then take my arm. We shall enact a processional but not more than ten feet. Anne, Freddy—prepare to do your best acting."

With that, Anne assumed her place behind the countess, and Freddy hastily jumped into his place behind his stunned father. Anne took Freddy's arm, the drapes were thrown wide, and the processional began.

Applause soon enveloped the room, but just as she had promised, Anne took no more than a few steps. She moaned loudly and said in a penetrating voice, "I feel very ill! Very ill, indeed! I am so sorry!"

With that, she fairly threw herself into Freddy's arms and collapsed.

Freddy, not being the strongest of gentlemen, had some difficulty supporting her, and for the barest moment she feared he would ruin all by dropping her on the floor. He rallied, however, and much to her surprise he was able to gather her up in his arms and carry her back to the antechamber. His arms were shaking by the time he dropped her onto the sofa. Anne struggled to keep from laughing as she bounced twice.

The countess had followed them and quickly drew the drapes. All three listened as Lord Lankhurst explained Anne had been feeling poorly all evening and that she had finally succumbed to a severe headache. A veritable melee of gossipy whispers ran about the chamber until the sound was a dull roar.

A moment more and Anne's mother and Kate entered the antechamber.

"Anne, what is the matter? What has happened?"

Kate, however, had appraised the situation more nearly and said, "The betrothal is off."

Mrs. Cassington glanced at Kate and frowned slightly. "Whatever do you mean?"

Anne, reclining on the sofa opposite the windows, begged Lady Lankhurst to fetch her twin. The countess left without the smallest hesitation.

She then addressed her mother. "Will you trust me if I tell you that I cannot wed Freddy and that he cannot marry me?"

Mrs. Cassington glanced from one to the other. "Is this so?" she asked of Freddy.

He nodded.

"Mama," Anne said softly. "All will be well. Lady Lankhurst understands the whole of it, I believe. Ask her and she will tell you. Kate, if I do not much mistake the matter, fully comprehends the rest."

"I do," Kate said confidently. "Come, Mama. Freddy and Anne have a great deal to discuss."

Mrs. Cassington allowed her second daughter to lead her away. She glanced back only once, at which time Anne gave her an encouraging smile.

Freddy drew a chair near and took her hand in his. "But are you certain, Anne? Can this be what you wish?"

Anne debated just how much she should tell him. To reveal that she had kissed Mercy's betrothed without knowing yet precisely the state of her sister's heart, would not be wise. "Freddy, though I do not wish to give you pain, I believe I would have come to break off the engagement regardless."

He seemed greatly shocked. "But why?"

"Perhaps for the very reason I have broken it off now, at least from my perspective. I had come to believe that you did not truly love me—at least not in a way that was pleasing to me. Do you know how often I longed to be kissed by you in precisely the way you have confessed to having kissed Mercy?"

"You told her?" a feminine voice called out.

Anne turned to see that Mercy had just passed through the heavy draperies. Before Freddy could give her answer, Anne said, "And I am so grateful that he did. I could think of nothing worse than continuing with a betrothal when one of the party no longer loved the other."

With that, Mercy sank into a chair at the foot of the sofa and burst into tears, her gloved hands covering her face.

"Go to her, Freddy," Anne said, giving him a push.

He did not hesitate, but moved close to Mercy and offered his kerchief. "Pray do not cry, my darling. I cannot bear it."

Anne could not help but smile. Freddy had never, in all these months, addressed her so tenderly. She watched as Mercy turned into him and buried her face in his coat in order to muffle her sobs.

Freddy consoled her with many encouraging words and after a few minutes, Mercy's tears ceased. She grew calmer and blew her nose. "What must you think of me?" she queried, regarding Anne over the edge of Freddy's kerchief.

"I think that you are wonderful," she said, smiling. "Only, I must know if you are in love with Freddy. Indeed, this information is of the utmost importance."

Mercy looked up at Freddy and smiled a watery smile. "I do not believe I understood what love was until I met him. I mean, I realize I am still betrothed to Lord Marecham and I did believe that I loved him, but I confess I was never comfortable in his society, not in the way I am with Freddy. Oh, dear, how am I to break Marecham's heart?" She looked at Freddy and new tears trickled down her cheeks. "I cannot do this," she cried. "I cannot break my engagement to him. I cannot break his heart. 'Twould be wrong, and if I did so and married you, I believe my perfidy, my disloyalty to him would harm our felicity together."

Anne now felt it was time to intervene. She rose from the sofa and crossed to them both. "Stuff and nonsense," she said sharply. "What compliment would it be to Marecham were you to wed him while loving another? What manner of kindness do you think this would be—or do you think him so lacking in intelligence that he would not one day discover the truth? I realize you wish to be honorable and noble, but to allow your betrothal to continue would be utter foolishness. Am I not right, Freddy?"

Freddy appeared appalled at being required to give answer. "I am afraid to agree with you merely because I cannot be objective. I believe you to be right, but my interests make it impossible for me to see clearly."

"Then allow me to make the judgment. Mercy, you should break off your engagement with Lord Marecham immediately."

Mercy's face crumpled. "I know you are right, but I cannot. You see, he has been particularly attentive to me these two days past and has made it evident that he desires more than anything to make me happy."

Anne considered what such conduct on his part might mean. She believed she understood, or at least she hoped she did. She decided it was time to own the truth. "There is something I believe I must tell you now, something of which I would be ashamed save that it all seems destined in some miraculous manner." She paused. Both Mercy and Freddy frowned at her, waiting.

"Of what are you speaking?" Freddy queried.

"I am speaking of Marecham," she said.

Mercy's face once more crumpled, but Anne drew close and touched her arm. "Indeed, you must listen to me and try to understand. Marecham kissed me four days past."

"What?" they cried in unison.

"Is that why you forgave me so easily and relinquished me without a tear?" Freddy asked, comprehension dawning swiftly.

"As much as I would like it to be otherwise, the answer is yes. It would seem I have fallen in love with Marecham.

Indeed, I met him by chance on the lane leading up to Lansdown Hill not quite a fortnight past. From that time, I was drawn to his company, perhaps in the same way you were drawn to my sister's."

Freddy turned to Mercy. Anne regarded her as well and saw an expression of supreme shock on her face. "Marecham k-kissed you?" she stammered.

"Yes." She swallowed hard. "More than once."

"More than once?" they intoned together again.

"I fear it is so. Again, I would repine, but it would seem it has turned out for the best for everyone."

"You must be mistaken," Mercy argued. "Marecham would not be unfaithful to me. It is not in his character."

"In the same way it was not in your character to allow Freddy to kiss you?" she asked gently.

At that, Mercy blushed quite deeply. "Oh, yes. I see now." She gave herself a shake. "Then he never loved me."

Anne laughed and took both her hands. "I know with all my heart that Freddy loved me and perhaps in his way still does. However, he found in you something more precious than what I was able to give him. I believe he has found a true friendship in you that he and I could never truly share." She glanced at Freddy and smiled. "We had many lovely moments together, but there it ends. Yet something far better begins. In the same way, Marecham and I were drawn to one another."

"You are being too generous, too kind," Mercy said.

Anne glanced at her. "You speak these words now, but I hope you remember that sentiment when you recall that I allowed your betrothed to kiss me as well. I hope you will find it in your heart to forgive me."

"How could I do otherwise?" she asked as one stunned. She blinked several times, nodding all the while. A larger understanding of the situation descended on her. "For look what has come to me because of you!"

Mercy settled her gaze on Freddy for a very long moment. He returned the tenderness of her expression and a moment later, in Anne's presence, he placed his lips on Mercy's, if briefly.

He drew back and laughed suddenly. His complexion was greatly heightened and, as was usual with him in such a state, his freckles stood out more brightly still. "I do beg your pardon, Anne. I had not meant or thought I would do that in front of you."

Anne rose to her feet. "There is something I would ask of you, however."

"Anything," Mercy responded.

"Would you be so good as to write a missive to Lord Marecham ending your engagement? I believe I shall call on him tomorrow, and I would like to give it to him at that time. Then I can explain everything that has happened. Would that be agreeable to you?"

"I feel I ought to speak with him myself," Mercy said. "Will it not seem paltry to leave the task to my sister?"

Anne could not help but smile. "Not by half, not when he learns it was my notion and not yours."

Freddy suddenly appeared quite serious. "Anne, you do not suppose you are mistaken in any manner about Marecham?"

Anne thought for a moment. She realized there was a possibility she was mistaken in him, in his regard for her, but she did not feel that these doubts signified at all, not when both Freddy and Mercy were staring at her so hopefully.

"Not in the least," she said seriously.

Though Freddy appeared prepared to argue the point, Mercy wisely intervened and asked him to fetch the much needed writing materials.

"Yes, of course, dearest," he responded promptly.

Within the quarter hour, Mercy's note was sanded, sealed, and in Anne's possession.

Anne again wished them every joy, but had a new inspiration. "There is one more thing you might do for me," she said.

"Anything," Mercy responded.

"Yes, anything," Freddy said.

She addressed Freddy, "Is there even the smallest possibility that your mother would be willing to exchange the gray kitten for the tabby?"

"Whatever for?" Freddy asked, surprised.

"Because I believe it would please Lord Marecham."

"Indeed?" he queried.

"Yes," Mercy said readily. "I recall now that he told me of some story of a gray cat from his childhood. I believe it was used to chase his dogs."

"That's right."

Freddy frowned and shook his head. "I fear that is not possible. I believe it would break my mother's heart."

A voice called from just beyond the draperies. "Of course it would not." Lady Lankhurst peeked her head through once more. "Do take the gray kitten with you, Miss Cassington, with my blessing. Tomorrow you may send a servant with the tabby."

"I should warn you that her name is Brutus."

Lady Lankhurst smiled broadly. "But how charming! A female cat named Brutus. I find I like the notion very much, indeed!"

"So what you are telling me," Mrs. Cassington said, as the coach bounced up the hill toward the Royal Crescent, "is that you and Mercy have decided to exchange beaus?"

"So it would seem," she said, smiling in the dark confines of the coach.

Kate merely cried out, "Huzzah!" She held the gray kitten on her lap in a small wicker basket. The kitten kept trying to climb out.

Anne laughed.

"Why do you crow, Katherine?" her mother asked.

"Because I have never thought Freddy would make Anne entirely happy. He is far too regimented and judgmental. I believe he would have driven her to distraction and eventually she would have plagued the life out of him as well."

"I believe you are right," Anne said, smiling still.

"So do you intend to wed Marecham?" Kate inquired.

Anne was surprised. "Why ever do you ask such a question?"

"Only because," Mrs. Cassington began, "the pair of you have been smelling of April and May since the moment you met."

"Oh, dear," she whispered. "So obvious, then?"

"Yes," her mother responded sympathetically. "What I could not imagine, however, was just how such a coil was to be undone. And so Freddy, our proper Lord Frederick, actually kissed Mercy?"

"They have both confessed it so."

"Marvelous. Absolutely marvelous."

Kate said, "So what do you intend to do now, Anne? Will you wait for Marecham to call on us or will you storm the Circus?"

Anne fingered Mercy's letter now hidden in her pocket. "Tomorrow, I shall take him the gray kitten, which he always preferred."

Mrs. Cassington chuckled. "A kitten would be a most unusual valentine."

"So it would," Anne cried. "I had nearly forgot that tomorrow was Valentine's Day."

"Quite appropriate, I think."

The remainder of the journey was spent in discussing just how the Lankhursts intended to manage the news that the betrothal had been called off. For the present, all that was known was that Anne had taken sick just before the announcement. Beyond that was a fountain of gossip to which Anne had already chosen not to pay the smallest heed.

Once arrived at the Royal Crescent, Anne sat before her own writing table and for the next hour contrived a valentine, which she meant to give to Marecham with both Mercy's note and the kitten. Within the valentine she inscribed a four-line poem that read:

With this kitten, pray receive
A Valentine that speaks my heart,
A twin to love and never leave,
A wish our lives will never part.
Anne

As she prepared the basket, Anne pondered Marecham. A myriad of doubts suddenly assailed her. Was she truly in love with him? Was he, indeed, in love with her, or was there merely an odd sort of flirtation between them? After all, they scarcely knew one another, having been acquainted now for only twelve days.

The deeper the shadows grew in her bedchamber as the moon descended beyond the hills, the more she began to worry that she had made some grave error in fairly forcing Mercy to break off her engagement with Marecham. What if he truly loved Mercy? What if, regardless of Mercy's feelings, he intended to marry her? What if—merciful heavens—what if he called Freddy out?"

With such lurid ruminations, she tossed and turned on her bed most of the night, falling asleep only as dawn was creeping up over the hills. She was awakened by a small purr.

She opened her eyes and saw that the gray kitten was beside her on her pillow. She looked up and Kate was frowning down at her. "Whatever is the matter?" she asked.

"Wake up, you goose! Do you not know that it is nearly ten? Should you not have already been in the Circus by now?"

Anne grabbed the kitten, though clasping it gently, and

sat bolt upright. "Yes! I must see to it at once! Mercy is depending upon me and should Marecham leave to visit her before I have even . . . no, I shan't think of that. Kate, help me to get ready on the instant!"

A half hour later, Anne was walking in the direction of the Circus. Slung over her arm was the basket containing her valentine, Mercy's letter, and the gray kitten. How her heart pounded in her breast. She could not credit how fearful she was suddenly that she might have completely mistaken Lord Marecham's advances. What if he was merely a rake disguised as a wonderful gentleman, who delighted in seducing maidens while betrothed to another?

She steeled her mind against such wretchedly unhappy thoughts. Her half boots made marching noises on the pavement below, a reflection of her mood. She softened her walk, laughing at herself. She was hardly going to war.

More than once, she nearly whirled on her heel to return home. What if he did not love her? What if he truly had desired above all things to wed Mercy? What if his kisses had been only the anxiety he was experiencing in having become engaged?

Useless, unhappy thoughts! She brought her mind to order again and again.

Fortunately, the Circus was not far from the Royal Crescent, or she was certain her courage eventually would have failed her. She made her way to the town house he had let for the winter and, with trembling fingers, she lifted the knocker and rapped three times. How loudly it echoed about the busy street. More than one coach passed by, the inmates regarding her with curiosity and interest. Bath was a small city, and she knew she was being gossiped about in every quarter given the events of last night. Her presence now as she stood before Marecham's town house could not help but cause more gabblemongering—although, since she was identical to Mercy, there would certainly be some conjecture as to which twin was actually demanding admittance to his house, and that without benefit of maid or chaperon.

The door opened and a self-important butler towered over her, a single brow raised as he looked beyond her for the maid or the chaperon. Seeing no one, he did not even address her, but rather lifted an imperious brow.

Anne grew irritated. "I wish to consult with Lord Marecham."

"Would he be expecting you, miss?"

Anne wondered if the servant had ever seen Mercy before and, if so, why he did not immediately allow her to come in. "Do you know who I am?" she asked.

The brow lowered. "I apprehend you must be Miss Cassington."

She was greatly surprised. "How would you know that?" she asked.

"You have a cleft in your chin. Miss Hencott does not."

Anne would have laughed, for she had supposed Marecham was the only person in the world who would be able to detect the difference. To have found such perception in his servant of the moment was quite disheartening, particularly when he gave every evidence of being disinclined to allow her admittance.

"You have guessed rightly," she said. "May I please speak with his lordship?"

"Lord Marecham is indisposed at present. I regret I have been given the strictest instructions that only Miss Hencott may enter."

"Very well," Anne replied. She stepped away from the door. "Which bedchamber is his?" she asked, glancing up at the windows.

She did not expect an answer, but immediately began crying out, "Lord Marecham! I have come to speak with you. Are you awake?"

"Miss," the butler cried on a harsh whisper. "Have you gone mad?"

"Indeed, I have not! I must speak with his lordship this

morning. Marecham! Will you not come to the window, at least?"

Heads began appearing in other windows and doorways.

"Lord Marecham!" she called at the top of her voice. The kitten mewed in response.

A very stately woman emerged from the doorway next to the viscount's. "What is going forward?" she asked severely.

Anne did not answer her, but rather glared at the butler. Though he scowled severely at her, he at last waved her into the house, though much put out.

Anne entered the foyer and extended the basket to the butler. "Will you take this to Marecham on the instant? I insist on waiting for an answer."

The butler did as he was bid and mounted the stairs.

Marecham covered his head with his pillow. The screeching sound had finally ended but there was so fierce a pounding in his head that had he had his hunting rifle close by he believed he could not have accounted for his actions.

He had had far too much brandy to drink last night.

"My lord," his butler screamed in his ear.

"Good God, Dawkins, must you yell?"

He squinted up at his servant who backed away slightly.

"I do beg your pardon, m'lord," he whispered. Even his whisperings were painful. "But this has arrived for you and the person who delivered it has requested an audience."

"Send him away," he stated firmly.

"*Her,* m'lord."

"Her as in she as in a woman?" Marecham asked. "What sort of woman makes deliveries and that to the front door?"

"A very improper sort, I have little doubt." He lifted his chin.

"What was all the shouting a minute ago?"

"That was the delivery person." An offended sniff followed.

"Well, you can see I am incapable of receiving anyone and I certainly have no wish of speaking with so vulgar a female. Do send her away. I do not wish to be disturbed by *anyone!*"

"What shall I do with this?"

Marecham opened his eyes sufficiently to determine his butler was holding a basket by the handle. "Leave it and go, for God's sake!"

"As you wish, m'lord."

He settled the basket on a chair near the bed and on his stately tread quit the room.

Marecham began drifting back into his troubled sleep. Decidedly too much brandy, he thought.

A soft squeaking noise disturbed him. He pulled the pillow about his ears. Everything hurt this morning, especially anything reaching his hearing.

Unfortunately, the sound penetrated even his pillow. What the deuce was that noise? He lifted his head and listened again. Another squeak, and so loud! It seemed to be coming from the basket that had been delivered to him.

He squinted at the basket, his head aching beyond bearing, and a gray head as small as his fist appeared at the top of the basket.

"By all that's wonderful!" he cried, then groaned so loudly that the kitten disappeared back into the basket.

He sat up, his stomach reeling. He pulled the basket onto his bed and lifted the kitten from his nest. He noticed two missives deep within and drew them out.

One, he recognized as Mercy's fair scrawl. The other . . . must belong to Anne!

His heart began to pound, which of course sent streaks of pain into the top of his head, but he did not care. He read Mercy's note first, then, as quickly, Anne's.

Exhilaration flooded him and the effects of his night's reckless drinking were swept away. He had but one thought as he rang for his valet. He must reach Anne as quickly as possible.

Oh, God, to think his ridiculous butler had sent her away! He felt ill all over again at the thought of what Dawkins might have said to Anne and how she might have interpreted it.

He went to his wardrobe and withdrew his coat of blue superfine, an embroidered waistcoat, buff pantaloons, and gleaming Hessians with silver tassels. Before even his valet arrived, he shrugged himself into his shirt and then his breeches. He was struggling with a neckcloth when his servant opened the door.

"Are you forgetting to shave?" Burcott cried, aghast.

Marecham glanced in the mirror. He looked like the devil. His eyes were wretchedly red-rimmed, and of course his stubble was thick and shadowed over his face. "This certainly will not do! But make haste, Burcott! I have a very important appointment within the quarter hour."

"Yes, m'lord."

Marecham did not know when he had spent so trying a ten minutes as those required to make him presentable. Betwixt times, he had summoned his butler and given him a severe dressing-down for his conduct toward Miss Cassington.

Dawkins took the lecture in stride and defended himself by saying, "She was not Miss Hencott and she was unaccompanied. You had already left strict instructions concerning Miss Hencott—that she was the only person you were willing to see. When Miss Cassington began shouting at your windows, I felt no compunction whatsoever in sending her away."

"Well, you will need to make your apologies, for she will very soon be mistress of Challow Park."

At that, Dawkins blanched. "I had no notion. How could I? Do forgive me, my lord."

Marecham looked at his butler. "You know, you are a

thousand times more agreeable in the country, and this is only Bath, hardly London at all!"

Dawkins sighed. "You have the right of it. I am quite useless here."

Lord Marecham, in the highest of spirits, said, "You may return to Challow Park today, if it pleases you."

Dawkins began to beam.

* * *

Anne continued to walk up Lansdown Hill. She had wept almost the entire way. Marecham's response to her presence in his home, delivered by way of his butler, had been succinct. "The only person his lordship wishes to see is Miss Hencott, as I told you before."

Anne now understood that she had erred greatly. She felt sick at the trouble she had created in assuming he would wish to have his betrothal to Mercy ended. She did not know how she was ever to face him once he learned she was the cause of all the mischief.

Beyond that, the knowledge that she had been so completely mistaken in him, in his regard for her, was unsettling in the extreme. Yet, to have rejected her so completely once he had read her poem . . . no, there could be no mistaking that she had, indeed, erred beyond belief.

The sound of an approaching horse caused her to move to the side of the lane and continue her uphill trudge. She swiped at another tear and then another. She would turn her face into the hedge when the stranger passed by so that her sadness could not be viewed from the road.

Only . . . the horse stopped. She wiped quickly at her face. Perhaps the rider was known to her.

When she felt presentable, she turned and gasped, for there was Marecham! "You!" she exclaimed. "But how did you find me?"

"When I called at your house, Kate told me you had returned a half hour earlier deeply distressed and had quit your town house almost as quickly with the intention of going for a long walk. The direction, I guessed."

"But . . . whatever are you doing here?" she cried, feeling ready to burst into tears all over again.

"I came, of course, to thank you for the gray kitten," he said smiling. "You have pleased me . . . beyond . . . my darling, why do you cry?" He dismounted his horse in a quick leap and secured him to the hedge. "I know what it is! Dawkins treated you abominably, but I promise you I gave him a severe dressing-down and then sent him back to Derbyshire."

"Y-you let him go on my account?"

"As heroic as that may sound, I merely sent him back to Challow Park, my country seat. He is much happier in the country and not so disposed to err as grievously as he did this morning." Without ceremony or so much as a by-your-leave, he took her in his arms and held her fast.

"Oh, thank God," she whispered, leaning into him. "Then I was completely mistaken in thinking you still loved Mercy and still wished to marry her?"

"Utterly and completely. I always loved your sister, but not as I do you. Only you must tell me if it is entirely true that she will be happy. I could not bear it were I to be the cause of her unhappiness in years to come."

Anne laughed a very watery laugh. "You will never guess at the actual truth."

"What would that be?" he murmured, gently wiping away another tear that trickled from her eye.

"Freddy kissed Mercy and she let him. That is how I discovered the truth last night. Just before the announcement of our betrothal, Freddy confessed his perfidy because his conscience would not allow him to continue. In that, he showed a great deal more character than I."

"And Mercy?" he asked, the expression in his eye troubled.

"She loves him. She said as much last night, and if you could have seen them together, you would have no doubts on that score whatsoever, I promise you."

"Then I will choose to believe you, for it seems to me to be so great a miracle that all has changed, and that so swiftly, that I can hardly credit it is true."

Anne needed to hear him speak his heart. "So you do love me?" she asked.

He drew her more fiercely against him. "More than you will ever know." With that, he kissed her warmly and deeply, holding nothing back.

Anne returned his passionate kiss, and as she always did in his arms, disappeared from this earthly realm. She entered a sublime place of extraordinary beauty and peace in which Marecham loved her and she loved him.

Could there have been a sweeter Valentine's Day in all the world than this one? she wondered. She thought not. Drawing back from him slightly, she asked, "So you liked my gift, then?"

He grinned. "The gray kitten?"

"Yes."

"I knew perfectly well that this was your way of giving a form to your affection for me. Had I been in doubt of your love, which I must confess I was a little, the presence of the kitten gave me complete confidence—that, of course, and your valentine. But however did you contrive to get the gray kitten? Had he not already been given to Lady Lankhurst?"

"That much is true, but she overheard my request and immediately agreed to trade the gray cat for the tabby. Besides, she seemed quite taken with the notion of having a female cat named Brutus."

"I am glad to hear it."

"All that remains now is to find a home for the black kitten."

"Unnecessary," he stated. "I mean to have them both."

"What of your housekeeper?"

"As to that," he said, "I shall promise to take both cats back to Derbyshire with me when I leave. She can have no objection then."

"I suppose not." She regarded him warmly and sighed quite profoundly. "How very critical you have become to my happiness. You can have no notion."

Marecham smiled at her quite lovingly in return. "My dear, sweet, Anne, how dearly I love you."

"And I, you," she murmured against his lips as once more he kissed her.

The Birthday Kitten

Cynthia Pratt

Chapter One

Johnna awoke early on the morning of her twentieth birthday, her hand tucked beneath her cheek. Cold rain tapped against her window. She snuggled deeper into her bedclothes to recapture sleep until a coil of steam sneaked in through a gap, the rich fragrance of tea beckoning to her. Her maid had brought in a tray without awakening either of them. Johnna smiled, still surprised and delighted with this service even after three months of marriage.

She rolled over to look at the gathered crimson silk canopy of her bed. Though she'd been sleeping here in the London house for the better part of a week, the gilded cherubs that held up the canopy never failed to bring a smile to her lips. She imagined she'd be smiling at their fat cheeks and absurdly small wings after twenty years of mornings, even if she grew used to having her breakfast appear as if brought by silent-footed spirits.

She moved her hand and arm beneath the cool linen, seeking her husband's warmth. Among the delights of marriage that were never discussed was not having to rely on one's own body heat alone on a February morning. She found his shoulder, solid and round, and he sighed contentedly. "I'd better go back to my own bed," Ramsey said.

"It's too early," Johnna said, remembering how he'd spoken the same words at about midnight. Her reply then had been that it was too late.

He must have remembered too, for he laughed sleepily and slipped his arm around her shoulders. She flipped her hair under her head so not to tickle him and lay against him, breathing his scent and enjoying the warmth not just of his body but of this closeness.

"What are your plans for the day?" Ramsey asked.

"Mother wants me to buy some gowns, but I can put it off if there's something you want to do."

"No, you should buy a few things. Can't have my wife out of the mode."

Johnna knew her clothes weren't of the best quality. How could they be, when there'd been so little money? Yet she'd rather hoped Ramsey hadn't noticed. She consoled herself with the idea that he had not married her for her clothes. "Mother says she's found an excellent dressmaker."

"Good. Don't be shocked by the prices. London modistes are famous for their outrageous charges. Have 'em send me the damages."

"Thank you, Ramsey."

"A pleasure," he said, forcing the words through a yawn. "Good Gad, is that the time?"

Johnna raised her head to let him pull his arm out from beneath her. "I'll get up too," she said.

"Nonsense. You go back to sleep. A lady doesn't rise before ten-thirty, or so I've been informed. She orders her household with a rod of iron and never permits her husband to spend the night."

"Alas, that I should be a failure already," Johnna said, pressing her hand to her heart with a great lack of sincerity.

Ramsey, half out of bed, turned back to kiss her hand

where it lay. She touched his thick, dark hair fleetingly. "You have time to grow into the role, my dear."

She watched him depart through the interconnecting dressing rooms that lay between their bedchambers, admiring his long body and broad shoulders. Lying back on the pillows, she sighed, well-content. Six months ago, she'd been a shy miss, destined to be the wife of a curate or a minor tradesman. Today, she was Lady Johnna Dillon, wife of the sixth Baron Dillon, a handsome gentleman of wealth and position. Her friends were delighted, her sisters astounded, her rivals sour with jealousy. Even now, she could hardly believe Ramsey had chosen her. She still did not know why he had.

When her friends had gushed that her romance was like a fairy tale, she had agreed. Yet what a curiously practical fairy tale it seemed, for she knew Ramsey did not love her. As for herself, what she felt for Ramsey was not love. She'd been in love before and never wanted to feel that much pain again.

A rap on her bedroom door made Johnna shut her eyes again. She should have known better than to hope this would be enough to ward off the inevitable.

A rapid tattoo of footsteps and the rattle of the curtain rings gave her a moment to pretend to awaken. "Good morning, Mama," she said.

"Good morning and happy birthday." Her mother turned from the window, the cold light of this rainy day showing up the silver gleams in her dark hair. A few inches shorter than her daughter, the modern taste for high waists and straight skirts did not become her. She herself said she resembled a sack of flour with a bow around it. Yet her carriage was so upright, her head carried with such conscious pride, that one hardly noticed her stocky figure.

Though she neither scolded nor frowned, Johnna had no doubt her mother was not pleased with her. Lying abed after daybreak led to all sorts of immoral behaviors beyond mere sloth. In Mrs. Feldon's house, daughters were expected to rise, wash, dress, and begin their before-breakfast tasks without any foot-dragging. Now that she but visited in her daughter's house, she couldn't say anything disparaging—but then, she hardly needed to. She'd had years to rule with no more than a curled lip or a raised brow.

Johnna sat up, pushing her long brown hair back from her shoulders. As usual, her cap had fallen off in the night. She sought for it discreetly under the covers. Across the room, set into the floor-to-ceiling sweep of chocolate and cream marble chimney piece, a gilded clock chimed the hour.

"Dear me, I have slept in," Johnna said, abandoning the search for her cap and throwing aside the coverlet. "And we were to have gone out early, Mama. Why didn't you awaken me earlier?"

"It's of no consequence. A great lady is permitted to keep her dressmaker waiting. Even expected to do so."

"I am no great lady, Mama. At least, I hope I am not." She peered at her face in the round mirror over her washstand. A flaw in the glass made her face waver as though underwater. First her eyes took prominence, then a queer angle of her cheek, followed by a swollen and bulging forehead. She shook her head at the sight, thinking that in the true glass on her dressing table, she was but little improved. She then washed her face briskly. The water in the jug was still hot. Wondrous service!

"You now bear a great name. You owe it to your husband's ancestry and posterity to support his title in a manner becoming to his rank."

Her mother had harped on this subject at every opportunity since Johnna and Ramsey's betrothal had been announced some months previously. Neither Johnna nor Mrs. Feldon had ever dreamed anything so wonderful would ever happen to them.

They had been making a summer visit at the home of Lady DePonsy, Ramsey's late mother's cousin. She had a daughter of her own, beautiful, blonde, vivacious. Johnna herself had no doubt she'd been invited only as a foil to Susanna DePonsy. A dark girl, quiet and plump, would serve to throw Susanna into greater prominence. Susanna had said so herself and then had proceeded to do all she could to avoid being alone with Ramsey. "He's a dear, dear man, and I don't say I wouldn't be tempted if it were not for two things. One, he is my cousin, and I simply can't marry a cousin."

"That's one reason," Johnna had said, tucking a last forget-me-not into Susanna's golden hair before they went down to the dance. "What is the other?"

Susanna glanced over her shoulder as if to be certain they were alone. "I'm in love with another man."

"Heavens, who?"

"I shan't say his name. The very walls have ears, and they all belong to my parents. But he is a very dear and gallant man and I shall have him no matter what."

"And Lord Dillon?"

"My cousin I leave to you, dear, darling Johnna. Keep him by you instead of chasing after me, and I shall adore you for it all the days of my life."

"Then the other man is here, tonight?"

Susanna smiled and fluttered down her lashes as if concealing her thoughts from any more interrogation. "Even if he were not, I should feel the same."

Then they'd gone downstairs to join the house party at a little impromptu dance and everything had happened. Everything had changed. She'd failed to give any more thought to what Susanna had said, so wrapped up as she was in the sudden wonder of her own existence. Though Susanna had attended their wedding, she'd never said another word about her mysterious lover. She was still unmarried.

Outside the dressmaker's shop an hour later, Mrs. Feldon

held Johnna back as she started up the steps to the shop. "Let me talk. I know how to handle these matters. You'll not be cheated, I promise you that!"

The visit to the modiste left Johnna feeling limp as a broken feather. Her mother had excellent taste. No one could deny it. Johnna encouraged her to choose gowns for herself. While Mrs. Feldon occupied the full attention of the owner of the shop and two seamstresses, Johnna made her own selections known to a junior needlewoman, quickly and decisively. Then she proposed a visit to a confectioners to recruit their strength after the rigors of the morning's work.

Once several buns had been tucked away, her mother turned from the subject of clothes. "You must rest before tonight, Johnna—your first evening as hostess in your London home to Ramsey's friends and your birthday to boot."

"Yes, I know. I've been trying not to think about that."

"I beg your pardon?" her mother asked absently, looking about her for the serving maid. "Did you say something?"

"No, Mother."

Mrs. Feldon leaned toward her, a twinkle in her eyes. "What do you think dear Ramsey will give you for your birthday?"

"I'm sure I don't know." She could not help but respond to her mother when in this mood. "Has he dropped any hints for you to pick up?"

"I don't like to say. A word might prove too much for such a clever girl as yourself."

"I'm not as clever as all that, Mama. Still, I suppose it depends on the word." More people than her mother thought of her now as 'the clever girl who ensnared Ramsey Dillon.' The role pinched her like a too-tight pair of shoes. She didn't feel clever; she felt fortunate, as if she'd been granted a wish by a mystic wizard. She wondered, too, when payment would be demanded. Magicians did not give such gifts without demanding their price.

In truth, it puzzled her very much as to why Ramsey had

married her or even what had attracted him to her in the first place. She hadn't liked to ask for fear it would look as if she were eager for compliments. He'd proposed the last night of the house party at the tail end of August, and they had married two weeks before Christmas. He'd seemed happy enough when she'd agreed, embracing her gently and kissing her cheek. Later, she'd heard rumors of another girl he'd pursued, but surely it couldn't be true that any sane woman would have refused his proposal. There could be no objections to *Ramsey,* of good family, with everything handsome about him. Her mother had been thrilled when he'd approached her for permission to propose.

"Are you all right, Johnna?" her mother said, her forehead creasing between her brows. "Is something amiss with your cheek? You haven't the toothache, I hope."

Johnna startled, lost in the past. She realized she had her elbow on the high table, her fingers lightly touching her cheek. "No, Mama. Are you ready to go?"

On returning to the house, Johnna smiled to see the red carpet already running down the half dozen steps between the door and the steps. The tall urns of gray stone flanking the door lost their somberness when overflowing with forced spring flowers. Though only four o'clock, the darkness had already advanced to the point where the windows threw forth welcoming beams of light.

"I must say, Ramsey's servants certainly know their business," Mrs. Feldon murmured as they walked up the steps.

"I'm glad they are already trained. I shouldn't know how to go about it." Johnna greeted the tall, thin butler as he opened the door. "Everything looks wonderful, Credley."

"Thank you, my lady," he said in a deep voice that, even after a week, seemed to belong to an entirely different man. "Shall I have refreshment sent to your rooms? Your maid is awaiting your pleasure."

"Thank you, Credley. Yes, a cup of tea would be wonderful. It's a trifle chilly this afternoon."

Credley bowed and closed the door behind them. As they continued up the staircase, Mrs. Feldon took her daughter's hand and patted it. "You do manage him beautifully," she said. "I'm sure I don't know how you've come by it."

"Credley doesn't need managing, Mama, and I'm sure I wouldn't dare to try if he did. He knows far more about running this household than I ever shall."

All the same, for form's sake, she came down after a half an hour's rest to inspect the arrangements for this evening. They were to entertain some dozen of Ramsey's friends at dinner, followed by a reception for ever so many more. The long table, set with silver, crystal, and crisp linen, sparkled mysteriously in the half-lit gloom of the dining salon. The candles were not yet lit, leaving the hothouse roses alone to perfume the air.

In the mirror-paneled ballroom, half a dozen musicians were settling in at the far end of the room, their white wigs piled on a gilt chair ready to hand. Here too were masses of flowers, hang the expense, interspersed with branches of the best quality pearl-white candles. A steadily played A hung in the air, the very sound of anticipation.

Everything was ready, except her. Johnna threw a last glance at herself, reflected in the mirrors like a thousand Cinderellas waiting for a prince. Time to put on her finery, to reassume the gown she'd worn for her wedding. She remembered the look in Ramsey's eyes when she'd walked toward him on her uncle's arm, how he'd smiled and nodded. Perhaps tonight she'd see a warmer expression yet in his warm brown eyes, now that they were no longer strangers to one another.

Several of the people who had accepted their invitation for this evening she'd met on her wedding day. Others were strangers to her, fashionable men and women, political couples, and old cronies of her husband's, some married, some not. She'd invited several young ladies she'd met during last Season, some successfully engaged, some not. It was said that a fox who had lost her tail wanted all other foxes to lose theirs as well, but she didn't want to match make. Perhaps her mother would continue to use her skills in that direction. A shame that her gifts in that direction would never benefit anyone else now that the last of her three daughters was married.

With her hair up and her gown fastened, Ramsey's mother's pearls in her ears and clasped around her throat, she waited for him. Their guests were due to arrive at seven. It wasn't the prospect of seeing all these fashionable people that made her body shake to each beat of her heart. When the long-expected rap sounded at her door, Johnna stood up, throwing her shoulders back. "Come in."

A little of the starch went out of her backbone when she saw her mother's face. "Johnna, dearest . . ."

"What's wrong?" she asked, coming toward her. It was no trick of the wavering candlelight that made Mrs. Feldon appear ghastly pale. A sudden horrible thought struck Johnna . . . *knocked down in the street . . . carriage accident . . . a load of bricks fell upon him. . . .* "What's happened to Ramsey?" she demanded, grasping her mother's wrists just as the door knocker sounded from below.

"He hasn't come home."

Ramsey would have denied being drunk. True, he'd accounted for the most part of a bottle, but it would take far more than that to turn his head. He knew that his abiding fault was his inability to refuse a conversational gambit. He'd entered his club at eleven o'clock in the morning, after visiting his bankers in the City. Since then, he'd talked politics, hunting, and racing. Afterward, he'd fallen into a long chat about the state of the American dollar with a retired governor of the London Mint, which had led, through tortuous paths, to a discussion of the latest Chinese diplomatic mess between two men with thick Scottish accents and a Russian officer. The Russian and the Scots polished off considerably more than one bottle each and somehow all four of them wound up weaving their way up St. James, singing—or attempting to sing—the *Hallelujah Chorus*.

Ramsey noted that while one Scot could still walk, if with a definite list to the right, the other one leaned heavily on the Russian while, at the same time, the Russian leaned heavily on him. Ramsey walked along with his hands in his greatcoat pockets, whistling a complicated passage and getting stuck endlessly on the third bar.

A carriage rattled past. Ramsey thought he recognized the horses by the glimmering yellow light of a street lamp. He paused to stare after it, and his comrades turned a corner and passed on without him. He started to follow them when the carriage stopped a hundred yards down the road with a clatter of hooves.

The door opened and a familiar figure filled the opening, beckoning. Ramsey approached with a shrug, hearing the strains of Handel fading in the distance.

"Good evening, cousin," Ramsey said.

"Would you care for a ride home?" Adrian Dillon was possessed of a considerable personal fortune, as were all the Dillon family. He owned a matched quartet of bay horses that were the envy of every gentleman, a town house that excelled in elegance, and frequented the company of exquisite mistresses. Yet he envied Ramsey his title. Should some evil befall him before he and Johnna should have an heir, Adrian would inherit.

Nevertheless, Ramsey had no qualms about accepting Adrian's offer. He had no fear that his cousin's envy would make him cross the line into crime. Adrian liked his comforts too well to risk ornamenting Tyburn Tree.

As Ramsey stepped up into the carriage, a memory tried to break through the wine and the lateness of the hour. The thought seemed connected in some way with Adrian, but only in the sense that a bookmark is connected to reading.

Adrian crossed his white hands on his knee. He was attired for a formal affair. "How have you been enjoying your evening, cousin?"

"Very well, thank you." Ramsey rubbed his forehead, feeling the advent of a headache.

"And your bride? She looked a trifle pale this evening—or so I thought."

"You called on Johnna this evening? That was kind of you."

"At her invitation. And yours. She said you'd been called away. Nothing—ah—serious, I trust?" Adrian sniffed slightly through his aquiline nose, undoubtedly placing the vintage of the burgundy Ramsey had downed.

"Called away? I haven't been any . . . oh. Oh. Oh, good God Almighty." He started to rub his temples.

Adrian nodded. "I see. You know I am not a sentimentalist, yet I confess I felt a certain respect for your lady wife when she dismissed your absence with a brave smile and a laugh. Your mother-in-law, on the other hand . . ."

"Yes?" Ramsey asked warily.

"Let me say that on your wedding day she struck me as a woman who did not conceal her feelings well. This evening confirmed my first impression."

He could just imagine. Mrs. Feldon had her own style of charm, mature and warm, but small setbacks seemed to disturb her out of proportion to their importance. He well remembered her blood-suffused face and high-pitched voice when the flowers in the church had not been precisely as she'd wished. He'd been confirmed in his decision to marry Johnna when he'd seen how she'd calmed her mother, fixed the flowers, and smiled at him despite his having defied tradition and seen her before the ceremony.

It had been her calm eyes that had first attracted him at the DePonsy home. Dispassionately considered, Susanna owned a greater share of beauty, Anne Leigh made him laugh with wit that often stung, and Evie Abell could both discuss art and kiss like a houri. Any of them would have made a fine wife. He didn't flatter himself particularly by admitting that any of them would have accepted him.

Only Johnna, however, brought him a sense of peace. He did not love her, for love, as he well knew, was just another word for chaos. He'd seen it from his earliest childhood, and his one desire was to avoid such a frenzy in his adult years.

Therefore, he felt doubly hesitant to return to his house. "Did she cause a scene?"

"Not for want of trying. Your wife kept her calm, smiling all the while."

Ramsey knew exactly the look he meant. He wondered if he'd ever see it again himself. Could she forgive him for forgetting to attend her first evening as hostess and her birthday party?

"I don't suppose there are any shops open at this hour?"

Adrian's fingers drummed once on his knee. "You didn't arrange for a gift?"

"Did you?"

"I gave her a fan. Ivory sticks, painted silk, a few spangles, nothing too tasteless."

Knowing Adrian, it meant the fan would have enthralled even a finicky collector. "That must have pleased her."

"She said all that was polite. Though I may not think Mrs. Feldon has perfect control over her emotions, she has raised her daughter well."

Ramsey chuckled despite his guilt feelings. "You're not seventy years old, Adrian. Nor, I think, a moralist."

His cousin smiled and suddenly looked his true age, twenty-seven, two years younger than himself. "What are you going to do?"

Ramsey shook his head, feeling his conscience prick like an itch he could not reach. "Grovel, I think. A solid, sustained grovel on my knees with plenty of begging, pleading, and abject apologies."

"Well, it's a start." Adrian rapped on the ceiling of his carriage with his silver-mounted stick. "I'll let you down here, shall I?"

Ramsey, looking out the window, saw that they'd reached the opening of his street. "Yes, this will do. Better go in quietly than come rattling up before the very door. No need to compound my crimes by waking up the whole street."

"Good luck, Ramsey. If you need a place to stay, I've an extra bedroom."

He reached out and shook Adrian by the hand. "I doubt it will come to that. I only hope she won't cry. I can't abide a crying woman." He did not add that he disliked it because having his heart turn to butter always made him feel ill.

After the carriage rattled off, Ramsey realized that he needn't have worried about waking the street. The dog barking wildly already shattered the nighttime calm. Something struck him as familiar in the hoarse, coughing barks. "King? King. Come here, boy!"

The barking stopped, but only for a moment. King resumed calling upon the gods of Dog to witness some foul and purposeful infraction of their laws. Ramsey picked up a loose cobblestone and strode off to investigate. If it proved to be some thief, a flying rock should discourage him.

He found King in the alley three doors down from his house, looking up at a windowsill and barking like a werewolf. The message he conveyed was clear: here was the vile abomination that must be utterly destroyed.

Already lights were moving in the house next door. Ramsey recalled that the owner of this house hadn't yet returned to town.

Ramsey strode up, dropping his rock. "King . . . come on, boy."

His dog, a spotted liver-and-white hunter, greeted him with a welcoming toss of the head. Then the pinkish nose swiveled, the brilliant brown eyes closed, and the barking started again, higher-pitched now that his master had come to lend assistance.

"King, no. Hush now, you daft beast." Ramsey caught the dog's silky jaw in his hand and gave his head a shake. "Hush now, before you wake all London."

King whimpered a little but was on the whole an obedient dog. He sat down with the air of a foot soldier handing off a duty to a superior officer.

"Now what are you on about?" Ramsey looked up at the bricked-over window, victim of a tax on window glass from fifty-odd years ago. He'd gutted and redecorated his house when he'd inherited it, along with the other properties, and had opened several such windows. He'd not liked the look of a blank wall with a windowsill protruding with no purpose.

But this one had a purpose, that of sanctuary. A triangular face peered over the edge, sky-blue eyes taking up a good third of available area. Seeing the dog, the kitten opened its mouth and hissed with defiance. King surged forward. Ramsey fought him back, exerting his strength against the dog's driving ancient instincts.

Ramsey bent down and hustled King down the few yards to his own house. He was doubly glad now that he'd insisted on constructing a five-foot wall around his garden, even though the neighbors had complained. He jerked open the dark green door and pushed King inside. The dog leaped up at the door. Ramsey could hear his claws scrabble against the wood as he barked sharply. Someone from within the house shouted in reply—his butler, by the bass notes of the voice.

Ramsey returned to the prisoner on the sill, wondering how the devil the kitten had gotten up there. A crate precariously balanced on an old barrel against the wall gave him the answer. The kitten must have leaped up to the barrel when surprised by King. Finding the dog could still reach it, it must have headed for yet higher ground.

He made a enticing noise between his teeth. "Sst, sst, sst . . ."

He looked up and saw that the kitten was giving itself the sort of wash-and-brush-up so necessary after trying circumstances. It looked up, pausing in the midst of a tricky lick around an extended ankle.

In addition to the natural extra helping of adorability given to small creatures, the kitten also possessed milk-white feet and bib, contrasting charmingly with dark gray fur. Ramsey was reminded of the pelisse Johnna had worn the afternoon they'd gone for a walk in silent snowy woods at the DePonsy home. It had been of an almost military cut, the close standup collar as brilliantly white as the sunlit snow above the dark gray velvet. Her hat had borne one white feather curling down to brush the lobe of her ear. He remembered that the cold had not turned her cheeks pink but made her pale. Only once, when she'd looked up unawares to find him steadily regarding her, had her cheeks brightened. She'd looked away, both frightened and smiling.

Ramsey stepped up onto the barrel and held his hands out to the kitten. "Don't you think it's time to come down from there? I think we can find a better place for you. A warm corner of the kitchen, perhaps. Or . . . how would you like to be a lap cat, petted and coddled within an inch of your life?"

The kitten sniffed at his fingers, its head delicately outstretched. With eyes closed to slits, it seemed to ask if this dog-smelling person could be trusted. Ramsey didn't know how to talk to cats, but he felt certain that Johnna would. It didn't seem eager to bite or scratch. Of course, it undoubtedly shipped a cargo of fleas. . . .

He reached out, his fingers sliding over the smooth fur, and scooped up the seemingly boneless kitten. Though it didn't purr, it didn't protest.

"Come on, birthday present."

Credley, opening the front door, found his master on the threshold, his arm held curiously across his body as if holding an injured limb. "My lord? Are you . . . quite well?"

"Entirely well. Where's her ladyship?"

"She retired half an hour ago, after the last of her guests departed."

The slight emphasis on 'her guests,' discernible only to one who knew him well, told Ramsey that here, too, he was in disgrace. "I see," Ramsey said. "Has her maid come down yet?"

"No, my lord. Reynolds has not yet descended."

"Good, then my lady is still awake. Here, take care of this for me, will you?"

Credley, instinctively holding out his hands, found one occupied by a ball of fluff. He drew back in alarm when a mouth opened, showing a mouth full of needles and a bright pink tongue. "My lord?"

"It's a kitten."

"So I observe."

"It's a present."

"No, thank you, my lord."

Ramsey laughed. "Comb it or wash it or whatever you must to make it presentable. Then bring it up to my lady's chambers. I'm sure she won't be asleep, but don't be longer than half an hour."

The battle between duty and revulsion showed plainly on Credley's face, but his training held. "Very good, my lord."

"Send my man up, if you please. With hot water. Oh, and King is in the garden. Please bring him in."

Ramsey took the stairs two at a time but quieted his steps as he walked past his mother-in-law's door. His room was in the middle of the upper floor, with Johnna's farther down. A connecting door between them led first to his dressing room and then to hers. It meant he didn't have to parade his intentions through the house whenever he wanted to visit his wife. Some of his other homes lacked this discretion, not that the servants didn't know everything that went on regardless of architecture. He never gave such things a second thought before his marriage, but Johnna was embarrassed by too much frankness. He smiled, thinking of her. In many ways, she was such an innocent.

Franklin, his man, appeared quickly enough with a brass can of steaming water. Ramsey hadn't done more than take off his greatcoat and tear loose his cravat. Even better than the water was the tray Franklin balanced on his other hand. "Coffee? God bless you."

"I thought, my lord, despite the lateness of the hour . . ."

"I'm not drunk, Franklin, nor even half-sprung. But as I fancy I may not sleep for an hour or so at least, a drop of coffee will not come amiss. Besides, I need all my wits about me." There was no reason to dissemble. The whole household knew he was in trouble.

"Yes, my lord," Franklin said darkly.

Ramsey rubbed his chin, wondering whether he should shave. He tended to look a trifle seedy by five o'clock. He drank, letting the heat and acidity scald the last of the wine from his system. "I'll shave."

"I'll bring the water up at once, my lord."

Clean, wrapped in his dressing gown over his shirt, he walked through the intervening spaces. The soft, spring-like fragrance Johnna wore permeated her clothing. Entering her dressing room, he paused just to breathe. The gown she'd worn lay flung over the straight-backed chair, her undergarments crumpled on the floor. Ramsey brushed his fingers over the cool silk, its smoothness like Johnna's skin, warming at his touch. He wished he could have seen her wearing it.

In a penitent mood, Ramsey knocked softly at Johnna's bedchamber door. He heard a mumble of voices, Johnna probably dismissing her maid. Ramsey waited a moment, then knocked again. Then one voice rose above the other, loudly and persistently. He recognized Mrs. Feldon and knew, before he tried the door, that it was locked.

Ramsey decided to retreat and take up a new tactical position. He walked back into his own room and stood by the window, drumming his fingers on the sill. When he saw the butler walk past his half-opened door, he called out to him. "Do you have it?"

"Yes, my lord."

He bore between his hands a basket, white wicker lined with pink silk. A large floppy bow adorned the handle, while a veil of the same fabric descended like a canopy, parted to show the gift within. The kitten lay on the silk, boneless forepaws folded out of sight beneath its chest. It rode in the basket like the Queen of Sheba on an elephant, ridiculously dignified considering the circumstances.

When the kitten saw Ramsey, it sat up and stretched out small paws, showing minuscule claws. A rumble like the sound of wheels over cobbles issued forth from a body that seemed too small to create such a resonant sound.

"It seems very friendly."

"Yes, indeed, my lord," Credley said. Only then did Ramsey notice the scratches marring each of the butler's fingers and the backs of his hands. Two or three bandages waved flag-like ends. "Shall I deliver the kitten to her ladyship? I believe we have eradicated all the fleas."

"Excellent work, Credley. I'll just follow you, then."

Ramsey put his hands in his pockets and sauntered down the hall like Credley's shadow. He halted short of the door, however, leaning against the wall just out of sight.

"It's Credley, my lady," the butler said in answer to a question from within. He turned the handle and entered, leaving the door ajar. Ramsey listened unabashedly.

"What is that?" Mrs. Feldon demanded.

Ramsey could imagine the stately bow, the regally raised eyebrow that gently reminded Mrs. Feldon to whom she was speaking. "A birthday present from his lordship to my lady, ma'am."

"Ugh. A cat."

"A kitten, ma'am."

"What did you say?" Johnna's voice came nearer as if she'd approached to see what was presented.

Ramsey turned so that he could look with one eye into the room. The butler stood with his back to the door, his bulk blocking most of Ramsey's view of his wife. Mrs. Feldon stood in an appalled attitude, her arms crossed and pressing hard against her waist, her mouth primmed up as if she were presented with a bad egg at breakfast. "Take the nasty thing away, Credley."

"No," Johnna said. "What a darling."

Ramsey wasn't sure if she meant the kitten or himself. Until the matter was clarified, he'd stay where he was. He only wished he could see Johnna's face. He liked how she looked when she was pleased, the soft light in her eyes, the trembling half smile that may have lacked confidence but made up for the difference in charm. He could have kicked himself for forgetting to return for this evening's celebration. Though she wouldn't have shown so much pleasure for every gift, there could have been a few occasions when she had looked like that. He would have enjoyed watching her.

Chapter Two

Johnna peered into the basket and found a pair of blue eyes peering back. She felt the tension in her back and throat release as she smiled down at the kitten. Ears like sails gave a piquancy to a triangular face. She held out her first two fingers. The kitten sniffed with the delicacy of a wine connoisseur making the initial appraisal of a bottle.

Accepted, Johnna reached into the basket and slid her hands under the front legs. The warm body was limp, hanging between her hands. A purr began to rise from the tiny form.

Johnna cradled the kitten against her bosom, enjoying the contrast between the softness of its body and its indomitable nature, for the tiny claws came out and it inched up to her shoulder, nuzzling at her earlobe.

"Are you hungry, little one?"

"Unlikely, my lady," Credley said. "She consumed a square of pâté de foie gras in the kitchen."

"She?"

"What difference does it make?" Mrs. Feldon demanded. "You're not planning to keep that creature?"

"Of course," Johnna took the kitten off her shoulder,

laughing a little as she freed the burr-like claws. "I wonder what I should call you? Where did Ramsey find her, Credley?"

"He did not confide in me, my lady."

Mrs. Feldon made a dismissive sound. "That's an alley cat if ever I saw one. It probably has fleas. Or worse."

"No, ma'am. I am willing to vouch for that," Credley said firmly. He walked to the bed and placed the basket into the corner between the bed and the wall. He paused a moment, turning the wickerwork an inch to the side in order to show it off to the best advantage.

"For heaven's sake, Johnna, you can't let the creature sleep in your bedroom! Keep it in the kitchen, if you must have such a thing in the house. If you take my advice, you'll put the creature out in the alley where it belongs."

"I can't do that, Mama. It's a present."

Johnna had been happy when she realized Ramsey's dog was an accepted member of the household. As a child, she'd longed for a pet. She'd fed a hedgehog in the yard for a few weeks until it had stopped appearing. A friend's mother had owned a wheezy white lapdog and had been delighted to turn him over for brushing whenever Johnna had come to her house. But her own mother had always been waiting with a vigorously wielded clothes brush the moment Johnna came home.

It was odd that Ramsey would have chosen a kitten as a birthday present. She'd never discussed her wish to have a cat of her own. There'd been no point. Her mother never would have permitted such a thing. This fact was so plain that there'd never been a need to so much as raise the matter.

"Just like a man," Mrs. Feldon said sharply. "No thought given to the practical side of things."

"What do you mean, Mama?"

"What about sanitary arrangements? Hmm? A cat isn't a dog; it can't be trained."

Johnna looked at Credley, who said, "My lady's maid has

no objection to escorting the creature outside at suitable periods, ma'am. There is a convenient sandy area at the bottom of the garden."

"Oh, his lordship's gardener will appreciate that!"

"Hempleford will do as he is instructed, ma'am. As do we all."

"Thank you, Credley," Johnna said. "You must be tired. There'll be nothing further tonight."

"Thank you, my lady." He bowed from the waist with no more than a discreet creak and held the door open, waiting.

"You must be tired as well, Mama. It's very late and you were awake and working so early. It was a lovely party; thank you for everything. I love the garnets you gave me." Johnna began walking toward the door. Her mother followed her automatically.

"But I wanted to tell you . . ."

"Yes?" Johnna waited.

Mrs. Feldon cast a wary glance at Credley, standing impassively by the door. He avoided her glance, not in any blatant way, Johnna noticed, but simply by seeming to be completely absorbed in the hand-printed wallpaper. "Never mind."

"Tell me in the morning." Johnna kissed her mother's powdered cheek, appreciating her special amber scent brought out only for special occasions.

"The morning will be too late. I know you, Johnna. A heart like butter."

"I doubt one night with a kitten in my room will lead to any serious consequences."

"It's not the kitten in your room that I'm worried about."

Johnna knew she meant Ramsey. As soon as her mother left, Johnna felt a little ashamed of herself for teasing her so. After all, no one could have stood by her more steadfastly or taken greater care of her. Her mother had rallied nobly as soon as it became clear that Ramsey would not appear. No seasoned diplomat could have invented a lie so quickly.

Johnna wondered how many of their guests had known it for a lie.

Certainly Adrian had guessed. He had looked into her eyes at table with a tenderness she would not have suspected lay behind his air of superiority. "Called away, was he?"

"Yes, so unexpectedly."

"No family emergency, I trust."

"No, indeed. Surely you would have been told."

"So I should hope," he said. "Then?"

Johnna had not been raised to lie. She had felt her cheeks flame as she smiled blandly. "To be frank, cousin, he told me, but I'm afraid I didn't pay as close attention as I should have. I was so disappointed that he couldn't be here."

He'd seemed to accept her feeble excuse and had begun to eat his soup. Johnna had turned to the gentleman on her left and asked him about his friendship with her husband.

Even now, Johnna couldn't be sure she was angry. Anger was not an emotion she knew very well. Proper young ladies weren't suppose to acknowledge strong feelings. To be uncontrolled was to be unladylike. When Credley had broken the news that Ramsey was not to be found, she'd been shocked, but anger had been her mother's portion.

The kitten meowed insistently. Johnna turned around to see it hanging by its claws halfway up the curtains. Laughing, she lifted it down, cuddling it under her chin. "What shall I call you? Or did Ramsey name you already?"

"No, I haven't."

She looked over her shoulder to see him standing in the doorway, the candlelight reflecting in his dark eyes. His carriage was no less erect than usual, yet somehow she received the impression of uneasiness. She couldn't keep from smiling at him—which, surprisingly, did not seem to reassure him.

"I love my present," she said, turning so he could see the kitten in her arms.

"I'm glad." He entered the room, closing the door behind

him. Johnna felt that strange flicker of excitement he always brought out in her, but he only held out his hand to the kitten.

It mewed excitedly and tried to launch through intervening space. Johnna caught it with a juggling motion. "Here now, slowly," she said. Its back claws had caught on her dressing gown. She drew breath between her teeth as one dug through her clothes and scratched her waist. Johnna tugged free the little claw and the kitten ran over her shoulder to fling itself on Ramsey.

"She likes you," she said, smiling at the picture he made, his hands so big, the kitten so small. Writhing over on its back, the kitten batted at Ramsey's chest. "She must remember you from when you bought her."

"I suppose so," he said, a bemused look on his face. "What will you name her?"

"Heavens, I don't know. I've never had a pet before. How did you decide on what to name King?"

When he laughed, she couldn't help laughing too. "When he was just a puppy, I pulled him out of the ornamental lake where he'd been chasing some geese. He was dripping with mud and a water lily was sliding off his back. My father said, 'Even King Solomon in all his glory was not arrayed like one of these' and since I didn't want to name him Solomon, I named him King."

"Your father sounds like he enjoyed a joke."

"Sometimes. Mind you, he wasn't too happy the pup went for that swim. He could have easily drowned if we hadn't been in that exact spot."

"How old was he?"

"A few months." He held up the kitten to look into her face. "Older than this little one. Her eyes are still blue."

"Is that how you tell how old it is?"

"That and the size. Didn't you know?"

Johnna shook her head. "I don't know very much about animals. We've never owned any, except for the horses."

"My father always had two or three hounds at his feet. Not to mention the peacocks, the hawks, and the jackdaw he'd tamed."

"Goodness," Johnna said, imagining what it must be like to have so much life around. "It must have been wonderful."

"A bit noisy at feeding time. The jackdaw used to sit behind Father's head at meals. He'd pass it tidbits from time to time."

"What on earth did your mother say?"

"Nothing. She . . . didn't care." He carried the kitten over to the bed and put it down in the middle of the coverlet. "Behave yourself while we think what to call you."

Tail high, the kitten began to stalk across the vast bed, exploring like a mountain lion across counterpane, blanket and pillows. Coming upon a suspiciously still tassel, it attacked, sparing neither tooth nor claw.

"Well," Johnna said, sitting down beside him, stifling the feeling that she was breaking some unwritten law, "if your dog is named for a king, perhaps my cat should be named for a queen?"

He nodded at her, taking her hand onto his thigh. "I like it. Which queen? Elizabeth?"

"No, my maid is Elizabeth. That would be too confusing."

"Mary, then?"

"That's not a cat's name."

"Besides, every Mary I ever met has a brother in dire need of some service only I can perform."

She wondered if he'd met a Mary tonight. Though no one had spoken of it to her directly, she knew men sometimes strayed. Now that she was married, other women did not guard their tongues so closely. She'd heard enough whispered innuendo to come to very clear conclusions. Her own mother, usually forthright, had only hinted that men were wild creatures, only partially tamed, and often roamed at night. A wise wife never asked those questions that would lead to heartbreaking answers.

She moved away from him, going to the basket. Down on her knees, she put the kitten on the silk. "My old nurse would say . . . oh, of course."

"I beg your pardon," Ramsey said, standing above her.

"My old nurse had many little sayings, some of which made little sense. Whenever my sisters or I looked particularly fine, she'd say, 'You needn't think yourself the Queen of Sheba, for handsome is as handsome does.' So I thought of her and then thought, if the dog is Solomon why shouldn't the cat be . . ."

"Sheba."

A little echoing mew came from the basket. Ramsey chuckled. "She approves."

He held out his hand to help his wife to her feet. Holding her hand, he looked into her eyes. "You must be very angry with me."

"Must I?"

"You needn't conceal it from me. I deserve your anger. I failed you and I have no excuse to offer. Rail at me if you wish. I will bear all your recriminations."

Johnna could not believe that her husband actually wanted to hear her complaints. She remembered how Gale would look at her with just such a tenderness, only to laugh at her for her naïveté. Then he'd steal a kiss . . . her heart twisted with remembered pain.

She withdrew her hand. "I'm not angry. I'm sure whatever kept you was of great importance."

He struggled visibly between letting her keep her illusion or breaking it. "I wish I could say it was," he said. "In truth, I simply forgot."

"I see."

"Let me make it up to you, Johnna. We'll hold another party, even grander, and I'll stay by your side every instant of the time."

"Won't that look a trifle obvious? Besides, no one knows you weren't called away as I claimed."

Ramsey bit his lip. "I'm afraid they will. I wasn't exactly in hiding. I was at my club and any one of a dozen fellows spoke to me. By noon tomorrow, all London will be commenting on my stupid piece of folly."

"Will anyone believe you—I mean, that you just forgot and weren't trying to embarrass me?"

"I hope no one will believe I was deliberately cruel! You don't, do you?"

Johnna saw the distress in his blue eyes. "Of course I don't. You aren't a cruel man." She'd known cruelty, not the sort that came with a fist but the sort that could laugh at another's pain. Why was she thinking so much of Gale? Ramsey wasn't like him at all, despite a tiny cynical voice whispering that all men were the same. She forced a laugh. "I suppose I should rest content that you remembered to appear on our wedding day."

Ramsey tapped his breast twice to signal a hit. "Touché, touché. I will purchase a memorandum book in the morning and write everything down from this day hence. It will be my constant companion, leaving me only at night. I'll rest it on the bedside table and check it last thing before I sleep and immediately upon waking."

"Stop," she said, laughing and holding up her hand.

He reached out to guide her fingers to his heart. "I promise I'll never treat you so badly again."

"It's all right," she said, feeling the steady beat beneath her palm. "I forgive you freely and fully. I don't know whether Mama will, but she likes you. I'm sure you'll resume your place in her good graces soon enough."

Ramsey kissed her cheek. "Thank you. Though I do think a memorandum book would be a good idea. I think I will buy one. They have some that fit in your pocket without ruining the set of your coat."

"You might start a fashion."

"I doubt it. Now, where would you like to go tomorrow for a belated birthday treat? You haven't seen any of the great lions of London yet, unless you visited such places during your Season?"

"Only Westminster and the Houses of Parliament. I've never seen the Tower."

"Then to the Tower we shall go. And if you want to chop my head off, there's a fine place to do it."

"Keep your head where it is, sir. I should look very foolish as a widow after only three months."

Johnna was glad he had dropped the notion of holding another party. She feared that if he'd married her looking for the perfect hostess, he was doomed to disappointment. Though she'd been trained to be always gracious and charming, she wasn't at ease meeting so many people and being responsible for their comfort. Perhaps once the Season was under way, after Easter, she'd grow more accustomed to that part of her new life.

Johnna sat down on the bed. "You must be tired," she said. "I know I am. I'm not used to such late hours."

"Yes, I am. What time is it?" He looked toward the gilded clock. "That can't say almost three."

He came to her and she felt that flicker of excitement within, like a candle's wick taking flame. But, to her disappointment, he only kissed her cheek and bid her good night. She wanted to close her hand on his sleeve, to keep him, but she reached out too late.

"Thank you again for my present," she said softly as he opened the dressing room door. "It's just what I always wanted."

He only waved silently as he closed the door behind him. Johnna shrugged off her dressing gown and climbed into her cold bed, the hot flannel-wrapped brick at the foot long since having lost all power to warm.

It was odd, come to think of it, that Ramsey had given her a pet, the one thing she'd longed for the most. Perhaps she could shrug off some of these doubts that possessed her, doubts about the reasons he'd married her and what he thought of her. *Wouldn't it be wonderful,* she thought, *if he really did understand me?*

She did not ask for love, but understanding was something she craved. To have another person know her without trying to control her or change her would be heavenly. Johnna wondered if she could possibly offer that to Ramsey. Could they ever reach a place where she could ask him to stay the night as unselfconsciously as she asked him to pass the salt?

Laughing at herself, she confessed that even such a simple action was a matter for debate. How loudly should she speak? Would it be better to ask for the salt before he used it or afterward? Would it discommode him if she were to ask for it twice?

After blowing out the branch of candles, leaving only the chamberstick alight behind a screen, Johnna rolled onto her side and watched little Sheba in the shadows. The kitten slept in a neat half bend, rather croissant-shaped. The tiny pink pads on her feet twitched as some dream rodent was stalked through the mists. Did a kitten realize how tiny she was when she hunted through the ancient memories of her larger, fiercer relations? Was kitten a smaller lion or a lion only a bigger kitten? She fell asleep and dreamed that a whole pride of tiny lions roared and tussled about her feet. She picked one up and held it on her palm. It began to grow and grow until it roared right in her face.

Though Ramsey had made no definite appointment as to time, Johnna ran downstairs extra early in order to be ready for her 'belated birthday treat' whenever he was. Since his lordship preferred breakfast at the table, the London house kept up the customs of the country. But when Johnna reached the breakfast room, only her mother was there.

"I hope you reconsidered and didn't keep that dirty creature in your room," Mrs. Feldon said.

"Good morning, Mama. Sheba passed a very restful night in her basket." She took an assortment from the sideboard and sat down.

"Excellent. The kitchen's the only place for such a thing. It'll earn its keep by destroying pests."

"The basket was beside my bed, Mama." She thought it best not to mention how Sheba had awakened her by purring very loudly in her ear while tickling her chin with her tail. They'd spent a lovely few minutes playing 'monster under the blanket' until the maid had come in to take Sheba out. Johnna trusted her mother's eyesight would not spy out the tiny scratches on the back of her hands.

Mrs. Feldon sighed. "I suppose, as it is a gift from your husband, that you must show that you like it."

"I do like it. I wonder if King will come to accept her."

"And if not? What will you do? Insist your husband's dog doesn't come into the house?"

"He doesn't come in very often as it is. But I'm sure Ramsey will be able to train him not to bite Sheba. I suppose it's possible. I'll have to ask him. Has he come down yet?"

Credley had entered to make sure all was correct. "His lordship went out an hour ago, my lady."

"Oh. Did he say when he would return?"

"No, my lady. But it is Wednesday. He has a long-standing appointment at Monsieur Duroc's Emporium du Fence every Wednesday morning."

"Of course. Do we have any bramble jelly, Credley? I'm not in the mood for marmalade."

"I shall ascertain, my lady."

"Thank you."

Her mother gave her a disapproving glance. "One mustn't cause the servants extra trouble, Johnna."

Some new impetus prodded her to speak. "They are my servants, Mama. If I daren't even to ask Credley for a different sort of jelly, then I'm a cipher in my own home."

Mrs. Feldon folded her serviette and dropped it on the

table. "If you are out of sorts with your husband, there's no need to take your ill temper out on me."

"Why should I be?"

"I know *I* have nothing to reproach myself with. I did my very best to keep you two apart until your heads had cooled. There need have been no quarrel if you'd listened to me."

"Ramsey and I did not quarrel."

"Then why did he leave the house at a far earlier hour than any gentleman would?" Mrs. Feldon said as if clinching the argument.

"You heard Credley."

"A fencing lesson. Indeed. I happen to know that fencing is quite passé among gentlemen of Ramsey's sort."

"Maybe he likes it. He must keep in condition some way when he can't ride point. I don't want him to give up any of his former pleasures just because he's married."

"Is that what you told him?" Mrs. Feldon rose to her feet, pushing her chair away. "I don't understand modern marriage. I only hope you won't live to regret such folly."

Johnna began to eat her breakfast with determination. She knew perfectly well that her mother was hinting that Ramsey hadn't come home last night because he was dallying with some former mistress. He'd undoubtedly forgotten all about going to see the Tower of London with her today. Well, so be it.

She thanked Credley for the bramble jelly when he brought it along with the morning's post. Among the messages from tradesmen inviting her custom were two letters from relatives, another one from an acquaintance from last season, and a letter from Susanna DePonsy. She picked it up and ran her finger under the seal. Then, as her eye fell idly on another letter, she paused as if turned by some spell into solid rock.

The handwriting was as familiar to her as her own, flowing L, dashing J, slanting Greek E, and all. The way the lines slanted up across the surface of the outer covering spoke of haste. Gale Farringdon might as well have scrawled his full name over every inch of the pale brown paper.

Without noticing, Johnna put down the letter she held in her hand and sat staring down at the other one as if someone had posted a venomous snake to her. She almost expected to see it writhe. But a snake could hardly be blamed for biting someone, for what evil could be imputed to a dumb creature? But Gale took great care to sting where it was most painful.

Johnna looked around for a candle to burn the letter unopened, but daylight streamed through the sheer curtains in the bay window. She'd have to take it to her room.

She heard her mother's quick steps behind her. With the speed of a pickpocket, Johnna swept Gale's letter off the table and under her napkin. Before her mother entered the room, she was eating her breakfast placidly.

Mrs. Feldon came to stand at the foot of the table, her hands twisting restlessly. This sort of aimless movement was very unlike her mother. Johnna looked at her in surprise.

"I . . . I don't want you to be angry with me. I only say these things because I care." Her eyes were shiny with unshed tears. "I hope you know how much I . . . I care."

Johnna stood up impulsively, serviette and all falling to the floor. "I know, Mama. Please. I'm not angry."

"You don't feel that I . . ."

Johnna put her hand over her mother's. "What is it?"

"If you are not happy with Ramsey . . ."

"What do you mean? Of course I'm happy. Perfectly happy. And I know how much of my present happiness I owe to you. I'll never forget it."

Her mother lost the strained look in her eyes and the vertical lines between her brows smoothed out. Her hand turned under Johnna's and clutched for an instant. "I didn't do anything. You'd made up your mind before I'd even seen Ramsey."

"But you encouraged me to hope when I thought he'd never call after we met at the DePonsys."

"Oh, I knew he'd try to see you again," Mrs. Feldon said with a wise look. "I'd been afraid I'd never see you so over the moon about a man again, not after that dreadful Farringdon man."

"Gale? What makes you think of him?" Johnna remembered the letter. Her mother wouldn't recognize Gale's handwriting—or would she? He had written Mrs. Feldon at least one letter after she had discovered that Johnna and Gale had been meeting in secret. Looking back now, Johnna found it hard to believe she'd been such a fool.

"Someone mentioned him last night."

"Who?"

"I'm not sure. They weren't speaking to me; I only overheard two men talking about gambling. And one of them mentioned 'Farringdon.' Now, perhaps there are several gentlemen by that name . . ."

"It's probably not him." Johnna tried to speak with confidence. She patted her mother's hand and let go. "I might meet him sometime, Mama, but please believe I want nothing to do with Gale Farringdon."

Mrs. Feldon glanced toward the doorway. "Did you ever tell Ramsey about him?" she asked in a lowered tone.

"It hasn't come up. Besides, there's nothing to tell. A boy-and-girl affair."

"He was thirty."

"And I was seventeen. I may not be so very much older, yet I have considerably more wisdom—I hope." She seated herself behind her breakfast. "If ever Ramsey and I choose to divulge the secrets of our respective pasts, I'll be honest. Yet I don't think he needs to know everything now. He knows my honor was unsmirched. I doubt he'll care I was once so foolishly in love."

For a moment, Mrs. Feldon pressed Johnna's shoulder before she left the room. Johnna waited a few moments, then leaned sideways from her chair. The letter had floated toward the far side of the table.

She went down on her knees and reached for the paper. It was a little out of reach. She stretched and felt stitches give in her shoulder seams.

"My lady?" Credley asked, just as Johnna achieved her goal. For an instant, she closed her eyes and prayed for ease, if not elegance. She rose with the assistance of the chair.

She gave the butler a dazzling smile. "Did his lordship say when he'd return?"

Credley's face was a credit to his training. No hint of surprise marred either eyebrow or voice. "He did intimate that he would not be long delayed."

"Excellent. Pray inform me when he comes home."

"Certainly, my lady. I shall send your maid to you directly when his lordship returns."

She purposefully did not try to hide the letter as she walked out of the breakfast room. However, she couldn't keep from racing up the staircase, reminding her of the days when she'd meet Gale behind the church. Realizing these reminiscent feelings of excitement and fear boded no good, Johnna slowed at the top of the stairs.

Walking into her room, she felt as though Ramsey were there. The thought of her husband steadied her. She took a deep breath and felt her tension ease. A bright fire burned on the hearth. Without a second thought, she strode over to it and held out the letter. Then the second thoughts struck.

She stood there, the fire heating her face, tapping the envelope against her thumbnail. After all, she was no longer seventeen. Gale could no longer harry her from blissful pillar to hopeless post.

This might be no more than a note of congratulations upon her marriage. Surely even the muddiest dregs of courage would suffice for the reading of such a message. Should it prove to be anything else, an attempt to play upon her heartstrings in some show of vile reminiscences or a message of recrimination for leaving him for a wealthier wooer, the fire waited.

She slid her finger under the blob of brownish wax impressed with a curling F. The bits of the wax dropped to the carpet. Johnna paused to collect the wax so that Sheba wouldn't eat it. She glanced toward the basket, where the kitten had been sleeping when she left to go downstairs. Now it was empty.

"Sheba? Here, kit-kit-kit."

She rang for her maid. Reynolds had probably taken the kitten outside and hadn't yet brought her back. Or the staff might be playing with her, though from certain words her maid had let drop, the cook shared Mrs. Feldon's opinions regarding animals in the house.

Thinking she heard a pathetic mew, Johnna bent to look under the bed. She couldn't see anything but it smelled dusty. "Kit-kit-kit?"

"My lady?"

"Reynolds, have you seen Sheba?"

The maid, a fresh-faced girl of twenty who had impressed Johnna as being remarkably intelligent for her age and class, glanced about her. "She was here this morning, my lady."

"When you made the bed?"

She nodded and got down on her knees to look under the bed as well. "Here, puss-puss. Shall I fetch a square of butter from the kitchen, my lady? She seemed awfully hungry even after she'd had her milk and liver."

"You like cats, Reynolds?"

"Oh, yes, my lady. My mother always had two or three around the house. For the mice, of course, but she liked them for their own sakes. She said they were more enjoyable than children, begging your pardon for speaking so free."

"More enjoyable than children? How so?"

"They showed gratitude for littlest favors and gave back more affection than they were given." Reynolds stood up and looked toward the canopy. "You don't suppose it climbed up there, do you, my lady? My mother's cats were always climbing up the curtains."

"I don't know. She's rather small."

"The smaller, the lighter, my lady. Shall I call one of the lads to come and see?"

The canopy descended from a wooden frame where the cupids sported amidst their gilded garlands. Johnna hiked up her skirts and stepped up onto the bed. Cautiously, she placed one slippered foot on the foot board. When she reached up to brace herself against the frame, she heard a few more stitches give up the ghost. Balancing on the balls of her feet on the narrow board, Johnna could just see the unadorned top of the box. It was also dusty but quite free from any trace of gray-and-white fur. She slowly lowered her raised heels. Glancing at Reynolds, she shook her head. "Not there."

A movement at the corner of her eye made her look round. Ramsey stood in the doorway, staring at her. Caught off balance, she wobbled, lost her hold on the frame, and fell, face first, onto the bed. Fortunately, the feather mattress absorbed her fall, leaving her to laugh at her own folly and the expression on her husband's face.

Chapter Three

Ramsey hurried to the bedside. When she rolled over, preceded by her laughter, he saw that her lightweight woolen dress was torn at the shoulder, her white skin as smooth as cream. "What on earth were you doing? You might have broken your neck."

A few giggles escaped her as she sat up, reaching for his hand. "You must think me quite mad. We . . . we . . ." She gestured to Reynolds, while wiping the tears from her cheeks with the heel of her left hand.

"The kitten seems to have disappeared, my lord," the girl said, dipping a curtsy. "My lady was looking for it."

"Disappeared? By magic?"

Johnna gulped down the last of her laughter. "I don't think so. Someone must have come in and left the door open."

"Oh, no, my lady. Mr. Credley's ever so strict about that. Says it's a slovenly habit."

They all three looked at the door, which Ramsey had left open. "And he's quite right, too." He walked over and closed it. "You've looked under the bed? What about that thing?"

'That thing' was a worktable with a long silken bag in a

virulent shade of green dropped through the middle of it. Johnna had not yet transferred her embroidery frames and pieces to it, another item which had belonged to Ramsey's mother. Reynolds opened the top and peeped in. "Nothing," she said.

None of the other furniture could have hidden a field mouse, let alone a whole cat, however small. The dressing table, the writing table, the several chairs, even the upholstered one, had no skirts or coverings under which Sheba could have hidden.

Ramsey tugged on the bellpull. "We'll order everyone to look for her," he said. "Reynolds?"

"Yes, my lord." The maid seemed to snap to attention like a guardsman.

"You retrace every step you took in here today. Maybe you let her out without thinking."

"It's possible, my lord. She was following me about. Seemed to like my duster."

Credley mustered his forces, two tall footmen for the tops of things, the boot boy for cupboards and wriggling under furniture, two maids for curtains, carpets, and cabinets. Even the gardener came in to search the cellar.

Credley, coming to report the search under way, frowned curiously at Reynolds. She polished mirrors without a cloth, pantomimed making an already tidy bed, and dusted six inches away from any surface. His master and mistress were watching this performance with what, under the circumstances, must have been critical attention. Ramsey held up his hand for silence when the butler would have spoken. "What was that?" he asked.

Johnna dropped her head to one side. "Was that my nightgown?"

"Yes, my lady. I folded it and now I'm taking it into the dressing room."

"Go ahead."

Reynolds carried the imaginary nightdress into the dressing room, leaving the door open behind her. Johnna and Ramsey exchanged a glance before following her.

"Was that door open?"

"I don't recall, my lord."

Just as Ramsey reached out, the handle turned. His valet stood there. "Would you come in, my lord, my lady?"

Ramsey's room had darker woods with crimson curtains. His bed did not have hangings, merely thick barley-twist posts ending in eagle finials. But the finishing touch among the heaped pillows was a gray and white kitten.

Johnna hastened over and picked the kitten up. "How did you get in here?"

But Sheba had seen Ramsey and squirmed so that Johnna let her down. She trotted across the floor to strop against his boots. When he picked her up, Johnna saw his valet wince as the kitten's fur marked his coat.

Credley touched the valet's arm and jerked his head toward the door. They collected Reynolds as they left.

Johnna smiled at her husband, his big hands contrasting with the littleness of the kitten. She knew how gentle his large hands could be. The memory made her turn her head away to hide a sudden blush.

"She must have found her way in here," Ramsey said, "and couldn't get out."

"I think she just likes you."

"If she does, I'm glad." He put Sheba down and reached into his pocket. "I imagine you'll want to change your dress before we go?"

"Go?"

He pulled out a small book, bound in red leather, and opened it to the first page. Holding it up before her eyes, he smiled. "Eleven a.m., the Tower with J."

* * *

The gray tower seemed as insubstantial as the mist rolling in from the Thames as they left their carriage to walk up to the impressive entrance. The yeoman warders were a bright scarlet reminder of England's past against the cold backdrops of stone and historical crime.

Neither February's misty chill or remembrances of judicial murder seemed as intense when she walked with her arm wrapped up in her husband's. She hardly needed her oversized muff as they strolled about and, in truth, she listened to the old stories with but half her attention. She smiled proudly at those few others who had braved the weather to visit the Tower. None had so handsome a companion.

The lions and other beasts were easily admired in their houses of stone. They looked healthy, though cramped, and their guide encouraged one of the tigresses, born in the Tower, to yowl for them. Johnna thought she'd never seen anything so elegant as the big cat pacing before the iron bars of its cage. "It moves just like Sheba," she said.

Ramsey nodded. "I'm sure when cats dream, they are tigers."

He asked if the yeoman warder would show them the Crown Jewels. A few minutes later, by the light of some dozen candles, Johnna admired the gleaming gold and shining gems while Ramsey stood apart with the middle-aged soldier in the Elizabethan uniform. She heard the chink of coins being offered and accepted.

"Take off your hat," Ramsey said in her ear. "And close your eyes."

Obediently, Johnna untied the ribbons of her upstanding bonnet and laid it aside on the desk in the room where the jewels were kept. She'd been surprised to learn that, though the room had no windows, the regalia itself was kept in a closet with quite an ordinary lock. Ramsey had written their names and address in a book before the jewels were brought out. "Just in case," the yeoman warder had said with a wink.

A moment later, she felt the weight and tightness of a crown around her brow. She gasped and opened her eyes, lifting wondering hands to touch cold metal and rounded gems. A clinking collar of gold, interspersed with enameled plaques, settled like a heavy snake over her shoulders. Ramsey laid Charles the Second's scepter in her hand while in the other he placed a huge, uncut ruby. Then he turned her by the shoulders to face a wall-hung mirror that the yeoman warder uncovered, grinning under his tall red hat.

Johnna stared at her glittering reflection until an incautious movement caused the crown to slip sideways to give her a rakish, even revolutionary, air. She laughed and doffed the crown, returning it to the yeoman warder with thanks. "Evidently, it takes some practice to wear one of those."

Ramsey helped her take off the rest of the regalia. "Are you sure you wouldn't like to keep it? I'm not ordinarily a braggart, as you know, but according to some accounts, my great-grandfather should have been offered the crown instead of Elector George."

"Your great-grandfather was the Old Pretender?" Johnna asked skeptically, tying her bonnet's ribbons, as they left the room and started down the stairs.

"No, no. Another fellow all together. After the fiasco of 1715, he chose not to pursue his claim. If the rightful Stuart king couldn't return, we Dillons had no chance."

"It's a good thing you didn't say that before witnesses, Ramsey. You could be hung for sedition. 'Rightful king,' indeed."

"Would you arrange my escape from this Tower if I were so foolish?"

"If I could. Has anyone ever managed it?"

"Oh, yes. Two or three times. One man climbed down a rope to a boat on the river and sailed away."

"What a delightful story. Please don't tell me what happened next."

"Don't tell you?"

"Sometimes it's better not to know, don't you think?"

"I'm afraid my curiosity always gets the better of me. What would you like to see now?"

"Everything," she said, "except the dungeons. I'm so glad it isn't a prison anymore."

"No. The last prisoners were removed two or three years ago. They say the animals will go one of these days. London needs a real zoological park."

Talking lightly of the future, arguing gently over the Regent and his tame architect's plans for the city, they strolled through the relicts of the past. Coming out from under the Bloody Tower, Johnna shivered, a reaction to both the infamies of the past and the thickening of the river's mist.

Ramsey stopped, facing her. A frown showed under the brim of his hat. "Why women's clothes are so flimsy . . ." he said, snugging her high collar closer around her throat. "You should have on thick boots and a fur-lined pelisse."

"I shall instruct my dressmaker as soon as I see her."

"The devil with that! Send one of the footmen with a note. These dreary February days can drag on into March, and I don't want to you come down with a catarrh."

"To hear is to obey, my lord."

"Precisely the attitude a wife should take," he said. She thought she saw a kiss in the depths of his eyes. As he pressed closer, she caught her breath, only to discover he was sheltering her from a heedless group of schoolboys racing through the narrow walkway, shouting to hear the echoes bouncing off the damp and ancient stone. When they'd gone by, he straightened. Yet the strange, intense look still glowed in his eyes. He brushed her cheek with his fingers.

"Cold as marble," he said, touching her lips with the pad of his thumb. "You write out your orders as soon as we are home."

"Yes, I will." They walked on, Johnna feeling a little disappointed. Between one step and the next, she abruptly remembered another letter, one that had completely slipped her memory. What had she done with Gale's note?

"Is something wrong? Johnna?"

"I beg your . . . oh, no. Nothing's wrong. But now that you have brought it up, I am rather cold. Not that I wish to go home yet. Not if you wish to stay."

"Never mind. We can go home at once." When she started to protest, he laughed. "They aren't dismantling the whole edifice next week and shipping it to America, you know, though I understand they've had offers. It will still be here in the spring. We'll visit again."

"I hope we will. I'd very much like to come back when the grass is green. The yeoman warder also said there'd be some newborn animals then, too." She tried to answer him lightly, as carelessly as they'd bantered before she'd remembered Gale's letter. She tried to remember when she'd had it last in her hand. How could she have forgotten about it? What if someone else found it? The servants might or, horrors, her mother.

She'd already broken the seal. Anyone could read what he'd written. Even innocuous statements could be twisted until they sounded like indications of infidelity. And Gale had a way of doing cruel things like that. If Ramsey discovered her folly, he might be kind, but could he ever forget her foolishness?

Ramsey sat beside her in the carriage. He'd taken her hand but, finding it chilled, he tucked it once more into her muff. Turning his head to look out the window, he suddenly rapped on the ceiling. "Hold up!"

The coachman maneuvered through the City traffic to pull up out of the way. "Wait here," Ramsey said and swung open the door. Johnna, curious, leaned forward to look out of the window, straining her eyes to follow his square form down the narrow pavement. Though night was coming on, overlaying the mist, she kept him in sight until he walked into a knot of passersby and vanished from her view. She could hear the coachman talking to the horses, reassuring them that this sudden stop wasn't anything to get nervous about. Johnna wished someone would talk like that to her.

She sat back among the squabs and waited, gazing idly out the window. They had stopped beside wrought-iron palings with an impressive guild building of white stone behind. Suddenly, Johnna recognized the unmistakable feeling of being watched. She looked about her swiftly.

There, between the carriage and the palings, stood a man, staring at her as if she were a vision. The coach lamps just illuminated him, so that she saw the pointed collar of his shirt first and then his face. His dark coat faded into the background. It was as if he had materialized out of the mist. He had a muffler wrapped around the lower part of his face so that she could not recognize him. Then he touched the brim of his hat with a flick of his fingers that was heart-stoppingly familiar, for she'd seen it a hundred times. "Gale," she said so softly that she herself hardly heard it.

He just stood there, making no move toward the carriage. Yet his stance, the way he held his head, told her that he was laughing at her in his odiously superior way. But why? Johnna felt sure his note would give her the answer. She was equally certain that she did not want to know. Yet if she refused to acknowledge his message, he might come to the house.

She turned her head, facing resolutely in the opposite direction. She did not need to see him to know he was still laughing. Then the coachman's voice penetrated, held close by the fog, "He's a-coming back. Get the door, boy."

Ramsey jumped into the carriage, the scent of roasting chestnuts coming with him. He held out the cone of twisted paper. "These will warm you up. He was just preparing to shut up shop for the night."

"It's lucky you saw him," she said, peeling a nut. The carriage rolled on. With considerable exertion of self-control,

Johnna did not look round as they passed the spot where Gale had been standing. If he was still there, let him see that she was protected and honored by her husband.

As if Gale had answered, she seemed to hear his voice asking, "But for how long?"

As they approached their home, Ramsey offered her the last of the chestnuts. Impulsively, she leaned toward him and kissed his slightly bristly cheek. He jerked back in surprise, then gave her a long look, his fingers touching the spot where her lips had pressed. "What a reward for courtesy," he said.

"Thank you for a lovely afternoon. I enjoyed myself very much."

"So did I. What would you like to do this evening? The theaters aren't open yet, but if you would care to accept some invitation or other . . ." He took her hand, his still warm from the cone of nuts. "I want to show the world that I am not so neglectful a husband as I seemed last night. Come, let's go to some card party or salon. There must be something. Or are you too tired?" he asked, perhaps feeling that her lack of instant response showed displeasure.

"No, I'm not tired. If you'd like to go out, of course, we will. For myself, however . . ."

"Yes?"

"Do you recall how we played dominoes at Mrs. DePonsy's in the evening?"

"I recall you beat me unmercifully. I'd plan my strategy with nigh on Napoleonic cunning and there'd you'd be with double blanks and double sixes like ranks of artillery blasting my hopes to perdition. Well, if it is to be my punishment, I should thank you for making it so light. Do you think your mother would like to play?"

"I'm sure she would. What shall we wager?"

"I am already too deep in your debt. We'll play for love."

* * *

In her room, Johnna searched high and low for the note. Just as Sheba, earlier in the day, had evaded her, so did the piece of paper. When Reynolds came in to help her change for the evening, she took her courage up and asked, as lightly as if the matter were of no particular importance.

"A letter, my lady?"

"Yes, on toast-colored paper. I had it after breakfast and, in all the confusion, I seem to have lost it."

"I can't say . . . a piece of paper usually shows up on a carpet like this," the maid said, glancing down at the figured turkey carpet that covered all but the edge of the floor. The pattern was a great mosaic of red and blue stylized lotus blossoms. What white or cream there might be was confined to small curved lines. A square of a light color would show up like . . . a white face against a dark background.

"Are you all right, my lady?"

Johnna realized she had shut her eyes against the swirling darkness that had overwhelmed her for a moment. "Yes, quite well," she said perfunctorily. "My hair looks very nice. Thank you, Reynolds."

"My pleasure, my lady. I never had a mistress with nicer hair," she said, giving a little pat to the nest of ringlets hanging down from Johnna's crown.

"I only wish it were a more interesting color."

"I could help you with that." The maid lowered her voice. "I could make a fortune, if I hadn't been sworn to secrecy by Miss Priddy. She's the one what taught me everything."

"Heavens, how mysterious."

"It's a secret mixture, handed down from one generation of maidservants to the next. It'll turn any head of hair into gold as pretty as a new sovereign."

"Golden hair, eh?" Johnna squinted at herself in the mirror, turning her head from side to side. Reynolds had threaded a blue ribbon through the curls in a shade that made her hair look somewhat less mousy. She thought of Ramsey's tousled hair in the morning, the candle awakening red gleams among the rich brown.

"No, thank you, Reynolds. I'd rather stay myself," she said lightly. "But if ever you feel like leaving our service to pursue a future in hair transformations, we'll give you our leave."

"Thank you, my lady. I'll ask among the staff about your letter."

Johnna reflected a moment. "Yes. Yes, please do. Now I think I should dress."

After dinner, Mrs. Feldon said that she'd rather embroider than play dominoes. She sat by the fire, a light over her shoulder, while Johnna and Ramsey played on a table in the middle of the room.

Ramsey liked to see the varied expressions on his wife's face, exultation when she made a good play, the almost feline flick of her eyes as she watched what pieces he laid down, waiting to pounce upon his every weakness. He also liked the golden light falling upon her rounded bosom in her low-cut evening dress. The rustling lustrous satin seemed to whisper of concealed delights, all the more alluring for being hidden. When she reached out to complete a run, leaning forward over the table, leaving him nothing to do but concede the game, he suddenly wished that they were quite alone.

"Mr. Adrian Dillon, my lord," Credley announced.

"Adrian? Delighted to see you, cousin," Ramsey said, getting up to shake his hand and bring him all the way into the room.

"Dominoes?" Adrian said, after greeting the ladies. "How domesticated of you, my dear Ramsey."

"We all come to it in time," Ramsey said with a lift of the shoulders.

"Would you like to play?" Johnna asked. Ramsey wasn't sure how he knew she was teasing, yet he could read that note in her expression. Some hint of a smile about her eyes, perhaps. He could also tell that Adrian, suave sophisticate though he might be, was taken aback.

"Draw up a chair for Mr. Dillon, please, Credley," Ramsey said. The butler snapped his fingers in their white gloves and the muffled sound summoned a footman.

"Mother, would you play too? I have a terrible time with three-handed games, as you may remember."

"I know we missed Nancy's company when she married Harlan. What point shall we play to?"

Evidently at a loss, Adrian took his seat at the gaming table. "What are the stakes?"

"We play for love," Ramsey said.

"And, of course, to win," Johnna added.

"How refreshing."

Ramsey laughed to himself. His cousin never sat down to whist except for bankruptcy-inducing stakes. To sit at a table without risking the loss of his shirt must be a novel experience.

The black counters with their golden dots snaked across the green leather surface of the table, keenly directed by all four players. Mrs. Feldon proved to be as eager a competitor as Johnna and accepted a kiss from both daughter and son-in-law when she won with a final slap of a double deuce. Adrian gravely saluted her fingertips. "Madam, it has been an honor to be defeated by you. Even more. An education."

After another round, Johnna rose to her feet. "Come, Mama. I'm sure Cousin Adrian did not come here tonight merely to play games with us. Let us leave the gentlemen to their talk."

Ramsey caught her hand as she passed his chair. "I won't be very long," he said, sure she would know this as a promise.

After the women had gone, he proposed that they adjourn to his study, where the chairs were more comfortable and the brandy uninhibited. "So what's amiss?" he asked when they were settled.

"I wonder if you would make me a small loan, cousin."

"Certainly. How much do you require?" He had the satisfaction of seeing Adrian out of countenance, for once.

"Don't you want to ask me what I need it for?"

"Considering that you have never applied to me before, I assume you find yourself in dire straits. It would be impertinent to inquire into your personal affairs."

Adrian laughed. "Did your father keep you on short strings, cousin? You have the air of a man who models himself on an ideal lender never yet found in nature."

"I confess freely that my allowance was never sufficient for my wants. My father's openhandedness was restricted to his friends and mistresses."

"I'd heard. *My* father didn't approve."

"*My* father would have damned *your* father's disapproval as a piece of insolence demanding satisfaction at Barn Elms. But we live in a more civilized era. Will five hundred suffice?"

"Very well indeed. Thank you, Ramsey." For once, Adrian's voice rang with sincerity. Evidently embarrassed, he went to the bookshelves and took down a volume at random.

Drinking from his glass as he walked, Ramsey crossed to his desk and pulled out a piece of paper. "I'll write you a draft on the Bank. In truth, as my heir, I should make you an allowance myself."

"Do and we part forever," Adrian said evenly, without looking up from his perusal.

"An occasional touch being of a different order?"

"I've never asked before. You were always my bank of last resort." He strolled over with his usual grace to collect the check that Ramsey held out. But as he reached for it, Ramsey flicked it back toward himself.

"Are you in more need than this?" he asked, his tone permitting no prevaricating.

"It will serve to stave off the most pressing debts. I played rather deep tonight with two gentlemen from the Isle of Wight, of all places. The five hundred is for them. The other fellow—one Farringdon—had worse luck even than I. Thank heaven for small mercies."

"Farringdon?"

"Yes, do you know him? He looked odd when I was introduced to him as Dillon."

"You must be used to that," Ramsey said with the careless wit between men who'd known each other as children. Behind the words, he thought furiously.

"Ah, but I think it was more to your address than mine, dear chap. He asked at once if I were related to you. Upon my shamefaced admission, he seemed almost on the point of asking questions but refrained before shattering his claim to be a member of the polite world."

"I believe Johnna may have known him," Ramsey said with seeming carelessness. "If it's the same man, they met when she lived in Canterbury."

"Canterbury? Odd. He impressed me as a most uncanonical man. I must reconsider my policy of playing with anyone who asks me provided they are in funds."

"You might reconsider playing at all."

"What should I do then?" Adrian asked with a bitter smile. "Settle down with a decent woman and play dominoes for the rest of my life?"

"You'll live longer."

"Alas, my dear cousin, it would only seem that way."

Ramsey kept Adrian with him for another half hour, hoping that a pursuit of several different subjects would wipe the mention of Gale Farringdon out of his cousin's thoughts. Adrian, so cool and controlled, would never be able to understand the black bile of jealousy.

After Adrian had gone, Ramsey returned to the study. He drank a little but the metallic taste in his mouth did evil things to the wine. The fireplace smoked a little, making his eyes sting. He supposed he should go up to Johnna. She must be waiting for him. Maybe her calmness would act as an antidote to the burning acridity of his thoughts.

He jerked the bellpull. "I'm going for a walk, Credley. I'll take King with me."

"Young Fred took the dog already . . . yes, my lord. At once."

The air was thick and cold, misty if not still foggy. Walking at the dog's pace, stopping frequently at fences, lampposts, and horse rings, Ramsey felt as if he could breathe again. It was not yet so late that every candle was extinguished, so even in the intervals between lamps, he could see well enough. In his heart, though, all was confusion and darkness.

He didn't even know when exactly he'd decided against love. Perhaps it was when he'd determined that his father's departures for London were the signal for his mother's retreat to her couch, where she would lie listlessly, crying a little. When he came home, the tears, shouting, and slamming of doors would begin all over again. The servants would gossip in front of him, assuming he was too young to understand. His nurse had been a great one for tittle-tattle. From her, eventually, Ramsey had learned his father's current mistress's name, address, and hair color. There had been more than one over the years.

When Ramsey's mother died in his thirteenth year, his father had retired to their country home, contrite too late. He'd confided in his son, hoping perhaps for the forgiveness he could not now request of his wife. Ramsey had been glad to return to school. Two years later, Lord Dillon had married a second time to a solid woman of his own age and class. He admitted that he did not feel for her the love he had for his first wife but that he did not wish to live alone any longer. Ramsey's stepmother had presided over a quiet, well-regulated household and showed no qualms at all when her husband took a mistress. She'd nursed him devotedly through his last illness and had retired to the warmer climate of Lisbon, where Ramsey sent her an allowance.

Small wonder then, when looking for a wife himself, he'd determined to choose for reasons other than love. He valued peace above all other possessions. He'd even—triple idiot that he was!—congratulated himself on finding a woman who was, quite probably, in love with someone else. He'd thought that would spare him from having to fend off the emotional entanglement of his own wife.

"Good evenin', sir," a passing lamplighter said, touching his cap.

Ramsey grunted and walked on.

Mrs. DePonsy had told him something about Johnna having been in love with an unsuitable man. "It didn't amount to very much. Her mother soon put a stop to it. She's had experience with libertines before. Her oldest girl had men around her like flies at an al fresco breakfast—though dear Johnna is not as spectacular as Ariana, by any means."

He could not, in chivalry, reply. Johnna wasn't a beauty, but she had countenance in a way that her prettier sister or Susanna DePonsy, for that matter, never would. Their beauty would flame and die to ashes while she remained a pleasure to look at even in age. Wide brows and classic bones do not wither at the touch of years.

Mrs. Feldon, too, had hinted that there was some 'boy-and-girl' folly in Johnna's past. What had she said one evening when Johnna was playing the piano while some couples danced? "Girls can be so foolish," was it? Or "girls can be made fools of"?

When he'd traveled to Canterbury, ostensibly to visit friends but really to see Johnna again, he'd spoken to their maid. An exchange of a few pounds bought him the whole story. An unsuitable man, an impressionable girl, the intercession of family, and a parting. "Oh, he never come to the house.

Mistress wouldn't a stood for it. But many's the time I stood outside the churchyard waiting for her. Ever so handsome, he was. Tall, like. But terrible cruel eyes, I thought. I said it to the cook, ten to one, I said, he's after her just for what he can get out of her or the mistress."

The Feldons weren't wealthy; Johnna was no heiress. Perhaps Gale Farringdon had loved her. Perhaps she'd loved him. But she'd married Ramsey. Did she regret it?

Unbuttoning his greatcoat, Ramsey reached into his coat pocket. He stopped under a lamp that burned a little more brightly than its fellows. King, sighing, sat down on the chilly pavement. "Good boy," Ramsey said absently.

He shook open the letter with one hand. His valet had picked it up from his bedroom floor that afternoon, seeing it peering out from under the coverlet edge. When Ramsey had gone up to change for dinner after his afternoon at the Tower, his man had given it to him. He couldn't read it now, the light was too yellow on the page, washing out the brownish ink, but he already knew what it said.

My dearest Johnna,

Such happiness to know that we are once more in the same city. Remembering those stolen hours we shared, those delightful moments we passed, makes me wish with fervor that they might be renewed. When shall I see you? Tomorrow at noon in your church? The usual place.

Yours eternally,
GF

It was dated yesterday. It must have arrived today. So tomorrow . . . what was he to do? Follow her like a jealous husband in a Restoration farce? Or confront her like a jealous husband in a French drama? Was there a more ridiculous character in all literature than the jealous husband?

Ramsey told himself that he was not jealous—or, if he was, in the sense that a man who owns a treasure would be angry when a thief tries to steal it. But he knew, in his heart, that he was more like a child screaming so loudly against being inoculated that he quite failed to notice the prick of the needle. For how could he be jealous—blackly, vilely, bitterly jealous—if he were not in love?

He crammed the paper back into his pocket and walked on, King patiently trotting along beside him. There was no proof, just this letter, that she even knew Farringdon was in London. But jealousy whispered cruelly that she *did* know and that she'd only been kind to him today because she would see her lover tomorrow. Ramsey learned that jealousy cannot be silenced by reason. Every argument he could muster was answered instantly by some new twisting of what Johnna had said and how she'd behaved. It was as if some part of him *wanted* to believe she was guilty.

"And to think I used to think Othello was too easily swayed," he said aloud. "Shakespeare was right, as always."

King's ears flicked back at the sound of his master's voice, but he'd discovered some interesting bits of rubbish and had no advice to offer.

If Johnna proved to be unfaithful, then he was right. Love was folly. Love was a lie. If she was guilty, then he need never risk telling her that he loved her.

Though they'd never spoken of it directly, there could be no doubt that they'd agreed to have a marriage that was companionable in feeling and correct in duty. Though her shyness had been an obstacle, she'd come ungrudgingly enough to the marriage bed. The charge that jealousy offered at that tender remembrance was instantly refuted. She'd been untouched.

To change the arrangement now was indeed a risk. She might be appalled. Worse yet, she might laugh. Or try to conceal her true feelings and pretend a response. Better to pretend himself. After all, he might be wrong. He might not love her.

He returned home, shocked when he saw that he'd been gone for almost two hours. As soon as the door opened, King trudged across the foyer and flopped down in front of the study fire with a sigh that seemed to come from all four feet.

"Her ladyship had some warm milk an hour ago, my lord," Credley volunteered, accepting Ramsey's greatcoat. His face seemed grave, not looking upon his master with his usual air of gracious approval.

"I won't disturb her, then. I'll retire at once. Send up my man."

"Very good, my lord."

After he'd changed and dismissed his valet, Ramsey looked at his bed and thought he'd never seen anything less appealing. The pillows were piled high, the thick coverlet turned back to expose soft linen sheets. He knew at least one hot brick lay hidden in the depths, suffusing warmth. Yet it repelled him because it was empty.

Taking his candle, he walked through the dressing rooms. He tapped lightly at his wife's door and listened for the reply. There wasn't one.

He opened the door and peeped in, his candle held low. Johnna's bed was a black mound, lit with a few golden gleams that were the carved putti and swags. He approached her side, the lights and shadows moving with him.

She slept on her side, curled around a pillow. All he could see of her face was her right eye, the lashes casting shadows on her cheek. She'd not yet torn off her nightcap and the bedding was pulled right up to her face. The light caressed her skin as if it fell on satin, spiraling down the single lock of hair that had escaped. Soon, she'd pull off her cap entirely and her hair would tumble out, spreading across the pillow. He'd often awakened, in the past three months, to the feather touch of her hair on his shoulder or face. It smelled always of chamomile.

Ramsey smiled as he looked at his sleeping wife, his love. He vowed that if she should prove innocent tomorrow, he'd tell her at once of his feelings. If not, there was one character in literature even more pathetic than the jealous husband—the loving husband of an unfaithful wife. If that was to be his role, he'd accept it, knowing no other than himself was the author of his misfortune.

Chapter Four

At breakfast the next morning, Johnna couldn't relax and enjoy her toast. She was waiting every moment for Credley to bring in the post. Mrs. Feldon was pouring coffee. Ramsey, siting across from Johnna, passed her the jelly when she asked for it. "What are you going to do today?" he asked in return.

"Oh! Mama and I are returning to the dressmaker's. My gown for tonight needs a final fitting."

"For tonight?"

"Yes, Madame Atwell's Valentine's Day ball. You told me it was a national institution."

He nodded. "Yes, it is. People actually come to London out of Season for it."

"That sounds like a lot of trouble," Mrs. Feldon said. "Why does she bother?"

"It commemorates her marriage. It was a—um—love match in the days when such things were even rarer than they are now."

"A runaway marriage, wasn't it?" Johnna said, wondering if he was feeling quite well. His cheeks were rather red.

"Oh, my." Mrs. Feldon tsk-tsked.

"Mr. Atwell wasn't yet a wealthy man. As a matter of fact, he didn't have two shillings to clink together. She was a gentleman's daughter. After they were married, Mr. Atwell invented some sort of steam engine that pumped fresh air into the tin mines."

"He must have made a fortune," Mrs. Feldon said, marveling.

"Yes," Ramsey agreed. "But he died before he was forty."

"And she holds this ball every year in memory of the day they met." Johnna smiled across at Ramsey, wondering if he felt the romance of the idea as much as she did. He met her gaze steadily but without smiling in return. Had she displeased him in some way? She hadn't been able to help falling asleep before he'd come up to bed. He'd been so late. Nor had he made any mention of the specialness of the day. Of course, neither had she. She opened her mouth to ask him to be her valentine when Credley came in with the morning's post.

Johnna watched him lay the letters beside her husband's plate. She wanted to ask if there was anything for her, but was afraid it would look odd. She'd never asked before.

Ramsey flipped through the cards and envelopes, laying aside invitations. These he handed across to Johnna. She also paged through them, looking for one particular hand. A sigh of relief escaped her lips when she realized Gale had not written again. No doubt it was only a note of congratulations upon her marriage.

Mrs. Feldon patted her lips with her serviette. "We should make an earlier rather than a later call upon your modiste. If there's anything amiss with the gown, the more time she has to correct it, the better."

"Yes, Mama. I'm so glad you're staying a few extra days."

"Are you leaving us, ma'am?" Ramsey asked.

"Yes. It's about time, don't you think?" She held up her hand when he would have spoken. "I shall refute your protests before you even make them, my dear Ramsey. It's time you and Johnna started your own lives without a meddling mother-in-law about. Never fear, I shall return when Johnna needs me. I only hope that day is not too far distant. A woman can't have too many grandchildren."

As Johnna came down the steps, fastening her glove, she saw her husband waiting for her at the foot. He, too, was dressed to go out, looking very handsome in a blue coat over a cream-colored waistcoat embroidered with vines in the same tone. His greatcoat, open over all, made him look very tall and somehow remote. "You look very fine," she declared. "Help me with this?"

He took her hand, bending over the small pearl buttons. "What time will you come home?" he asked.

"I'm not certain. Did you want me?"

"Not for anything of great importance. I thought we might have luncheon together. At noon, perhaps."

"Noon? That's rather early, isn't it? Do you have an appointment in the City?"

"No . . . I mean, yes. I must visit my banker. What color is your gown?"

"Silver blue," she said, surprised that he would even inquire.

"There's a set of pearls and sapphires that might do for that. I should really bring all the jewelry here, shouldn't I? It's all yours now, and you should really know what's there. You might find a use for them . . . someday."

"I'd would like to see your mother's jewelry, but I don't think we should keep it in the house, do you? Reynolds will give you that topaz set to put back at the bank. Everyone admired it the other evening, but I wouldn't feel safe with such things here. What if we were burgled some night?"

"King would bark and Credley would bite," he said with something like his usual humor. Yet there was a sad downward twist to his mouth as he looked at her.

Johnna reached for his hand. "Are you feeling well? You seem . . ."

Somehow his hand was not there. Before she'd completed reaching out, he'd moved it, pulling out his watch. "Is it eleven o'clock already? You'd better be on your way."

"Yes, thank you, Ramsey. As soon as Mama comes down . . . ."

"Here I am," Mrs. Feldon called, trotting down the steps like a girl. "Are we to drop you somewhere, Ramsey?"

"No, thank you. I shall walk to the corner and find a cab. I haven't very far to go."

In the carriage, Johnna sat silently until her mother asked her what was amiss. "Ramsey said he was going into the City to visit his bankers. Then he said he didn't have far to go when you asked if he was coming with us. That doesn't make sense."

"Maybe he was being polite. Or . . ."

"Or, Mama?"

She moved restlessly on the cushions. "You've been married three, almost four, months. You can't expect a man of the world to be content forever."

A few months ago, Johnna would have been at a loss. Now she understood such hints. She could laugh at them too. "No, Mama. I don't think Ramsey will ever be unfaithful to me."

"You don't? Child, you're living in a dream."

"No, I'm not. He has very strong views on fidelity."

"Most men hold such views—for their wives. For themselves, it is something else again."

"Ramsey is an exceptional man, Mama. He told me once—shortly after we met—that if a man's honor demands he should walk through fire to discharge a gambling debt, then he should strive just as hard to keep trust with the woman he marries."

"You discussed such things before you were married?" Mrs. Feldon's tone was shocked.

"We discussed marriage very general terms the second time we met."

"He must have been thinking of marrying you even then. I wouldn't have believed it. Even Ariana's husband didn't want to marry her until he'd known her a year, and he apologized for being so impetuous!"

The fitting, thank heaven, didn't take very long. The dressmaker promised to have the trifling alterations done at once and the dress would be delivered, without fail, that afternoon. "Where shall we go now?" Mrs. Feldon asked. "I understand they have excellent kid gloves at the Burlington Arcade. It's not far from here, I think."

"Take the carriage if you wish, Mama. I think I shall go home."

"Go home? Alone?"

"Yes, why not? If Ramsey can hire a cab, why can't I? Or, if you don't mind, take me home and then go on yourself. I'll place it at your disposal for the day."

"Oh, I don't want to rattle all the way across town and back again. Have the coachman drop me at the Arcade and then drive you home. He can come back for me in an hour or so. I'll have no trouble amusing myself there!"

"I suppose there must be a dozen things you want to buy before you go home. Presents for my sisters? And Mrs. Palmer's always so grateful for any little remembrance. Maybe one of those china pug dogs we saw at that shop . . ."

"Exactly."

So Johnna came home by herself. The coachman promised faithfully to collect Mrs. Feldon in an hour and a half, giving them time to rest the horses. Johnna waved her thanks and went into the house. Credley met her at the door. "This came by messenger an hour ago, my lady. I hope it is nothing urgent."

Johnna hesitated before taking up the envelope he offered on a salver. "No, nothing of importance. Is the boy waiting for an answer?"

"No, my lady."

"Thank you," she said absently, looking at the writing. "Has my husband come back?"

"No, my lady. But I expect him shortly. He said he would return just after noon, and it is five-and-twenty past."

Johnna passed into the morning room, knowing that she would be undisturbed there now that her mother was out. The wavering sunshine seemed warmer there, influenced by the yellow wallpaper and botanical prints. But there was a coldness at her heart no sunshine could reach as she seated herself on the settee. There seemed to be some sort of fuss going on outside in the garden but Johnna ignored it.

Using the ruthless speed of a person pulling out their own tooth, Johnna ripped open the envelope, not fussing with the wax seal this time. She spread out the page and turned pale as she read the word scratched into the paper with a vicious pen.

My dear Johnna,

You may have already learned, during your short stay in Town, that people are censorious, determined always to put the worst possible interpretation on what they see or read. For evidence, I present your recent abandonment by your husband at your birthday party and, secondly, those sweet letters you wrote to me during our friendship.

Though I had vowed to burn them, upon rereading them, I could not bring myself to put them on the fire. If you wish them to be burned, you shall have to do it yourself. I trust you will acquire them soon. If a third party were to read them, I doubt he would see the innocence and only believe he had been deceived before ever being made happy.

Yours, in anticipation
of a profitable meeting,
GF

She was about to crumple the letter despairingly in her hands when she espied a faint postscript.

I have procured an invitation to Madame Atwell's famous ball. I will see you there.

What hurt wasn't that he was a scoundrel; she'd guessed that early in their friendship. What hurt was that he could be a scoundrel to her. Even when he'd boasted of his former bad behavior under the guise of confession, she'd been secretly thrilled that he'd confided in her. She'd believed she could change him into the man she dreamed of, dashing, dangerous, and yet safe.

Is that what he'd seen in her? Someone to hero worship him and yet be too stupid or innocent to understand that he never would change? Remembering how he'd kissed her, laughed at her, and teased her, she realized he'd been playing a game, flattering his self-conceit, enlivening a few boring months spent in a social backwater while he recouped his funds.

How long before it would have palled for him? Looking back, she knew he'd already begun to find her pallid virginity boring even before her mother had interfered. If Mrs. Feldon hadn't broken it off, he would have, breaking her heart into the bargain, for he would not have been kind. And now he meant to hold her letters over her head, making demands for money, for she knew perfectly well that it was never high water with him for long.

Johnna couldn't recall with any precision what she'd written. Girlish effusion and no more, for she hadn't known what more there could possibly be until after her marriage. Ramsey might not think the worst of her, but that was a risk she could not take. His good opinion meant more to her than she'd ever hoped. For that reason, she didn't dare confess, either.

She heard a commotion somewhere in the house—raised voices, a sharp exclamation. Johnna got up and shut the door, thinking furiously.

She wished her mother was at home. Mama would scold

and say I told you so, but she'd have advice to offer as well. One could always rely on her for steady good sense.

The voices penetrated even the closed door. Johnna, disturbed, went to see what the trouble was. She met Credley and Reynolds outside. The butler seemed shaken out of his Augustan composure. The maid stood with her hands on her hips, evidently giving as good as she got. The instant they saw her, they were silenced and resumed the perfect posture of good servants. "Yes?" Johnna said.

"Through an unfortunate oversight," Credley said, "my lady's kitten has escaped the house."

"Escaped . . . you mean she's outside? Where?"

"In the garden. With the dog."

"The dog? Oh, my goodness." Hastily, Johnna stuffed the letter into its envelope, then tucked it for safety into her bosom. "Show me."

The garden in the rear of the house was centered on a long sandy path with the beds along each side quartered by hedges. It formed a sort of loose knot garden. At this season, of course, there were no plants in bloom, but the sticks of rose bushes and the naked branches of some low shrubs showed where the color and fragrance would be come the spring. At the far end, on either side of the alley's gate, stood two sheds. Latticework was nailed to every visible surface so that vines could be trained to conceal these utilitarian objects.

All the maids belonging to the household as well as the seldom-seen cook were standing before the right-hand shed, gazing up. Some made beseeching noises. The tweeny held up a saucer of milk while the cook had a small sausage extended toward the roof as if supplicating some god above the clouds. The dog sat on his haunches watching the cook, apparently more interested in the sausage than in the cat.

Sheba sat as upright as a basalt statue of an Egyptian cat, her forelegs close together and her tail wrapped as far around her ankles as it could reach. She gazed without enthusiasm t the multitude below. When she saw Johnna, however, she nloosed her tail, walked to the edge of the shed roof and newed plaintively.

"She cain't get down, my lady," a maid she did not recog-ize said.

Another one dipped a curtsy first. "She's ever so scared, num."

Credley, shocked by this lèse-majesté, silenced them with terrible frown. "As you may observe, my lady, your kitten, pon finding the dog present, chose to retreat to higher ground. Now, unfortunately, it seems unwilling to muster the courage to come down. In my opinion, we should leave it where it is until it becomes hungry. It will then descend of its own free will."

The maids murmured protests against this sensible, if hard-hearted, attitude.

"Return to your posts at once," the butler thundered awe-somely.

Instead of scurrying away as they should under such a command, the maids and the cook walked slowly toward the door, with many a dagger look and grumble. An anonymous voice rose slightly above the crowd. *"Vive la revolution."* The French accent was execrable; the sentiment heartfelt.

"Who said that?" When Credley would have stormed off to interrogate the maids, Johnna restrained him.

"How are we to get the cat down? Isn't the gardener here?"

"No, my lady. He left yesterday for his holidays."

"And the groom and coachman?"

"After they brought you back, they went out for refresh-ment—but not, it seems, at their usual public house."

"The footmen?"

"On their half day, my lady. They go together, as they are brothers."

"The boot boy?"

"Running a small errand and will not be back for another hour at least, knowing him," he added darkly.

"Very well, Credley. You take out the ladder and I shall climb it."

"My lady?"

Ramsey waited at the church from eleven-thirty, at first at the main doors and then, fearing they'd enter by another way inside the building. He'd managed to avoid being seen by the Reverend Mr. Precox, not wanting conversation. Not only did Johnna not appear, but no other man seemed to be waiting for her. Either he'd misunderstood the note—perhaps the words 'your church' had meant a different building—or they'd communicated by other means. If Johnna hadn't read the note, she would not have come, naturally enough. But why wouldn't Farringdon show up? He couldn't have known that Ramsey had read it.

Ramsey came home at one o'clock, hungry and confused. A night had brought no better counsel than his walk. Johnna had seemed so natural at breakfast, not at all like a person with a guilty conscience. Maybe she did not yet have anything to be guilty about. That 'yet' tortured him.

Credley was not there to take his coat. Ramsey hung it up himself. Catching a stray maid in the hall, he asked for the butler. "Oh, my lord. Oh, my lord," she said in evident distress.

"Are you talking to me or to God?" he inquired politely, not wanting to intrude on her prayers.

After a little while, the maid told him that his wife was in the garden and that the kitten was on the roof. Ramsey went outside at once. King got up from where he was lying and trotted over to his master. Ramsey patted the dog's smooth head absently, his attention on the tableau at the bottom of the garden path.

"It's my duty, my lady," Credley said.

"I cannot hold the ladder for you, so you must hold it for

ıe." So saying, Johnna began to climb up, the undersides of er small shoes showing.

The butler, looking around wildly, saw his master. But amsey held up his hand when the other man would have poken. If Johnna was disturbed, she might fall—and the hed roof was just high enough that she might have dangerusly hurt herself.

"Come along, Sheba," she said, when her head topped the oof. "Come to me." Johnna held something out to the kitten n her fingertips, some tempting morsel, no doubt.

The kitten, just out of grabbing range, sniffed disdainully. Ignoring Johnna, she gave some needed attention to ıer ears and whiskers.

Johnna sought to rise one more step, but that would put ıer almost at the top of the ladder. Ramsey strode forward. He gave more support to the ladder. His wife looked down at him and gave him such a warm smile that his doubts bent before it. They did not, however, break.

"Come down, please," he said. "I'll go up for her. Credley can hold the ladder for me."

"Gladly, my lord."

"I can almost reach her." She leaned over the rough roof, but the kitten had gone farther out of reach. Her right foot kicked up so that she was standing only on the toes of the other one. She tried to reach farther than her arm's length, imperiling the stitching of yet another dress, and the ladder shuddered against the side of the shed.

"Johnna, please come down. You're making me very nervous."

"All right."

While the butler looked the other way, Johnna descended. "I can't imagine how she got up there unless she climbed the lattice."

"Cats have levitating powers left over from when they were worshipped by the Egyptians," Ramsey said.

While she stood under him, helping the butler hold th ladder, Ramsey climbed up. Sheba came to him instantl Ramsey scooped her up in one hand and turned to let h down into Johnna's waiting arm. She cooed over the kitte telling her what a bad girl she'd been in tones so loving th Ramsey wished she use them to him. He had just that one in stant to whisk another letter out of sight. It must have bee in her bodice and fallen out when she leaned forward.

He wanted to be alone to read it, feeling that shamefu things should be done in privacy. Luncheon was ready, an not before time. Johnna was more vivacious than he'd eve seen her, grateful for his assistance, though confident sh could have succeeded. "I'm so happy Sheba likes you s much. You must have saved her from something terrible."

"No more terrible than King," he admitted, then told he how Sheba had come into their lives.

"You are a hero to her," Johnna said. "And to me, as well."

"I didn't rescue you."

"Oh, but you did." She didn't say any more and the letter seemed to burn in his pocket. "Have you been to your bank yet?"

"What? No, no. I had another errand to see to this morning."

"Would you mind if I accompany you? As I said earlier, I don't like having very valuable gems in the house. If I could choose at the bank, then you wouldn't need to transport everything here."

"Certainly. I want to introduce you to my man of affairs there anyway. In case I am ever out of London and you need assistance."

"I hope you'll never leave without me," she said, dropping her lashes.

Ramsey supposed he could have escaped to the most private place of all, but somehow his eagerness to read the new letter had evaporated. Besides, it was too dark in there to read. He even toyed with the idea of giving the letter back to her, oh so casually. When she ran up to get her hat, he took it out and studied it. This envelope was ripped open, the seal intact, the letter rumpled. Obviously she had read this one.

Ramsey slipped his finger under the folded edge of the letter and began to inch it out. The front door opened behind him. "Good afternoon, Ramsey," his mother-in-law said. "Where's Johnna? I must show her my purchases."

"We are about to go out," he said.

"Again? You'll confuse people. First a neglectful husband, then an attentive one. I hope to goodness you don't change back."

"If I do, it won't be my fault."

Johnna came flying down the steps like a young girl. He didn't know whether to hope that Mrs. Feldon would pull out her 'purchases' then and there, giving him a few moments alone, or not. Not, as it turned out.

They returned home just in time to change for the ball. Ramsey noticed that Johnna was subdued on the drive home. "Are you too tired to go tonight?" he asked.

"Oh, no," she said, straightening up and forcing a smile. "I wouldn't miss it."

Johnna sat before her mirror, her head dropped forward as she massaged her temples. "I must be losing my mind in addition to everything else," she muttered.

"What, dearest?" her mother asked.

"Nothing, Mama. It just seems that every time I pick up a piece of paper these days, I lose it."

"Oh, what have you to do with papers? Let your husband handle those sorts of details."

"Not these sorts."

"What, dearest?" Her mother, at least, was in high spirits.

Johnna leaned forward to look in the mirror. Outwardly, she seemed just as usual, except for a slight heaviness about her eyes. She patted rose water into the puffiness and thought it improved. A few minutes later, she was dressed, sapphires about her neck and hanging from her ears. Remembering how Ramsey had placed a king's crown on her head, she smiled giddily, helplessly.

She drew on her white gloves, thanked Reynolds for draping her cape around her shoulders, and she and her mother went downstairs. She waited for Ramsey to notice her. When he did, his lips curved in a smile but his eyes did not light. If anything, he looked sad—as if he looked at a portrait of someone very dear who was lost to him.

In the carriage, she sat close beside him. Daringly, she put her arm through his. She wanted to rest her head on his shoulder but was afraid to mark his black coat with the rice powder she'd put on her face. He kept his gaze turned toward the window. In truth, she didn't know if he knew she was there. Thank heaven her mother was with them or the ride would have been accomplished in total silence.

Once they passed through the crush of carriages to step down in front of the grand mansion, Johnna's nerves began to play tricks on her. Every second gentleman seemed to have Gale's thick black hair or his height or his mannerisms. Once she thought she heard him laugh, but it was someone completely different.

Quite a few gazes, she noticed, were turned toward them as they were announced and approached their hostess. Johnna felt so proud to have Ramsey beside her, quelling the rumors that he was a bad husband. There was many a worse crime than forgetting her birthday. Didn't he arrange special treats for her almost every day? Everything from the flowers she carried to the jewels about her neck was his gift. She kept her head up and met questioning glances with the blandest possible smile.

And he was all she could have wished. He opened the ball with her and asked for every waltz. He waited for her when she came back from dances with other men, most of them elderly, and procured refreshment without being asked. He could have been her lover instead of her husband.

"Why are you blushing?" he asked, as she moved into his arms for another waltz.

"It's hot in here," she said, not wanting to confess that she'd been remembering their wedding night.

"Yes, it is rather. Did I forget to mention that you look like an angel in that gown? I like the flowers in your hair. Are they silk? They look real."

"Yes, they're silk."

In the next turn of the dance, she felt him pluck a flower from her hair, so in rhythm to the music that no one else noticed. He placed it in his pocket and looked at her as if he'd like to kiss her.

After that, she felt as though her feet didn't even touch the ground. There was only one snake in all this Garden, but as the moments passed without his appearance, she began to wonder whether he'd forgotten. Or perhaps it had just been a cruel joke to cut up her peace. That would be like Gale.

Then she saw him, standing behind the row of dowagers near the floor. He was bending low to speak to one of them, a lock of his hair falling into his eyes. It was only a miracle that Johnna did not slip on the polished floor.

"All right?" Ramsey asked.

"Yes, just a little breathless. Dancing is such exercise."

"Do you remember the first time we danced together?"

"I shall never forget it. You were wrong to ask me when Susanna was standing there. She was your cousin."

"Was Susanna there? After I looked at you, I couldn't see anyone else."

She looked at him perplexedly as the music came to an end. They joined in the polite applause for the orchestra. The leader turned to the ballroom and announced that the world-famous soprano Madame Rinaldi would sing love arias in honor of the day.

"Good," Ramsey said in her ear. "We can rest a little while. Would you care for another glass of champagne?"

"Do they have lemonade? More than one glass of champagne makes me dizzy. I think it's the bubbles."

As soon as he left, she wished he were back again. She felt exposed even among such a mass of people, as if they were all standing back on the other side of a circle she didn't remember drawing. They all faced the stage, where a tall and slender woman had just come out to enthusiastic applause.

Then, also standing apart, she saw Gale. He flicked up his chin, signaling her to follow him. She glanced around for Ramsey. He was not in sight. With luck, she would say what she had to and return before he knew she'd gone.

Outside the ballroom, a door stood ajar. A quiet drawing room waited beyond, decorated in shades of blue that harmonized well with the Chinese pottery on the shelves. A pleasant, tasteful room turned horrible by its occupant. "Come in, Johnna," Gale said.

Once she'd thought she knew every shading of that voice, from the melting to the mocking. This was different yet. A hard metallic ring underlay each word. "You're looking well, my dear. Marriage agrees with you. You've lost that pinched look you used to have."

"I received your letters." She kept her tone very level. Gale enjoyed evoking the emotions in others that he wanted them to feel. She might pay him for her letters, but she wouldn't give him the satisfaction of making her show feeling.

"Indeed. You didn't meet me yesterday. This public meeting could have been avoided if you'd followed your instructions."

"I didn't read your first letter, Gale."

That surprised him. "But you read my second one."

"Yes."

He smiled, showing his small teeth, as if she'd been a trained dog who'd performed a trick. Johnna decided she'd rather be a cat. They were unpredictable. "Good."

"You're thinner, Gale. It's very becoming." The lines that had given his face character were sharper now. He seemed to have aged more rapidly than she. There were creases around his eyes that had not been there two years ago.

"Such a nice child. I've always thought so. It pains me to meet you under such mercenary circumstances, but my windmill has dwindled to a nutmeg. I need money, Johnna. In such times, a man must look to his assets."

"My letters?"

"Precisely. To show my good faith, I brought one with me. Do you remember this?" He held up a page before her eyes, covered with girlish effusions in a neat, round hand.

"I always had excellent handwriting."

"Then you admit it's yours. I'm pleased. I was afraid I should have to deal with your entreaties and tears. You were such an emotional child." He flipped the page over and began to read. *"I long to see you again, to taste the sweetness of life that you have shown me* . . . did your mother know you were reading those sorts of books, Johnna? Or were you sneaking Byron up to your bedroom?"

"What do you want, Gale?" she asked. When she saw the flicker of triumph in his eyes, she knew her feelings had shown through for a moment. "I don't have any money to speak of. The allowance my husband gives me is generous but I haven't drawn it yet. I've only been married a few months."

"I'm sure we can think of something. That necklace, for instance."

She touched the cool weight nestling around her throat. "It's not mine."

"Come now. Give it to me, I give you the letters, and you claim to have lost the necklace somewhere in the crowd."

"You have my letters here?"

"No, I'll send them to you tomorrow," he said, but he'd fleetingly touched his right-hand pocket.

"Very well." Johnna turned her back to him. "You'll have to help me with the clasp. It's complex."

He stepped up close behind her. She felt the warmth of his body, the touch of his fingers on the nape of her neck, and felt nothing. The necklace slid over her collarbones and into Gale's hands. "Thank you," he said with a horrible travesty of a bow. "You wait here a few minutes until I can get away. We mustn't let you be compromised."

She watched him walk out, bearing both his prizes. As soon as he closed the door behind him, she closed her eyes and let her head droop forward. Then, an instant afterward, she heard a grunt and a slam as something struck the door outside.

The door opened, slowly, and Gale Farringdon fell backward into the room, apparently unconscious. Ramsey followed, his fists clenched. Standing over the fallen man, he looked sharply at Johnna. "Are you all right?"

"What are you doing?"

He seized Gale by the collar and dragged him into the room, ignoring the sound of tearing cloth. He kicked the door shut. "Did he take your necklace?"

"Yes. No. What are you doing?" she asked again.

Bending down, Ramsey went through Gale's pockets. He found the necklace at once and, on the other side, pulled out the letters.

"No," Johnna said, going over to him. "Please give me those, Ramsey."

"Certainly, my dear. May I suggest the fireplace?"

She clutched the packet, some half dozen screeds she'd written in the haste of infatuation. "You know what these are?"

"Letters to him," Ramsey said, straddling the fallen villain. "He'll come around in a minute or two. Thank goodness. I wouldn't care to explain this scene."

"Here," Johnna said, holding out the packet. "Please read them. I want you to."

"I've read enough letters over the last two days to last me for years. You'd better add these two to the pile."

She gaped at the familiar toast-colored paper. "You had them?"

"I'm sorry I read what wasn't for my eyes. Blame it on the cat." She could only gaze at him, befuddled. "In the future, though, Johnna, I hope you'll come to me with these kinds of problems. What's a husband for?"

"There won't be any more problems. I've only ever been so foolish once."

She dropped the packet on the fire. All the letters burned brightly for a moment, then were smoke. Ignoring Gale, Ramsey came over to stand beside her, gazing down into the flames. "Johnna . . ."

"Ramsey, I'm so sorry. I . . ."

He took her hands, his eyes so bright that they seemed to shine. "Johnna, will you be foolish with me? Write me love letters. Lots of love letters. Love me, Johnna. Love *me*."

"I . . . I do. I've never loved anybody else. I never could love anybody else."

Ramsey kissed her with a passion that would have frightened her yesterday. Now she returned it, touching his face, his throat, his shoulders. He placed her necklace around her throat, and she shivered at the brush of his fingers on her neck. "You go back to the ballroom," he said, kissing her forehead. "I'll take care of Mr. Farringdon."

"What will you do to him?"

"Nothing. Merely quote the Duke of Wellington." She shook her head, uncomprehendingly. " 'Be damned.' " As if in echo, Gale groaned as consciousness returned.

* * *

Sheba went for a walk across the bedroom floor. The claw on her back right foot caught in a loose thread and she dragged a silk stocking behind her until she shook it off. The fine blue coat was still warm with the scent of the man, wringing a purr from her throat. Sheba stumbled a little as the pair of shoes under the coat shifted as she walked on them. She batted at a fringe hanging off the bed. Then a hand came down and plucked her from the floor.

She nestled down among the humans, purring with contentment as she realized that those most unrestful creatures were not likely to move for quite some time. They showed her the attention she deserved, scratching her ears, smoothing her fur, while they talked in low voices. She'd almost fallen asleep when they moved her once again to the floor. Offended, she stalked back to her basket while those strange sounds that had awakened her began again.

Discover the Romances of

Hannah Howell

__**My Valiant Knight**	0-8217-5186-7	$5.50US/$7.00CAN
__**Only for You**	0-8217-5943-4	$5.99US/$7.50CAN
__**Unconquered**	0-8217-5417-3	$5.99US/$7.50CAN
__**A Taste of Fire**	0-8217-7133-7	$5.99US/$7.50CAN
__**A Stockingful of Joy**	0-8217-6754-2	$5.99US/$7.50CAN
__**Highland Destiny**	0-8217-5921-3	$5.99US/$7.50CAN
__**Highland Honor**	0-8217-6095-5	$5.99US/$7.50CAN
__**Highland Promise**	0-8217-6254-0	$5.99US/$7.50CAN
__**Highland Vow**	0-8217-6614-7	$5.99US/$7.50CAN
__**Highland Knight**	0-8217-6817-4	$5.99US/$7.50CAN
__**Highland Hearts**	0-8217-6925-1	$5.99US/$7.50CAN
__**Highland Bride**	0-8217-7397-6	$6.50US/$8.99CAN
__**Highland Angel**	0-8217-7426-3	$6.50US/$8.99CAN

Available Wherever Books Are Sold!

Visit our website at **www.kensingtonbooks.com.**